FRENEMY

DON'T TURN YOUR BACK FOR ONE SECOND

THE DARK HEARTS SERIES

MARIA FRANKLAND

AUTONOMY
PRESS

First published by Autonomy Press 2022

This novel is entirely a work of fiction. The names, characters and incidents portrayed in it are the work of the author's imagination. Any resemblance to actual persons, living or dead, events or localities is entirely coincidental.

Maria Frankland asserts the moral right to be identified as the author of this work.

First edition

*I dedicate this book
to Vicky Sykes,
my longest and oldest friendship.*

JOIN MY KEEP IN TOUCH LIST

If you'd like to be kept in the loop about new books and special offers, join my 'keep in touch list' by visiting <u>www.mariafrankland.co.uk</u>

You will receive a free novella as a thank you for joining!

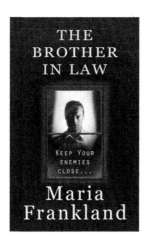

ALSO AVAILABLE IN THE DARK HEARTS SERIES

PROLOGUE

I STEP BACK from the door, and look up at the house. The upstairs is in darkness, but the flickering TV is visible between the cracks of a downstairs blind. Is she *hiding* in there? Ignoring the door? She wouldn't have known I'd be calling tonight, so it can't be that.

I lift the flap of the letterbox and peer inside. Nothing. I check up and down the street. Deserted. I brush beads of sweat from my brow before creeping around the side of the house, picking my way through the bins and stepping over plant pots. The gate creaks as I push it open.

Curtains curl out of the open patio doors. As I start in that direction, my attention is diverted to a dark shape at the side of the shed.

It's... She's...

I drop into a crouch beside her. I reach for her hand. As my fingers search her wrist, I see a halo of darkness surrounding her head. Blood. Her hair flutters in the breeze. Her eyes stare back.

Dead.

PART I

LOU

1

NOW

WHEN I SEE who's calling, I stifle a groan. I don't have the time *or* energy for Donna right now. I sweep my gaze over my classroom, which always looks messier when it gets to this point in the school year. And I've got so much to do before the kids come back in.

I let it ring off, silently promising that I'll call her back after school. But she's not giving up. As usual. She leaves a voicemail. Then a text. Finally, I snatch up the phone. *What on earth is wrong with her?* I spoke to her for nearly an hour last night. She seemed alright by the time we'd finished talking.

> I need to talk to you hon. Everything's in such a mess.

I hit the call button, knowing I won't be able to focus this afternoon if I don't. *Yes,* Donna leans heavily on me, but that's what friends are for. She'd do the same for me if roles were reversed. She *has* done the same. As she never tires of reminding me.

"Lou. At last."

She sounds so relieved to hear my voice that I feel guilty for my hesitation. And my irritation. Mum's voice pops into my mind. *Set your boundaries Louisa. Learn to say no.* She says I'm a *people pleaser*, though she means it in the nicest possible way.

"What's up?" I refrain from adding the words *this time.* "I've only got a couple of minutes before the bell, I'm afraid."

"He's ignoring me," she blurts out, the edge to her voice turning from the relief at me answering, into despair. "It's been two-and-a-half days now. He won't even reply to my texts."

"Are we talking about the *widower*?" Balancing the phone under my chin, I gather dry paintings from the washing line in our art corner. I love the smell of the paint we use. It takes me back to my own childhood.

"Don't call him that. His name's Owen. And I told you he'd gone all funny on me."

In chapter and verse, I also refrain from adding, sighing as I imagine Donna's eyes full of tears. She has the same sort of luck with men as a gambling addict has with slot machines.

"He's probably just feeling guilty. You told me yourself it's not even been six months since his wife died."

"But he was up for it. I even asked him if he was sure before we went upstairs."

"It was too soon." I wander around the classroom, placing paintings on the children's desks. "He was probably lonely. From what you've shown me of his Facebook page, he looked happily married before..." My voice trails off.

"She's bloody *everywhere* in that house." Donna's voice takes on a harsher tone. "In photographs... and her things are all over the place. You'd think he'd get rid of them. I mean, who'd want someone who's died staring at them everywhere they look?"

"Everyone handles these things in their own way."

"And I forgot to tell you, when I stayed, I asked if he had something I could brush my hair with, you know, the morning after, and he gave me *her* hairbrush. It still had her hair in it."

"Bloody hell." I close my eyes, knowing it's too late for *I told*

6

you so's, much as I feel like them. I told her until I was blue in the face to leave it for a while with him. "Were their kids around the next morning?"

"They're *his* kids now. *She's* gone, hasn't she? Not that you'd know that. No. Thankfully. They were staying with Owen's mum. She was apparently the one who'd persuaded him to have a night out. Oh Lou, what have I gone and done?"

I wave at Georgia, my teaching assistant, as she pops her head around the classroom door and I mouth the words *two minutes* at her.

"Sorry," she whispers, and disappears again.

"Look, what's done is done. You've slept together. End of. You can't turn the clock back." I move towards the book-bags. I can stuff them with the letters from the school secretary whilst I'm on the phone.

"But I don't want it to be the *end of.* I've fancied Owen for years. You know I have. And he's available now."

"Except he's not, is he? The poor bloke was married for nearly ten years. He's grieving."

"Whose side are you on?"

"Yours - of course I am. But you keep going after men who are only ever going to hurt you. You need to look at this. Seriously."

"But Owen's not like that. I thought he was my friend. I thought he liked me."

"But you've crossed that line now. And there's no going back." I wave at one of my pupils through the window. I'd quite like to be out there, enjoying the sunshine with them instead of listening to my best friend weeping down the phone. As usual. "You can't *un-sleep* with him."

"Why do you always have to be so reasonable Lou? And sensible. It does my head in. Why can't you understand how it is for me?" Her voice sounds strangled. I can't tell if it's with anger, or whether she's crying. Either way, I need to get her off the phone.

"I *do* understand. Where are you, anyway?" Perhaps if I bring her attention back to the here and now.

"At work, of course. For the moment, anyway." Yes, she's definitely crying. "I feel like going home, to be honest. My head's in absolute bits with all this."

"What about Jacob? Who'll look after him if you cry off? Surely you can just get through this afternoon?"

"The other learning mentor has already taken him out to play. I told her I wasn't feeling well."

"You'd be better staying at work. Keeping busy. Look Donna." I glance at the clock. "My TA needs to speak with me, and the bell's going any second. I'm going to have to go."

"Yes, *Miss Important.* I suppose I'd better hang up then. What are you doing later?"

Oh no. She's not going to like this. I'll have to let her down gently. "I'm going for a meal with Scott." A flicker of excitement dances in my belly as I picture the new dress hung on the back of my wardrobe door.

"Great." The anger behind Donna's single word is tangible. "I thought we agreed never to dump each other when a man came along."

"We were seventeen years old." I force a laugh. It's not the first time she's reminded me of our longstanding promise to each other.

"Please Lou. Don't leave me sitting at home on a Friday night. Not with all I've got going on. I need you more than *Scott* does."

She sounds like Charlie when she's hankering after new trainers. My heart plummets at the choice she's asking me to make. I know she's miserable but... *No.* Mum's face pops into my mind. "Scott's booked a table tonight. I've been looking forward to it all week."

"You've been seeing him for all of five minutes and suddenly he's more important than me?" She sounds even more like Charlie.

"Five months actually, and no, of course he's not more important. But he's *as* important. I really like him – you know I do."

"And you'd rather spend this evening with him, instead of with me. If you were in my position, I'd drop anything and everything for you."

"Look." I swallow, knowing I'll have to see her. "I'll ask Scott to move the table booking back slightly and if he can sort it, I'll meet you for a drink before I meet him. How's that?"

She falls silent for a moment. "I suppose I should be grateful that you're shoehorning me into your busy schedule."

I let a long breath out, relieved that she appears to be accepting my compromise. The bell jolts me back into the present, and out of the corner of my eye, I notice my class lining up at the cloakroom door. Georgia is nowhere to be seen. "I'll have to go. The kids are coming in and my TA's vanished. I'll drop you a text later."

"But..." She starts to say something, however I lower the phone from my ear and cut her off. That's my lunchtime gone. I'll have to get Georgia to do the register so I can eat my sandwich.

"Another week done." Georgia slumps onto the beanbag beside me in our book corner. "Only two more until the summer holidays."

"Not that we're counting, of course." I playfully push her shoulder. "We love being here with our little darlings. I'm just going to have five minutes to myself before I set up for Monday."

"Anything you want me to do? I've got ten minutes before I clock off. Not that I'm in any rush to get home," she adds. "All my parents are going on about at the moment is my stupid brother."

"Paint and glue pots." I laugh as she groans. It's her least favourite job. I should probably ask her about her brother. It's the third time she's mentioned him this week and I get the impression she'd like to talk. But with Donna to contend with, I've hardly got the capacity to take on anyone else's woes.

As Georgia clatters around with the paint pots, I reach to the side of my chair and tug my phone from my handbag. I really never get a minute's peace. In less than two hours, I've had five missed calls and seven text messages. I hope Scott isn't going to cancel. It feels like ages since I've seen him.

True to her word, Donna must have bunked off sick this afternoon. All the calls were from her. Not all the texts are though. Only three.

> Don't forget to text me about tonight. I could really do with a chat.

> Have you sorted it yet? With Scott?

> Call me as soon as you get this. I'm at home now.

I scroll down the others.

> Do I really have to stay at Grandma's tonight Mum? Can't I stay at home?

Yes you do!

I'm not ready for Charlie to meet Scott yet. Nearly, but not quite. The last thing I want is for their first meeting to be bumping into each other en route to the bathroom in the middle of the night.

> What time are you dropping Charlotte off?

Mum must be telepathic.

> Can't wait to see you tonight.

I smile at Scott's text, relieved that he isn't cancelling.

> Five days is far too long.

Then the last one.

> I need to speak to you about maintenance money. I'm a bit short this month.

I'll deal with my errant ex, Darren, later. He always wants to speak to me about maintenance money, or lack of it. He seems to have no idea how much thirteen-year-old girls cost to look after. No doubt his dreadful wife Liz will be behind this text. She resents every penny he pays towards Charlie. Not that he pays very many.

I text Scott back first.

> Any chance we can make the meal an hour later?

Three waving dots appear on the screen almost immediately. I like this about him. He never keeps me waiting or wondering. I know exactly where I am with him, though I can't seem to relax into our new relationship. Donna's never-ending drama with men has made me edgy.

How come? I was hoping you'd be pining for me by now!

I need to see Donna first. She's in a bit of a state.

Again?

Sorry.

I'll see what I can do.

2

THEN

"ALL DRESSED up and nowhere to go." Donna smiled at me from where she sat, cross-legged, amongst the make-up we'd been trying on.

"Like we need to go out to have a good time." I swigged from the bottle and passed it to her. "We have just as much fun staying in."

She didn't take her eyes from me as she raised the bottle to her crimson lips. Constance Carroll's latest colour.

"What's up?"

"I was just thinking..."

"About what?"

"I hope it's always like this. Me and you, I mean." She pointed at herself, then at me as she spoke.

"Of course it will. Why wouldn't it?" She was always extra clingy with a bit of Lambrini inside her.

"One of us could move away, or meet someone. Things change, don't they?"

"*We* won't." I reached over the mound of make-up in between us and squeezed her arm.

"I hate it when someone gets a new boyfriend, and then dumps all their mates. Don't you?"

"We won't ever let a man come between us. Don't you worry. Boyfriends come and go, but friends are there forever."

"I'll drink to that." She grimaced as she swallowed from the bottle, then passed it back to me.

3

NOW

"I don't see why I even need a babysitter." Charlie glares at me from beneath her barely-there blonde eyebrows as we pull up outside Mum's.

"Grandma's not *babysitting* you! She just loves you spending time together." I yank the handbrake on and turn to her. "But you're not old enough to be left on your own late at night yet either."

"When are you going to stop treating me like a kid?" She drags her bag from the back seat onto her lap.

"When you stop acting like one." I wave back at Mum as her head pops up at the window. I can't get used to her being grey since she decided, in her words, to *grow old disgracefully*. She still looks ten years younger than she is though. I open the door.

"Now make sure you behave when you get in there," I say across the car roof. "Grandma would be mortified if she thought you didn't want to be here." She really would. As her only grandchild, Charlie's always been her world. I think this is why she's liking the idea of my growing relationship with Scott so much – she might sense the possibility of another grandchild in the future. Maybe...

"Well, I don't want to be here. I just want to chill at home." Charlie drags her feet as we make our way up the drive. "It's not fair. Just so you can go out with some stupid man called Scott."

"How do you know about him?"

"Not telling." She gives me one of her looks. "Hi Grandma."

"Where's my hug Charlotte?" Mum grabs hold of her as she attempts to squeeze past her into the hallway. "You'll never be too old to give me a hug when you arrive, you know."

"Sorry Grandma. But I wish you'd stop calling me Charlotte."

"Never." She smooths her hand over Charlie's hair as she leans into her. "Gosh, you're growing up far too fast."

"I'll dump my stuff." Charlie heads towards the foot of the stairs.

I follow Mum to the kitchen, coveting the denim dress she's wearing. I'll have to borrow that. "Have *you* told Charlie about Scott? She's just mentioned him."

"Of course not. I thought you weren't ready to introduce them yet."

"It must be Donna who told her. She's the only other person who knows. Though I asked her not to." I pull a chair out from under the table with a scrape.

"I wouldn't trust that Donna one with anything like that." Mum sniffs as she fills the kettle. "You should have learned that long ago."

"She's my best friend." I shake my head as I fiddle with the edge of the tablecloth. "You've never liked her." It's the one subject that always comes between Mum and me. *Donna.*

"I had a bad feeling about her from the moment we met." She slides the kettle onto the hob. "There was something about her. There still is."

"Alright Mum. Let's not go down that road again."

"Is she still with that man? The engaged one?" She turns to look at me, her eyebrows raised in curiosity. "You should really limit the time Charlotte spends with Donna you know. At her age, she's very impressionable."

It's not the first time she's said this, but I duck it and comment on the question about the man. "Nope. He saw sense and broke it off." I squint in the late afternoon sunshine as Mum moves away from the window. This time of year is my favourite, particularly when we get a heatwave like we're having at the moment. I can't wait to wear my new dress tonight.

"So, it's all back on with his wedding then?"

"As far as I know. I don't really know him. Only to say hello to at the gym."

Mum wipes her hands on a towel. "I bet Donna's happy about that then? Or has she moved onto the next one by now?"

"Yeah, there's someone else." I decide against telling her he's a newly-widowed man with two small boys. Mum would have a fit.

"You want to watch this new man of yours around her." She wags her finger at me.

"Donna's a lot of things." I laugh. "But she'd *never* do that to me. We have boundaries, you know. Lines we'd never cross."

"She'd cross any line." Mum frowns. "You mark my words. So, when do I get to meet this Scott anyway?"

"I was thinking of introducing him to you and Charlie at the same time."

"That's a good idea." Her face relaxes into a smile. I know they'll get on. Scott's such easy company, I can't imagine anyone not liking him.

"Yeah, I was thinking it wouldn't be so intense if it's the four of us at once, rather than introducing you separately. Maybe dinner at mine? Now that Charlie knows, we might as well get on with it. How about this Sunday if it's OK with him?"

"Sounds good to me. He seems like a nice chap."

"You're a bit dressed up, aren't you?" Donna eyes me with what looks like suspicion as I emerge through the crowd at the doorway of The Black Horse.

"I told you I'm going for a meal after we've had a drink." I have to shout over the raucous laughter of the women next to us.

"You could have called it off." Donna pouts as she tosses her hair behind one shoulder. In her short dress and sandals, she's done up like she's out for the whole evening, not just an hour.

I shake my head. "Sorry." Though why I'm apologising is anyone's guess.

"Swanky restaurant, is it?" There's no getting away from the venom in her voice. I wish she could just be happy for me.

"Something like that. Anyway, Scott's deferred the table for an hour."

"So you've only got an hour with me? Why thank you." She gives me a mock-sweet smile. Donna really can be a cow when she doesn't get her own way. "I expect I should be grateful."

I feel bad at the slump of her shoulders as I stand next to her at the bar. Once upon a time, I might have cancelled my evening when she was feeling so down, but I can't bear to miss out on seeing Scott.

"I'm sorry Don. I'll make it up to you." I nudge her. "Promise."

"Well, you can start by getting the drinks in." She turns to the man behind the bar. "Two large white wines when you're ready."

"Make mine a small one with soda water please," I call over her shoulder. "I don't want to be drunk before I get to the restaurant, do I?"

"Suit yourself." She shrugs as we watch the barman slide two glasses from the shelf above him.

"I take it Owen still hasn't been in touch?" I might as well get the conversation started. After all, I really only have an hour and it's what she'll want to talk about.

Her head bows and her eyes glisten with tears at the mere mention of his name. "Nothing. Not a thing. I texted him to see if he wanted to come out tonight. He's read it too. *And* he's been active on social media." She waves her phone in the air. "He obviously can't be bothered replying to me. I'm pig sick of men treating me like this Lou. What am I going to do?"

"Look Donna. He's been married for ten years and has probably never been near another woman other than his wife until he slept with you." I lower my voice as the barman gives us a funny look. "No doubt he feels as though he's betrayed her."

"She's dead, for goodness sake. How can he betray her?"

Blimey, she just doesn't get it at all. "If I were you, I'd give him some space for a few days."

"I've given him space for the last two days."

"But that's just it - you haven't. You've been ringing and texting him. Let him get his head around things and if he likes you, he'll come running."

"Do you reckon?" She looks at me with large eyes, as though really needing me to help her feel better.

I nod as I hold my payment card against the machine and thank the man.

"Surely the fact he's slept with me *must* mean he likes me?" She reaches for her wine glass. "Thanks."

"You don't need me to tell you it doesn't work like that. We both know what men can be like. You've played your best card too soon Donna. I'm always telling you to hang fire."

"Like *you* do?" Her voice is dripping with sarcasm.

"I made Scott wait four months, actually."

"Four months!" She shrieks above the buzz of conversation. "I'm surprised he stuck around."

19

"Anyway, we're talking about you, not me." I move to one side to let someone pass.

"So what am I supposed to do then?"

"Like I said, leave him be. Let him wonder what you're up to. Allow him to be the one who does the chasing." I almost laugh at myself. I probably sound pious. Just because I've met someone decent doesn't make me a sudden authority.

"And what if he doesn't? *Chase me,* I mean?" Her face falls even further.

"Then at least you'll know." I give her what I hope is a sympathetic expression. "And there's plenty more where he came from."

"But it's *him* I want."

"Then listen to me."

"OK. I'll try not to text him anymore." She follows my gaze to the clock behind the bar. "As if Lou! You're with me and you're clock watching. Cheers." She pouts and looks down at her glass. "I can't believe you're going to dump me in an hour either. Can't I come with you?"

"I'm going on a date." I can't keep the exasperation from my voice. *As if!*

"What am I supposed to do when you go?" Then her face brightens. "Who's looking after Charlie? Maybe I could go round to yours and wait for you there? She'll be well chuffed to see me."

"She's at my mum's and no, you can't - sorry. I think me and Scott are off back to mine, if you know what I mean." I wink at her. "Why do you think I got Charlie out of the way?"

"It really is alright for you, isn't it?" She scowls. "I mean, what have *you* got that I haven't?" She sounds so exasperated, I half expect her to stamp her foot.

"Oh, come on." A group of women get up from the table opposite so I reach for my drink. "Let's bag that table. My shoes are rubbing. You're gorgeous – you know you are. Just relax. You'll be snapped up by someone decent before you know it."

"You've been saying that since I split with Aiden." Her face darkens. "Bloody four years ago. I'm sick of being on my own. And now my best friend would rather shack up with some man she's only known for five minutes instead of me."

"Come on. Before someone else gets that table." One subject I want to steer clear of is Donna's ex-husband who she lured from someone else. Women should stick together and have each other's backs, not go around pinching each other's husbands. However, she was to get a taste of what it felt like. She was shocked beyond belief when Aiden ran off with the florist from their wedding. They'd only been married a few months when she found out. She'd taken some real propping up through all that.

We slide into the seats on either side of the table, facing each other.

"Are you at the gym in the morning?" I ask. I was miffed when she first joined the gym I've been going to for years. There are gyms much closer to where she lives. The first time she planted her mat beside me in a pilates class, it felt as though my precious 'me time' was being encroached upon. I've since got used to the idea, and at least it gives me some time to spend with her now that I'm seeing Scott. Not that I get a lot of spare time these days. My job literally swallows me up.

"Yeah." She jerks her head from staring into her drink towards looking at me. "Are you going to meet me there? Or will you be too busy with lover boy?"

"I'll be there." I do mental calculations about how and when I'm going to get Scott to leave. Not that I want to, but it's a fair bargain for having to leave Donna on her own tonight. If I can get Mum to drop Charlie off, then I'll have enough time to fit everything in tomorrow.

"I don't even know how I'm going to get home tonight."

Donna takes a big sip of her wine. "I don't get paid till next week. I shouldn't really be out." At least she has the grace to look apologetic.

"Bloody hell. As if you can't get home!"

"It's OK for you to say with your *head of department* job. Us minions have more month than money."

"I've got a teenager to feed and clothe, you know. On my own too." I sigh as I reach for my purse, recalling Darren's earlier text that I'll be getting no maintenance yet again this month. "Do you need me to sub you?" I have to shout above the DJ that's started up. I do feel bad. It's shaping up to be a good night in here and I'm dumping Donna when she's upset. But no way am I standing Scott up.

4

THEN

"Mum. Donna. Donna. Mum."

"Call me Carole." Mum wiped her hands on a towel as she turned from the sink. "I've heard lots about you."

Donna laughed as she slid onto the breakfast bar stool. There was a hint of nerves in there. "All good, I hope."

"Mostly." Mum laughed too. "Can I get you girls a drink?"

I felt nervous too as I sat beside Donna. Especially since I'd recounted to Mum several tales of scrapes Donna had got into since we'd been friends. Usually involving a boy. She could win anyone over though. Even Mum, I hoped.

"So what do you do Donna?" Mum placed two glasses of orange juice in front of us.

"What do you mean?"

"School? Work? College?"

"Oh right." She laughed again. "I've just dropped out of sixth form actually. I only went so my mum could keep claiming child benefit for me."

I nudged her with my knee. I wanted Mum to like her and that was not the right thing to say. My mother and her mother could even become friends. Maybe.

"What does your mum do?"

"Erm. Well. She's just split up with my dad, so…"

Seriously awkward. Why does Mum always have to grill people? Just because she's a social worker shouldn't mean she has to act like one when she's at home.

"It's a lovely house you've got here." Donna glanced behind her to the garden visible through the conservatory. I knew what was going through her head. She'd be comparing it to the tiny terrace she shared with her mum.

"We like it."

"If I lived somewhere like this, I'd never want to go out."

5

NOW

"Well, look at you."

The appreciative expression on Scott's face as he leans against the wall is worth my uncomfortable shoes and the price I paid for this dress. He whistles.

"Sorry I'm late."

"I suppose I can forgive you. Looking like that." He stands up straight and kisses me hard on the lips. I catch a whiff of his aftershave. "Sorry Lou, but we'd better get in there, much as I'd like to greet you properly. They've just let me know that another five minutes, and they'd be giving the table away. I thought I might be eating alone!" He reaches for my hand, and we head towards the restaurant door. "Did you meet your friend?"

"Yeah. She's hopefully on her way home now."

"Is she OK?" He looks back over his shoulder as we walk in. He looks pretty good as well. I've always liked a man in a white shirt.

"Yeah, man trouble."

"We're a horrible lot, aren't we?" He grins as the waiter comes towards us.

. . .

"Do I have to confiscate that phone?" Scott smiles but irritation creeps into it.

He's right. I'd be miffed if it was the other way around. "Sorry. It's just..."

"Your friend?"

I nod. "Look. I'm really sorry. You're absolutely right – I was just checking she's got home OK."

"She's a big girl, isn't she? Although your concern for her is very endearing."

"Of course she is. She's just... I'm sorry. I'll turn it off." I slide the phone into my clutch bag. "I'm meeting her in the morning anyway."

"Aww. Does that mean you'll be turfing me out early doors then?" He takes a big swig from his glass, then brushes froth from his beard. I don't usually like a man with a beard, but it looks good on him. I can't imagine him without it.

"Not that early. Don't worry. I've got lots of plans for you."

"I was rather hoping we could make a day of it. Go somewhere. Do something."

"I wish." I shake my head sadly. "But duty calls. Between Donna, lesson prep for next week and Charlie, I'm afraid I just don't have a day spare right now. But I'll make it up to you." This seems to have become my most used phrase. *I'll make it up to you.* When I die, perhaps it will be the inscription on my headstone.

"You don't have to make anything up to me." Scott reaches across the table for my hand. "But it's interesting that you named Donna first in your list of responsibilities. Even before your daughter."

I drum my fingers on the table, unable to think of an immediate response to his comment.

"So, did you have a good night, then?" Donna sniffs as we stand in line at the gate to the gym, poised to swipe our cards.

Her expression tells me she's not asking out of genuine curiosity, but as more of a chance to make the comparison with her own evening. That's what she does. I hope she's not going to make me feel guilty.

"Yeah, great thanks. When I finally got there, that is."

"Pardon me for existing." She sounds as huffy as she looks. It seems I can't win at the moment.

"Did you manage to stop yourself from contacting Owen?" I ask as we reach the door to the changing room.

She turns to look back at me, her expression darkening some more. "Well, if I hadn't been so royally dumped by you last night, my mind might not have been on him."

"Donna," I say as I slide my rucksack into the locker. "I did *not* royally dump you. I said from the off that I had plans."

"Alright. Alright. Anyway. It's not good." She presses a button on her phone and hands it to me. "Read these."

I tuck my hair behind my ear and look down at the screen.

> Hi Donna. I'm sorry for not answering your calls and texts but my head's all over the place. The other night was a mistake. A big one. I'm not ready to get involved with another woman so soon after losing my wife. I don't know if I ever will be, to be honest. It's not an excuse, but you got me at a bad time. I was drunk. And lonely. I'm really sorry.

"That's a long message. Especially for a bloke. But at least he's been straight with you." I hand the phone back.

"There's more." She bows her head and pushes it back at me.

I sink to the seat below the locker. "Shall I read on? Are you sure you want me to?"

She nods and slumps beside me.

> I thought you liked me. I can help you get through it all. You shouldn't be on your own at a time like this. How can you call what happened between us a mistake? It was wonderful.

> I'm sorry Donna. I just need to focus on my boys right now. It's not you. It's me.

> Do you know how many times I've heard that?

> You're a nice lass and in another life things might have been different. Like I said, I'm really sorry.

> Come on Owen. You've not even given us a chance. We'd be great together.

I sigh and glance up at her, resisting the urge to say *desperation.com*. I'll never understand her. She could have her pick of boyfriends if she went after the right ones.

> Look I don't want to hurt you, but I'm a mess right now. Please try to understand.

> But I don't understand. And I've liked you since we were at school. You must have been able to tell. You're single now. I'm single. If it's time you need, then we'll just take it slowly.

> Please. Look. I've got to go. I'm with my boys at the moment.

> Can I come round? You might feel differently if you see me.

I need you to leave me alone.

"His tone's suddenly changed, hasn't it?" I glance up at Donna. She's watching me intently as she nods.

What do you mean? I thought we were friends.

Friends don't hound people like you're doing.

I'm not hounding you. I just want to be with you.

"Oh Donna." I shake my head.

"If you'd been there for me last night," she snaps. "It's not as though I could even ring you."

I might have known I'd get the blame for this.

Well, I don't want to be with you, and if you keep this up, I'll have to block you.

Block me. What are you going on about? Look how about I leave you alone for a few days?

I want you to leave me alone - full stop.

But you weren't saying that when you were getting into my knickers a few days ago. You've completely used me.

"Is that it?" I hand the phone back to her. Tears are leaking from her eyes.

She nods, her ponytail bobbing up and down with the motion. "I should have listened to you. He's blocked me on everything. I mean, what did I do so bad?"

"Like *he* said. It's not *you*. It's him. He's probably eaten up with guilt."

"But why? We're both consenting adults."

"It's been what, five or six months since his wife died. It takes much longer than that to get over losing someone."

"What makes *you* such an expert?"

"I'm not. I just remember my mum when my dad died. She was a mess for ages."

"Yeah. Sorry. I forgot about that. Do you think *she'll* ever meet someone else?"

"I doubt it. Dad was the love of her life." I recall, with a pang, how they'd always sit together on the sofa, and always hold hands when out walking. Hopefully that's the sort of connection I've found with Scott.

"I want to be someone's *love of their life*. Why can't I find someone who wants me?"

Her wail bounces off the walls of the wooden locker room. I glance around us, thankful there's only the two of us in here. There's normally a few more people in on a Saturday morning. But in the middle of a heatwave, who wants to go to the gym? Most people with any sense are walking or cycling on a day like this. I'm only here to keep Donna company. And I deserve a *friend of the year* award, tearing myself away from Scott this morning. I don't think he was too impressed.

"Men can sense desperation." I realise my voice is sharp, so I attempt to soften it. "You need to be happy on your own first. Then you'll attract someone you deserve. Someone who *really* wants to be with you." I nudge her. "Listen to me."

"Hark at you." She looks at me and smiles, but it doesn't reach her eyes. "It's not fair." She playfully slaps me on the shoulder. "You always have all the luck. And for your information, I'm not desperate, alright?"

"Come on." I rise from the bench. If I don't move soon, I'll end up in the coffee bar instead. "Getting rid of your angst in the gym will make you feel better than having a pop at me."

"Nothing will make me feel better. I'm just so pissed off." She brushes a tear away. "I don't know what to do anymore."

I sigh as I reach into my pocket. Full-blown waterworks I do not need. I pass her a tissue.

I really can't be bothered with the gym today – we should have just met for a coffee. Before the end of next week, I've got twenty-nine reports to write. Plus, I've arranged to cook a Sunday lunch tomorrow. Scott's got the afternoon free, so I'm going to introduce him to Mum and Charlie. But I've got a terrible sense of foreboding about it and can't understand why. Maybe it's just nerves.

Hoping to distract Donna from her woes, I tell her how nervous I am as we stride towards the exercise bikes to get warmed up. It's our usual routine before we hit the weights.

"Why would you be nervous?" She threads her blonde ponytail through the back of her cap. Only Donna could look good in a baseball cap. "Especially if he's as perfect as you make him out to be?"

"Ah, you know. I'm hoping Charlie gets on with him, mainly. And that she doesn't feel threatened. She's at a funny age." I rub the tops of my arms. It's so cold in here with the air conditioning that I've got goose bumps. It certainly doesn't feel as though there's a heatwave outside.

"She seems alright to me." Donna always claims to know Charlie better than I do. She opens up to her more than she does to me. When someone is not your parent, it is easier. I have to monitor it though. Mum's right. Donna's not always the most appropriate example. And occasionally I have to fight not to feel left out of their cosy little union.

"It's just, you know, after what she's been through with Liz." I swing my leg over the bike. "I knew it would be tough for her when Darren got re-married, but it's been a nightmare. He could have at least ended up with someone half decent."

"That woman wants stringing up." Donna presses the buttons on her bike. "I can't believe she's so threatened by Charlie. I mean, she's such a good kid too."

"Not that Liz will ever see that. I've no idea what her problem is. She won't even let Charlie leave any of her stuff there. And some of the texts I've had off her…"

"Like what?"

"Oh, I've had the lot, things like telling me she's not a glorified babysitter when I want to bugger off at weekends, name calling, she was calling me a grasping bitch last month when I had the cheek to chase Darren for all the maintenance he owes me."

She shakes her head. "It wouldn't bother me in the slightest if I met a bloke with kids."

At least my woes seem to have taken her mind off Owen. We start pedalling, on our roads to nowhere. My thoughts drift to visions of Scott and I pedalling along a country road. We could stop for lunch, walk by the stream, we could…

"So, am I invited to this dinner you're having tomorrow?"

"Erm." Shit. She's got that look. The one that works with nearly everyone she wants something from. "Not this time Don. I want to introduce him to Mum and Charlie first. Then I'll arrange something with you as well."

"But you might as well get it over with in one go, hadn't you? Mum, daughter *and* best friend." Her breath quickens as she pedals faster. "I'm not doing anything tomorrow. And I'd love to meet him too."

The way she says *I'd love to meet him* sets off warning bells. She's *never*, to my knowledge, made a move on a man I've been involved with, so I don't know why a knot of dread has suddenly tightened within my belly. Probably because Scott means more to me than any other man I've dated since Darren moved out.

"No really. I'm sorry. Look. I'll sort something soon, I promise." I follow her gaze towards the treadmills. "Anyway what, or should I say, *who* are you looking at?"

"See them over there…" She smiles for the first time since I met her in the car park. It's good to see her perk up, and I'm glad that something has diverted her attention from wanting to come for dinner. "They're checking us out." She smooths her hand down her ponytail.

"Hmmm. Yes. I suppose so." I try not to look as I continue pedalling.

After a few minutes, she swings her leg over the exercise bike. "Come on, let's go over."

"I can't. No. Donna. We're not here for that." *Here we go.*

"Don't be boring Lou. It doesn't suit you." Out of the corner of my eye I see them speaking to each other, then looking back at us.

"But I've got a boyfriend now."

"Don't I bloody know it?" She leans across and hits the stop button on my exercise bike. "We're only going to say hello. Come on. Live a little."

"What if I don't want to?" I fold my arms and stare at her.

"For me Lou? Please."

"No. You go. I'll stay here if you don't mind."

She steps towards me, fury written all over her face. "Do you know something Lou?" She leans her elbows onto the handlebars of my bike. "You've become utterly boring since you started seeing Scott."

"I haven't. It's just…"

"I mean it. You used to be fun in situations like this. What the hell's happened to you?"

6

THEN

"THAT'S my round taken care of." Donna plonked the pints of lager and lime at the edge of the table, ignoring the dirty looks the girls already sitting at the table gave us. "See him over there." She waved at a dorky-looking lad who wore his fringe in curtains. "Him and his friend want us to go over. He's just asked me."

"But I like this song. You promised me no lads tonight. I thought we were out to have a laugh. And a dance for a change." I pointed towards the DJ as the introduction of 'All Together Now' played. Everyone was flocking to the dance floor, including the girls from what would now become our table. I sighed as I sat down, wishing I had the guts to dance on my own.

"Over here." She beckoned to where one of the lads stood watching us from the bar. He nudged his mate, an even dorkier looking individual who, with his collar length hair, looked as though he needed reminding we were no longer in the eighties. There would be no prizes for guessing which of the two Donna would have her eye on. And what Donna wanted, she usually got.

Still, it would mean a few free drinks and a laugh. Hopefully that would be enough for her.

7

NOW

"He's here! Oh my God. Best behaviour you two." I point from Charlie to Mum, putting on a mock-stern face.

"Of course." Mum winks at Charlie, who gives me her best wide-eyed expression of innocence. "You can count on us. Well, go on then. Let him in."

I rake my fingers through my hair as I rise from the chair.

"Look at Mum." Charlie laughs. "Sprucing herself up for him."

Butterflies flap within me as I stride towards the front door. But it's not his six-foot frame I see silhouetted in the frosted glass. Instead, it's a shape I know only too well. I frown as I throw the door open to Donna.

"What are you doing here?"

With her hair plaited onto one shoulder and a long, flowing summer dress, she looks amazing. I wipe sweat from my top lip. After slaving over a Sunday roast for the past two hours, I look anything but amazing. My make-up has probably slid from my face.

"Is that any way to greet your best friend?" Her laugh is

tinkly as she pushes past me. "You said you were nervous, so I thought I'd come along and offer some moral support."

This is all I need. Mum won't be happy either. There'll be an atmosphere. There always is when they're in the same room. Especially when Charlie's there too. "I'm fine, honestly."

"Where is everyone then?"

I turn in the doorway to face her in the hallway. "Look, I'm sorry. I haven't cooked enough."

"You always cook too much." She laughs again. Besides, I'll just have a drink if you haven't got enough to go around."

"Donna!" Charlie darts from the kitchen at the same time as Scott's Mercedes pulls up at the end of my drive. "I thought I heard your voice." She looks delighted, as always, to see her. Mum appears behind her, looking puzzled as she glances from Donna to me.

"Go in there, will you?" I hiss. "He's here."

"Don't be snogging him Mum." Charlie and Donna laugh.

I give Donna the fiercest look I can muster as I jerk my head in the direction of the kitchen. "Go on then." She doesn't move, so I pull the front door behind me and stride towards Scott's car as he gets out.

"Wow. I don't usually get a welcoming committee." He grins as he looks from me, towards the front door which Donna's opened again. I'm fuming, but I can't let it show in front of Scott. I turn back to him.

"This is for you." He thrusts a bottle of wine at me. "And this is for Charlie. The air conditioning in the car has kept it cool." He gives me a huge bar of chocolate. "And these," he leans into his back seat and pulls out a bouquet. "Are for your mum."

"Aww, she'll like them. I think it's safe to say flowers are a good start!"

He locks the car, and we head towards the door where

37

Donna's leaning into the doorframe, arms folded. "So what have you brought for me then?"

He laughs. "Sorry. I don't think we've met before. I'm Scott."

"Obviously. And I'm Donna." She holds her hand out, which he takes in his. "No doubt you'll have heard lots about me." She gives him the same look as she did those men at the gym yesterday. No man is safe with her around.

"Of course. Nice to meet you. I wasn't expecting to - not today."

"Me neither." I grit my teeth as I look at their hands, still clasped. I feel like forcing them apart. She's always at her worst when a relationship has just gone wrong. It's as though she's looking for extra validation that she can't find from looking inside herself. "Shall we?" I gesture into the hallway.

"Come through Scott," Donna says as though she owns the place. "Is something burning in there?"

I dash past them where lo and behold, the carrots have boiled dry in the pan. The bottom half of the pan's contents have been reduced to charcoal.

"Didn't you smell burning, either of you?" I call to Mum and Charlie, who've taken themselves out onto the patio.

"Not from out here," Mum calls back. "Sorry love."

"And no one even noticed the plumes of black smoke. I guess carrots are off the menu then."

"It's a good job I can see in the dark just fine then, isn't it?" Scott winks at me. "Can I help with anything?"

I blush, wishing it *was* just me and him in the dark. "No, you go through whilst I sort this out." I open the fridge and pass him a beer. "Mum and Charlie are looking forward to meeting you. I'll be out in a minute when I've sorted these carrots."

By the time I've salvaged what I can of them, all the introductions seem to have been made. Mum and Scott are chatting like they've known each other for years. Donna keeps trying to get a word in edgeways, and Charlie watches on, quiet for a change. I can tell from her expression that she's trying to suss him out. Probably making sure he won't treat her like her dad's wife does. Over my dead body.

Donna's taken the seat next to Scott, so I loiter around for a moment in the doorway. I'll have to get another chair. And a glass of wine is in order. I don't know why I've got this feeling of utter gloom deep in the pit of my belly. It's a beautiful sunny afternoon and I'm here with my four favourite people in the world, albeit without carrots.

"I'd better see to dinner," I say as I set the chair down. I want to put it between Donna and Scott, but I'll only make myself look stupid. "Shall we eat out here?"

"It's certainly warm enough." Mum gets to her feet. "I'll set the table, shall I?" She follows me back to the patio door.

"I didn't realise Donna was invited today." Pulling the cutlery draw open, she raises an eyebrow.

"Me neither. But she's at a loose end." If I tell Mum that I *asked* her not to come, she'll end up saying something.

"You mean she's between boyfriends?"

"There'll be enough food to go round." I ignore her remark. "We've got starters and puddings too."

"Oooh. Starters and puddings. You must be trying to impress." Mum squeezes my shoulder. "He's a nice chap. I like him." She turns to the patio doors. "So does Donna, by the looks of it." I glance over at them. She's talking animatedly, throwing her hands around. When she's not doing that, she's fiddling with her plait, twisting it in her fingers. Charlie still watches on. I'll have to ask her later what she thinks of him. She's not giving anything away. The bar of chocolate is more than Liz has ever given her though.

"This is lovely Lou." Donna points at her plate. "Thanks for inviting me to stay."

There's the tiniest hint of sarcasm in her voice, but I can't read her expression as her large sunglasses are hiding her eyes. It's on the tip of my tongue to say *I didn't,* but that would be rotten. Instead, I give her my sweetest smile and say, "you're welcome."

"What do you do Scott?" Mum asks her stock question.

"I've told you what Scott does before, haven't I? I must have done."

"Not in a way that makes much sense!" She pours herself a glass of water from the jug.

"I don't think Lou understands what I do either." Scott laughs as he stabs at a roast potato. His eyes crinkle up at the corners when he laughs. I wish we were sitting together. "She thinks I just tinker about with computers all day."

"Well, isn't that true?" I catch his eye.

"Actually, I maintain all the systems in all the primary schools in this region." He puts his nose in the air in mock-grandiosity. "It's a very important job."

"He even has the word *engineer* in his job title," I add.

Mum smiles. "So that's how the two of you met? At your school?"

"Mum! Don't you listen to anything I tell you!"

Donna laughs. "Maybe she's getting him confused with another of your boyfriends."

Charlie laughs at this. I suppose she would. Though she's been very quiet throughout this meal. I'll have to speak to her later. Make sure she's alright. Nothing and no one will ever come between me and my daughter.

Thankfully Scott ignores her comment. "The first Tuesday afternoon of the month became my favourite time - when I'm at Lou's school. Also coinciding with when she has her planning time."

"Not that I get much planning done!" I recall the time we spent in the early days. The two hours when we were both supposed to be working would slip by as we chatted about anything and everything. We'd both end up having to work late then to make up for lost time. I also remember the desolation I'd felt those first few times when we parted company, knowing I wouldn't see him for another month. Luckily by the fourth month, he asked me out for a drink.

Donna seemed happy for me to start with but, became sour about the whole thing as mine and Scott's dates became regular. To use her words, *I wouldn't shut up about him.* Yet it's alright for her to give me chapter and verse about the men she hooks up with.

"That's how the best relationships start." Mum squints at Scott in the sunlight as she looks across the table at him. "As friendships, I mean. It was like that for me and Lou's dad, wasn't it Lou?"

I laugh then. "Yes, so you say. I wasn't there, was I?"

"I'd love to see a picture of him sometime." Scott puts his fork down. "Although I can see where Lou gets her looks from." He nods towards Mum. Judging by the look on her face, this was the right thing for him to say. It will be good for them to get on. Darren became such a waste of space toward the end of our marriage that she could barely bring herself to give him the time of day.

I notice Donna nudge Charlie and I'm convinced I hear her whisper the word *creep* before they both dissolve into giggles. If Scott hears, he doesn't let on. Instead, he reaches for the wine in the centre of the table.

"Where do you get *your* looks from then Scott?" Mum tucks her hair behind one ear.

"Oh, erm." He looks uncomfortable as he tops his glass up. "You'd have to ask Lou that. Who do I look like, my mum or dad?"

"Well, I've only met them once, but I'd say you've got your dad's looks and your mum's personality."

"You never mentioned you'd met his parents." Donna pulls a face. "I thought you told me *everything.*"

"I hope not." Scott tops my glass up too. It's probably not the best thing for him to say in front of Mum and Charlie. Too much innuendo. It's no wonder I was feeling so nervous about this meeting. Though at least it's done now.

"So will you be breaking up for the holidays soon as well Scott?" Mum pushes her plate away. "It was lovely, that was love." She smiles at me.

"I wish," he laughs. "No. I'm only paid for term time, so I do consultancy work through the holidays."

"You must be loaded." Donna's eyes bulge. "No wonder you snapped him up." She giggles as she holds her glass towards him. "I'll have a refill as well, if you don't mind."

"Will you get *any* time off during the six weeks?" As he puts the bottle down, I turn to him. I had visions of him winning Charlie over, and the three of us then being able to go off somewhere, or better still, Scott and I going somewhere alone together, if Charlie ends up going off for a few days with her friend's family like she did last year. It's not as if I can send her to her dad and Liz.

"Well, I can pick and choose if I want time off," he replies, "so feel free to come up with an offer anytime!"

"Donna thinks *we* should have a holiday Mum." It's the first time Charlie's spoken throughout the meal. "We were on about it the other day. Do you remember Donna?"

"Oh? Who's *we?*" I'm not sure how I'd feel about Donna taking Charlie on holiday. Not on her own. Once she gets her head turned by someone...

"The three of us, of course. I've been looking at the South of France, actually." Donna takes her glasses off and looks straight at me.

"We'll see." I'm not exactly jumping for joy at the idea, but this isn't the time to debate it. Nor is it the time for me to ask how she would pay for it.

Charlie is evidently far more enthused than I am. "Oh, can we, can we? Please Mum. We could go to Antibes. My friend from school has just been there and I've seen her pictures. It's really warm, and the sea is bright blue. It looks amazing. *Can we?*"

Donna, who by her own admission, always has too much month left at the end of the money, shouldn't be making wild promises like this to Charlie. I want to change the subject before I get railroaded into something.

"We'll talk about it later," I say. "Now who wants pudding?"

"I'll drop you off," Mum nods towards Donna who looks to be falling asleep on the sun lounger. "Can you be ready to go in ten minutes?"

It's been a scorching afternoon, and we're all full of too much food. And wine, apart from Mum. I certainly am. It took two large glasses to dampen the wrath that bubbled up inside me earlier. Try as I might, I can't forgive Donna for ignoring my wishes. I wanted this afternoon to be about me introducing my new boyfriend to my mum and my daughter. It's gone as well as I could have hoped for though. Everyone has got on with Scott, and Donna has kept things drama-free apart from a couple of barbed comments towards me, and flirtatious remarks towards him. Sometimes, when the wine gets hold of her, anything can happen. She hasn't looked at her phone since she got here, so it seems she's accepted that Owen's not going to come running back. She'll be onto her next one within a few days.

"I might just stay here tonight actually." Donna shields her eyes from the sun as she blinks at Mum. "I always leave a couple of changes of clothes here, just in case. Prepared for all eventualities, as they say."

"To be honest, it's probably best if Mum drops you off. I've got a lot to do."

"But Scott's still here." She smiles at him. "If you've got schoolwork and stuff, I could keep him entertained until you get done."

"Erm no. No thanks." I reply, as though she's offered to do me a favour. "I've got an early start tomorrow. You go with Mum."

"I'm off to finish my homework." Charlie stands from her sun lounger with a yawn. "I'm tired."

"Nice to meet you Charlie," Scott calls after her. She doesn't reply.

"Give her time," I say. "She's had a very rough ride with her dad's wife. To say she's not very welcome in their house is an understatement. I can tell she likes you though."

"Who wouldn't?" Donna looks sidewards at Scott. I bristle with anger, vowing to keep them apart. It's the first time she's ever done this with someone I'm seeing. In front of me anyway.

Mum must notice it too. "Right then," she says, in a voice normally reserved for Charlie. "I've got an early start in the morning as well."

"Well I could just…"

"No." Mum says even more firmly. I could literally kiss her, as Donna finally sighs and gets to her feet. She's given in with less of a fight than I feared. It's moments like this I wonder why I'm even friends with her.

"Finally." Scott reaches across the table for my hand. "I've got you all to myself. Fancy a top-up?"

I hold my glass towards him and glance over the garden,

relieved beyond measure that the meal is over and done with. They've all met each other now.

"They all seemed to like you." I raise the glass to my lips, hoping he'll respond with his first impressions of the three most important women in my life.

"And I liked them too. Hopefully your daughter will come out of her shell with me in time." He points to the sun lounger where Charlie was sitting.

"She will. She was just sussing you out."

He pulls a face. "She and your friend seem close."

"Yeah. Well, she's her godmother. She was the first person to see her after she was born. My ex was too squeamish to be in there."

"I see what you mean about her though."

"Who? Donna? How do you mean?" A cold hand of fear clutches at my throat as I wait for his reply. I hope he's not going to say how pretty she is, or similar. When men first meet us when we're out and about, they always go for her. It rarely bothers me, but this time it's different.

He pauses, as though uncertain whether to continue. "I'm not trying to cause trouble between you, but she was incredibly flirty with me. You must have noticed it."

"She's like that with everyone," I blurt. "It's just how she is." I don't add that men are usually drawn to her like bees to a honeypot. Though the way I'm feeling right now, I could easily use the analogy of flies, rather than bees. Mum *has* used this in the past.

He shakes his head. "Nah, it was more than that. In fact, when you and your mum were inside, she was saying how lucky you are to have met me. Amongst other things."

I smile through my fury. *She just can't help herself.* "Well, I am lucky."

"Anyway, I told her *I'm* the lucky one." He shifts his feet forward under the table and cups my bare foot between his.

"Well, that's true as well."

He pauses, his face saying he's uncertain whether to continue. His brow is furrowed to the point that I could rest a pencil in the groove it's made.

"What is it?"

"It's, well, she made a comment that I'm just going to come out and repeat to you."

Still, he pauses. Waiting to hear what he's got to say is maddening.

"She said that she wished *she'd* found me before you did." He rakes his fingers through his hair. "That she'd been the one to *snap me up.*"

"Are you serious? She said that?" Though I know she will have done. *Snapped up* is an expression she uses.

"I thought she was your friend?"

"She is. She's just got too little sense of acceptable limits."

He nods. "Look I didn't know whether to tell you. But I decided you've got the right to know." The muscles of his arms bulge beneath his t-shirt. She'll have noticed them too.

"I'll speak to her."

"I wouldn't bother. Just have it for... information, I guess. And just for the record. I wouldn't touch her with that."

I laugh as he gestures towards the clothes prop against the washing line.

"You're in the minority," I say. "She certainly attracts the men."

"She's too needy." He strokes the top of my hand with his thumb. "I could sense that a mile off. And nowhere near as interesting and intelligent as you are."

Interesting and intelligent?? I want him to use words like *beautiful.* Or *sexy.* Damn Donna. I'm going to have to watch her like a hawk around him.

8

THEN

CAN I HOLD HER? Donna stretched her arms towards the midwife.

"We'll pass her to Mum first."

I accepted the wrapped bundle that was my new daughter onto my chest as Donna looked on. She was not happy. How on earth could she expect to hold the baby before me? Or Darren?

Although, she had been nothing short of awesome throughout my entire labour. After my waters had broken, Darren became paler and paler. He'd have passed out if he'd have stayed in there, which is why I swapped him with Donna.

"Look what we did." She excitedly clasped her hands together. "Are you still going to call her Charlotte?"

"Of course." I smoothed the crook of my finger over her perfect skin. Part of me wished Donna would leave us for a few minutes. I wanted it to be just me and my baby.

"Hello Charlie." Donna's finger touched mine on the top of Charlotte's head. "We're going to have so much fun together."

"I'm not sure about you calling her Charlie," I said, not taking my eyes from Charlotte's perfect face. "Let's just stick with Charlotte for now."

"Dad wants to come in," the midwife called from the doorway. "And your mum's just arrived. We can only have one visitor in here at a time whilst you're in the delivery suite. You can have two when you're moved to the ward."

"But I'm not a visitor. I'm practically family." Donna looked from the midwife back to me. "Tell her. I haven't even held Charlie yet."

"Why don't you get a coffee? You've certainly earned one after all you've done for us. And no doubt you'll want to wet the baby's head tonight."

"Now I've served my purpose you mean." Her face darkened. "I've supported you through having her, and now you want rid of me."

"It's not like that at all. Don't be stupid." I returned my gaze to Charlotte. "I just want Darren to come in and meet his daughter."

"Most dads wouldn't have missed their baby's birth for the world, regardless of some so-called blood phobia. It shows how little he thinks of you, if you ask me."

"Well, I didn't ask you." I suddenly felt on the verge of tears. Why was she being like this? "I've known since I met him about his hematophobia. He'd have been useless if he'd stayed in here."

Saying nothing else, she flounced past the midwife who momentarily seemed unable to contain her shock at our altercation. However, she quickly straightened her face and called Darren in.

9

NOW

MONDAY VANISHES in the blink of an eye. After Georgia leaves, I sink to the chair behind my desk to tackle a few more of these wretched reports. I've let Georgia go early; she's been preoccupied all day and checking her phone every five minutes. She said she couldn't talk about it when I asked her what was wrong.

It's nice to have some peace now – there's the distant echo of the rounders after-school club, but other than that, I can get on with these reports. Copy and paste is a wonderful thing, especially for the concluding parts of the reports. I only hope the parents of my class never read each others and realise some paragraphs are the same.

I wonder if Scott will ring me tonight. My hangover from Sunday lunch in the sunshine has dissipated. However, I can't help feeling down, and it's not the usual teacher-related Monday blues. Nor is it a knock-on effect from Georgia's subdued mood all day. It's more than that.

Bloody Donna has completely marred any time I've had with Scott. Our meal on Friday, waking up together on Saturday, and then introducing him to Mum and Charlie yesterday. Now I won't see him again until Friday. No way will I let her sabotage my weekend next time. In fact, I might even see if Mum will have Charlie, and I'll suggest Scott and I go off overnight somewhere. And I'll be switching my phone off. That's if I get these reports done. I can't go anywhere if I don't.

The intercom buzzes behind me. Sighing, I push my chair back with a scrape. I'm usually left alone after school's finished - until the caretaker throws me out anyway. The school secretary should have left by now, so I don't know who could be buzzing me.

"There's someone in reception to see you," she says, her voice laced with impatience.

"Who?"

"I didn't get a name. And I'm just on my way home. You'll have to come through and find out for yourself."

"OK. I'll be along in a moment."

I'm barely out of the classroom door when I see Donna sauntering along the corridor, her heels clicking against the parquet floor.

"How did you get in?" It's an odd sight, her being in my place of work. She applied for a job here once as a learning mentor to a year five boy with ADHD, but she was pipped at the post by Dougie, who I've got to know pretty well since he's worked here. The lad with ADHD is definitely better with a male mentor. He'd have made mincemeat of Donna. He was bad enough when I had him in reception class.

"The caretaker let me through." She stops in her tracks and stares at me. "I've been trying to ring you all afternoon."

"Why? What's happened now?" I'm aware of my sharp tone, but the words are out before I can do much about it.

"Why haven't you been answering?" She juts her chin out as she looks at me, her expression almost accusatory. "I haven't done anything wrong, have I?"

I won't go down the road of mentioning her flirtatious

behaviour towards Scott. Not now. Not here. Besides, I've got so much to do. Donna is the last person I need to see at the moment.

"Sorry. I haven't looked at my phone since lunchtime. I haven't had a chance."

"Shall we?" She ushers me back into the classroom, reminding me of yesterday, when she acted like my house was hers. Now she thinks she can do the same with my classroom.

I resume my position behind the desk, and she sits facing me, sweeping her gaze around the room.

"Nice. I wish I had this." There's a sigh in her voice.

"You could always train? You'd get accepted with your mentoring experience."

"Nah. I can't afford it. And, at least I can bugger off at the end of the school day. I'm not married to my work like you are."

She's kind of right, but I can't be bothered going into the whys and wherefores of being a teacher. "You shouldn't really be in here. The head wouldn't be happy if he saw you."

"I thought you were the head of your department." Even wearing her sensible work clothes, she still looks perfect. She doesn't have pens poked into her ponytail and sweat patches under the arms of her blouse. Not like me.

"I'm only head of foundation stage. Not the whole school."

"What's the problem? I'm all police checked, aren't I?" She waves her arms around as she speaks.

"You still haven't told me why you're here." I glance at my computer screen as it drops into sleep mode. It looks like I might have to abandon this until later.

"You're being a bit off Lou." If Donna was someone who wore glasses, right now she'd be peering at me over the top of them. "What's up?"

"Nothing. I'm just tired."

"It's this job. You should take it easier. Anyway, I'm here

because I've got the chance to get out of that poxy flat of mine. A house has come up."

"Oh right. That's good. You've been wanting to move for ages." Not that she's explained what that's got to do with her sitting in my classroom.

"I can't tell you how excited I am. It's perfect. In fact, it's everything I could want. So I've accepted the place, subject to a few details."

"Such as?" A sense of foreboding creeps over me as I survey the eagerness in her eyes. This is going to involve me. I just know it.

"Well, that's where you come in." She looks sheepish for a moment. "You see..." She pauses and I instantly know what's coming. "I've got the first month's rent, but I need to raise another five hundred quid for the bond. And I need a guarantor as well."

"I can't." The words are out before I've even thought about them. "I'm a single parent, for God's sake Donna."

"Five hundred quid is pocket change to you Lou." Donna narrows her eyes. "You forget I know what you've got squirrelled away. It'd only be a loan anyway."

I wish I'd never told her about my savings. I could kick myself every time she needs subbing and throws them in my face. "OK, suppose I agree to the money side of it..." I sigh, knowing I'll have to help her. It's what friends do. "But being a guarantor? Why do you need one anyway?"

"I've only had my job since September, haven't I? Plus, I'm punching slightly above my weight with the rent. The guarantor thing is just a formality though."

"Why? How big is the house you're after?"

"It's just a two bedroomed, but it's got a back garden, and a porch, and a shed... It's even got a utility room. Lou, it's gorgeous. I want it so bad. I need to get out of that flat. Please say you'll help me. I'd do the same for you. Look at how many scrapes I've got you out of. It's how we met, after all." She barely pauses for breath as she pushes at all the buttons she knows will work with me.

"But what if something happens? And you can't make your rent. I know I've got savings put by. But I've got a daughter to support. It's not as though I can rely on her father. Besides, the savings I have are for Charlie's future, not for me to lend to my friends."

"It'll only be for a year. Once I've been in my job for two years, I can take the tenancy on myself."

I can't believe what she's asking of me. But she's like a pit bull when she wants something. She's got me around the neck and is unlikely to let go.

"So I'd have to actually sign a tenancy agreement? Bloody hell Donna. I've already got my mortgage to pay."

"You're on triple what I earn Lou. I've seen your payslips."

Really, I want to tell her to mind her own business. What I earn is nothing to do with her.

"That's not the point here. The point is about me taking on a financial obligation that isn't mine."

"But I'm your best friend." Her eyes widen like Charlie's would when imploring me for extra pocket money. "How long have you known me Lou? We're practically family. We're *sisters from another mother*, remember?"

"I suppose." She's going to sit there begging at me until I agree to this. I don't know what else I can do. Something within me gives way. I'm sure it will be fine. It's not as if she isn't working.

"And you know you can trust me," she continues.

Do I? I want to say but bite my lip. What can I trust her more with? My man or my money?

"You will then?" Her voice rises. "Help me, I mean?"

"I'm literally putting my name to it Donna. Nothing else. If you let me down with keeping the payments..."

"I won't. Thank you." She leaps from her chair around to my side of the desk. "Let me give you a hug. I knew you'd say yes."

As she lets me go, she grabs her phone from her pocket. "They've already pencilled us in for five o'clock. I'll let them know we'll *definitely* be there."

"What for?" Gosh. She really *knew* I'd say yes. She's already made the appointment. What a pushover I am.

"To sign all the forms, of course. And pay the money. The house is empty. I can move in as soon as I want." Her eyes shine as she looks at me.

"Wouldn't it make sense to wait until the start of the school holidays?"

"You know I don't do making sense." She lifts the phone to her ear. "Yes hello. It's Donna Meers speaking. I was in at lunchtime about the house – erm 17 Chestnut Grove, Farndale. I'm just ringing to confirm that my guarantor and I will be in to sign everything up at five pm, like I said... Yes... All sorted... Yes... See you soon."

"But..." I stare at her. "*Chestnut Grove? Farndale?* That's only around the corner from me."

"We'll be neighbours." She grins back at me. "It'll be awesome."

"I don't like the sound of that. *Living around the corner?*" Mum folds a tea towel into quarters. "She already leans on you far too heavily."

"I don't know how I feel about it either," I say. I'm not going to mention anything about the money or the guarantor setup. Mum will go spare. "Especially now I'm seeing Scott. I love Donna to bits you know I do. It's just..."

"I know. I can see it gets claustrophobic. It was hard enough to get her to go home the other night. And once she's living around the corner, she'll be at yours every five minutes unless you set some ground rules from the get-go."

"Oh Mum. I feel dreadful for moaning about it. I know how badly she wants to move. She's been stuck in a flat above a motorcycle shop for ages. It's just..." I need to change the subject. I'm driving myself mad with all this. "Anyway, thanks for giving Charlie her dinner. I don't know what I'd do without you." I tilt my phone towards me as it beeps.

> I'd love a night away.

Scott has replied to my earlier text to him.

> Only one??

> Are you wanting two?

> Of course!

"Mu-um."

She jerks her head towards me from where she stands at the sink. Her earrings swing from side to side with the movement. "I know that tone. What are you after?"

"What are you up to this weekend?"

She looks out of the window as if gathering her thoughts. "I'm working in the charity shop for a few hours on Saturday morning. Oh, and book club here on Friday evening. That's it as far as I know. Why?"

"I want to go away with Scott for a couple of nights."

"Do you indeed?" Mum laughs. "And you want me to have Charlotte, I take it?"

"If that's OK? She does her own thing mostly, so you'll barely know you've got her."

"I know my granddaughter love. But she'll have to come here to me, because of book club."

"That's fine." Excitement builds within me at the prospect of two uninterrupted days and nights with Scott. Even if it means I'm up till three in the morning every night in the run up to then, to keep on top of my work. I'll have some bribing to do with Charlie since I'm making her stay at her Grandma's again. Trainers it might have to be. She wouldn't have minded at all if Mum was staying at ours with her. But it would take an absolute emergency, loss of an arm or someone dropping dead for Mum to miss her book club. She always lets me know when they're talking about the sort of books I read. If I have time, I go along, though there's not a great deal of book talk after the first hour. Plenty of wine flows instead.

> I'm free for two nights. You sort the hotel. I've sorted the teenager.

He sends me a kiss emoji, then my phone beeps again.

> I've arranged a van for Sunday. It was the only day they had. Will you drive it for me?

"Bloody hell." I drop my phone onto the table.

"What's up?" Mum slides a mug in front of me, her bangles rattling on her arms with the motion.

"Donna wants me to help her move now. This Sunday."

"She's not messing about is she?" Mum sits facing me. "Doesn't she have to give notice on her flat?"

I shrug. "I've no idea. If the new house is empty, I expect she'll just want to get in there as quick as she can."

"What help does she want?"

"For me to drive the van. And to help her lug her stuff, I guess."

"Can't she drive the van herself?" It's clear from Mum's tone that she disapproves of the whole thing.

56

"Probably not. She only passed her test last year."

"But, surely on Sunday you'll still be away."

My phone bleeps.

> Answer me Lou. I need to get this sorted. I'm at the van place now.

"If we're not going too far, I'll just have to set off back early on Sunday morning, won't I?" Something dips within me as I imagine Scott's reaction. Maybe he'll be OK with it. He seems to understand that I'm Donna's *go-to* in life. There really isn't anyone else to have her back. Her mum's moved away not that they were ever close.

"So you're going to let your friend hijack your life again?" Mum frowns. I know she's right, but if I say no, Donna will just hound me.

> I've paid the deposit on the van. They were closing up. You just need to take your licence and proof of address.

I'm going away this weekend. Is there no one else you can ask?

> You know there isn't. And I need help to move stuff too. Please Lou.

I don't know when I'll be back.

> Where are you going anyway?

Just somewhere with Scott.

> Great. I'm sidelined for your bf yet again.

You're not.

> When are you going?

> Friday till Sunday.

> What time are you back on Sunday?

> I don't know.

> Well, I'll just change the booking until the afternoon then. Problem solved.

Mum's watching as I text with Donna. "I know you've been friends a long time love, but you're not responsible for her. You never have been."

"I know. But we've been through a lot together. And she's been there for me when I've been at my lowest ebb. All the stuff that went on with Darren... And the troubles I've had with Liz."

"As I'm sure Donna frequently reminds you." Mum gives me a knowing look. "And now you're going to be neighbours. You really, really need to set some boundaries love."

Something sinks further within me as the feeling that she'll be borrowing a lot more than a cup of sugar envelops me.

10

THEN

I LOITERED in the cloakroom for as long as I could.

"Haven't you got a home to go to?" The caretaker emptied a bin of paper towels into a liner.

I tried to smile at him. Look normal. "I'm going in a minute. I'm just waiting for someone."

"There's no one else here. Go on. You should be at home by now, revising for those GCSEs of yours. Not long to go now, eh." The caretaker was a friend of Mum's. No way could I tell him why I was too scared to leave the cloakroom. He'd tell her. And she was coping with enough grief after losing Dad.

I'd been sitting in the school canteen earlier getting a quick sandwich before the Science exam, on my own, as usual, when they'd plonked themselves on the table next to me. The school witches. They were the main reason I would not be staying on into the sixth form but was going to college to do my A-levels instead. They'd bullied me right through secondary school and I was nearly free of them.

Even my dad's recent death from cancer hadn't softened

them towards me, rather it made me stand out even more as I struggled from one day to the next, probably with a face like the world was about to end. I'd never felt more alone.

"What did you do for Father's Day Lucie?" One had said to another. I froze. It was obvious the conversation was for my benefit.

"We went for a meal. How about you?"

"I bought him a new wallet. He loves it."

"What did you get your dad for Father's Day Louisa?" One of them called over to me as the others laughed. Tears stung my eyes as I pretended to ignore them.

"Perhaps she bought him a coffin." Then they all started coughing loudly.

"Leave me alone," I'd shouted. "Fucking bitches."

"What did you call us?" The ringleader, Joanne, slid into the chair opposite me.

I sprang to my feet and grabbed my bag.

"After that exam finishes." She gave me a knowing look. "You'd better watch yourself. Nobody calls me a bitch and gets away with it."

"Come on," the caretaker continued. "Or do I need to chase you out with my broom? Your mum will be wondering where you are."

"She's still at work," I replied.

"Yes. I expect she'd want to get back to normal. Though how she deals with everyone else's problems all day with what she's going through..."

"See you later," I called back over my shoulder. The last thing I wanted was to get into conversation about my dad with the caretaker.

I heaved a sigh of relief at the sight of the deserted school gates and began walking towards them. Just two more exams and I'd never have to face the school witches ever again. Then, as I approached the bus shelter, one by one they emerged from behind it.

"You took your time," Joanne grinned. "Right, let's show you what happens to someone who calls us names."

I turned to run back, but they were faster than me. Several pairs of hands pulled me to the ground. I screamed out as I tried to get back up several times before being pushed back down. One of them laid the boot into my back. I yowled and curled into a ball on the ground. All I could do was pray someone would drive past and stop them.

"Get off her!" Heavy footsteps pounded towards us and a girl and boy who I'd never seen before were holding empty glass coke bottles aloft. The girl smashed hers against the fence and was left holding half of it by the neck.

"Yeah, and what ya going to do with that?"

"Go near her again and you'll find out." She held the bottle in front of her, pointing it at them. "I mean it."

As one by one, my assailants backed away, I raised my eyes to hers. Judging from her expression, she'd have had no hesitation in using the bottle as a weapon. The witches must have realised this too as within seconds, they'd scattered like seeds in the wind.

I cried in pain as the girl helped me to a sitting position whilst the boy gave chase. "And don't come near her again," he yelled after them.

"Are you OK?"

I looked past her to where a clump of my hair was drifting down the road in the breeze. I nodded. "Thanks for helping me."

"It's not a problem. I'm Donna by the way."

11

NOW

"I'll have to get this." I give Scott my most apologetic look. "It's my mum."

He lifts his arm away from where it's resting along the back of my shoulders. "At least it's not Donna this time." He shakes his head, then looks out across the lake. I'm glad he's got his sunglasses on, and I only have to imagine the look that will be in his eyes. I should have switched my phone off like I'd promised myself I would this weekend. Mum was right. I really have allowed myself to feel responsible for Donna, and it's getting worse as the years go on. Hopefully, she'll shift her focus one day and I'll get a bit of peace. I suspect it might take a man to come along and actually stay with her for me to get my life back.

"It's only me. I'm really sorry to interrupt your weekend away love. Can you talk for a few minutes?"

"Yes. I'm just on a boat in the middle of Windermere. Is Charlie alright?" I can't think of any other reason Mum would ring me whilst I'm away.

"She's fine, don't worry. It's something else." Her voice is hesitant. "Something I thought you should know about before you get back."

"What?" I glance at Scott. He really, really doesn't look happy. Although my phone has been quiet for the last couple of hours, prior to that Donna was bombarding me with texts and calls. There'd been a mix up with the van booking. Her back door key for the new house didn't work, and she'd had a row with her old landlord. What she expects me to do from where I am, I don't know, but she's always come to me with *everything*. Scott has only recently come on the scene, so I can't expect him to understand the sort of friendship she and I have. I'm not even sure that I understand it myself anymore. I still can't get my head around the fact that she's about to live a two-minute walk from me, and I really hope she won't be on my doorstep every five minutes.

"Did you leave Donna with a key?"

"Where for?"

"Where do you think? Your house."

"No."

"Do you leave a spare anywhere?"

"Only with the next door neighbour. Why? We have a key to each other's houses. For emergencies. She's always at home, so it's useful if Charlie ever locks herself out."

"Donna was in your house when I got there." Mum sounds stressed. I hope they haven't been arguing. Suddenly the tranquillity of the sunlight dancing on the lake has been lost.

"Really? Hang on. How come you were there as well? I thought Charlie was staying at your house whilst I'm away?"

"Charlotte was nagging at me to stay back at home tonight. She said she needed to be on her own computer to get her homework done. She was going on and on, and on, so I gave in."

"Yeah, right." I laugh. "More like she wants Jess round. So anyway – Donna. I'll check with my neighbour – I don't know how else she could have got a key. Really, Helen shouldn't be giving my key to *anyone* other than me or Charlie. That's what I told her."

"Well, you know how persuasive Donna can be. Anyway, she was upstairs when I got there Louisa." Her voice dips as it always does when she's imparting something salacious. "And so was some man she was *entertaining*."

"What do you mean, *entertaining*?"

Scott turns his attention from the lake to my conversation.

"You know. Surely I don't need to spell it out?"

"Did you actually catch them at it?" Bloody hell. I'm going to kill her for this.

"She reckoned to be using the bathroom when she first saw me, but I knew she was lying. It was written all over her face."

"She shouldn't have been in my house in the first place."

"I know that. Then a man came down the stairs."

"Who was it?"

"I've no idea. Does it matter? Anyway, he just left, through the front door, plain as day, right under my nose. I saw him with my own eyes."

"Alright Mum. I get the picture."

Her voice rises some more. "He even had the cheek to say hello to me Louisa. I'll admit it was one of those rare occasions when I couldn't speak."

Normally a comment like this would amuse me. "Wait till I see her. How dare she bring some man into our home? What did she have to say for herself?"

The passengers in front turn around, making no attempt to disguise the fact they're eavesdropping. I suppose I am speaking loudly and it's quite a meaty conversation. I look down, studying the nails I've had painted cerise at the salon, especially for this weekend.

"She says he's a friend. One with benefits, by the looks of it. Did you close your bedroom blind before you left yesterday?"

"No."

"Well, it was closed when we pulled up outside. You definitely need to speak to her."

I attempt to lower my voice along with my gaze. "Too right. Did Charlie see it all as well? The man coming down our stairs?"

"I'm afraid so. Some example she's being set. I don't know why you ever chose her to be Charlotte's godmother. I've said to you time and time again that you should limit Charlotte being around her."

"I'll speak to her when I get home. And Donna, obviously. I'll get to the bottom of it."

Great. I've got that to look forward to now. And if she thinks I'm helping her move after this, she can think again.

"I just thought I should let you know."

"I appreciate it. Thanks Mum."

Scott's pulling a face as I drop my phone back into my bag. "I gather your friend has been making the most of your absence."

"You could say that. I'm going to kill her." If only Scott would put his arm back around me. I'm eighty miles away from Donna, and she's still interfering with my weekend.

Her battered Polo is outside my house as Scott pulls up behind it. She's got some nerve being here after how she's behaved. I wonder if she even knows that Mum's been in touch with me.

"Do you want me to come in with you?" *I wish,* I think to myself. What I'd give for the rest of my Sunday to be spent leisurely with Scott. I've got a right week coming up at work with all the assessments to get finished ready to pass on to their year one teacher.

"No. I need to speak to her on my own, I think."

"Are you still going to help her move? I'd offer to help Lou, but I can't lie – I'm not overly keen on her."

"Neither am I right now." Despite how stressed I feel, I laugh. "I don't know about the move. I guess I'll see what she has to say for herself first."

What I don't tell him is how I'm already signed up as the guarantor for a six-month tenancy and I've transferred five hundred pounds to her for the deposit. He'd think I'm barmy. Which, of course, I am. After I've done this, I'm going to pull back from her. It's time, and as Mum's told me before, I'm probably not doing Donna any favours in the long term by always giving in to her.

"Thanks for a lovely weekend." He cups his hand over mine. "Apart from the barrage of phone calls. You should talk to her about that as well. I'd like you all to myself from time to time."

"I know. I'm sorry."

"Stop saying sorry. Really. It's your friend who should be apologising. And don't be putting up with any crap from her when you go in there."

To say he's only known me a matter of months and has only met Donna once, he's incredibly informed about our friendship. And me.

"Where's my mum?"

Donna sits at my kitchen table with her hands wrapped around a mug. Her face is bare of makeup and she's wearing the jumper Mum bought me last Christmas. Mum will have noticed that, too. And will not be happy.

"She's gone. She said you were on your way back and that she needed to get to the supermarket."

"And Charlie? Where's she?" I face Donna across the table.

"At the park with a couple of her friends. Your mum made her take her phone, don't worry."

"Right. Well, I'm actually glad it's just us." I'm strangely calm to say I'm about to confront her for having sex with some random man in my bed. I once caught her with someone on Mum's lounge carpet when we were nineteen, but at least that was only on the carpet, rather than one of our beds. I could never have sex in someone else's bed. Evidently Donna can. "Apparently you've had some man in my house? *Had*, being the operative word."

She doesn't flinch. She was probably expecting this. "I take it your mum told you? After she'd thrown me out of here. I still can't believe she did that. Right in front of Charlie as well."

"I'd have thrown you out if I'd caught you. What were you playing at?"

She hangs her head and her hair covers her face like a blonde curtain. "I'm sorry."

"You had no right bringing *anyone* round here without asking me." My voice echoes around the kitchen. "Who was he anyway?"

"It was Jason. So it wasn't just *anyone*. It's not as though you don't know him." She sips from her cup.

"The *Jason* you dumped? *After* you broke up his marriage?"

"It's not *me* who did anything wrong. I wasn't the one who was unfaithful to someone." She cocks her head to one side, almost defiantly. "He was. He's the one who was married, not me!"

"I thought he'd gone back to her anyway?" I rise from my seat to fill a glass of water. It's a wonder I'm not pouring the wine.

"He has." Still, there's no emotion from her. No sign of regret. I can't look at her right now.

"You didn't want him when he risked *everything* for you." I bang my glass down onto the draining board, "but now he's

67

returned to his family, you've reeled him back in. What's wrong with you?" I turn towards her.

"I just wanted to feel better." Tears fill her eyes. I don't feel any sympathy this time. "After how Owen treated me. I've a right to be happy too."

"Oh, for God's sake." I'm almost shouting, but I don't care. "You had no right having sex with someone in my house. How did you even get in here?"

She points to the left. "Helen next door. I had a coffee with her and asked her for the key. Then I messaged Jason."

"I didn't realise you even knew her. And how do you know she has a key?"

"You've mentioned it before. Or Charlie has – I can't remember. I was at the new house and she walked past with her dog. We just got talking."

I can't help but feel uncomfortable. Not only is she muscling in on the place where I live but also having cosy cuppas with my neighbours? Especially nosy next door neighbour Helen!

Or am I being unreasonable here? Donna's entitled to live where she wants and talk to whoever she wants, after all. But she's not entitled to bring married men into my house for sex when I'm away.

"I'm sorry." She drops her head into her hands. "I really am. I was selfish and stupid. The only reason I invited him here was because I was feeling so crappy about myself. It was a moment of madness."

"So you actually...?" I look at her. "Mum wasn't sure at what point she'd interrupted you."

She raises her head, saying nothing.

"In my bed?"

A flush is rising up her neck. "On it. Not in it. Not for long though. Your mum and Charlie turned up, didn't they?"

"Why *my* house though? That's what I don't understand. Why not your new one?"

She shrugs. "I don't know."

I let a long sigh out. "I'm well pissed off with you. I really am."

She stares at her hands, clasped in front of her on the table. "You've every right to be. I'll make it up to you, I promise."

"Where's my key?"

"Your mum took it off me. You'll have to ask her for it. Look Lou. Please forgive me. You know I can't stand it when we fall out."

"You mean there's a van you want me to drive this afternoon?"

"There is that." She tilts her wrist towards her face. "The place shuts at four. I really wanted to get into the house today. Especially after the do with the landlord. He reckons I'm not giving enough notice and says he'll sue me for three months' rent."

I'm not even going there with that conversation. She can sort it out herself.

"Have you packed everything?" I'm going to have to do it. Much as I can hardly bear to look at her right now, she'll give me hell if I try to back out.

"Yeah. I'm moving from one furnished place to another, so it wasn't too much of a job."

"Why the van then?"

"You know, there's my bike, and my computer desk, oh and my dishwasher. There isn't one in the new house. Plus, it means I can do the move in one go rather than umpteen ten mile trips. I don't even know if my car would make it at the moment."

I sigh again. "We'd better get on with it I suppose."

"Thanks Lou. I'm so lucky to have a friend like you."

Everything is always about Donna. She hasn't even asked me if I had a good time this weekend.

12

THEN

"The only alcohol I could find in the house is my mum's wine." I pushed the door open with my elbow, balancing glasses and the bottle as I went in. "Oh. Shit. Sorry."

Donna and the lad from the club were spreadeagled on the carpet. I stepped back into the hallway and allowed the door to close again. Mum would have an absolute fit if she knew lads were even in the house whilst she was away, let alone one getting to grips with my friend on her lounge carpet.

Then I heard retching coming from upstairs. "What the hell are you doing up there?"

"I'm sorry," he called back. "I've had one too many."

I took the stairs two at a time and started banging on the bathroom door. "You'd better be hitting the toilet. Look, you'll have to go. Where do you live?"

I paced the landing until his next round of retching had passed, trying to ignore the moaning noises emanating from the lounge. Some night out it had turned into.

"I can walk it from here," he eventually said.

"Well, get on your way then. And take your bloody mate with you."

"I don't think I'll be able to tear the two of them apart." He finally emerged from the bathroom looking like a ghost. "They were snogging each other's faces off before. His girlfriend will be gutted."

"They've gone further than snogging now." I follow him down the stairs. "I've just walked in on them."

"Luke!" The lad hammered on the lounge door. "I'm not going in there if they're..."

"Just a minute."

"Never mind just a minute." I hammered on the door then. "I want you out. Both of you. All of you."

After a few more minutes and a bit of scuffling and belt rattling, they emerged from the lounge. Him shamefaced, her looking gleeful.

"Get out. I mean it."

"We're off. I'm going to..."

"Get him out of here. And you..." I turned to Donna. "I'll ring you a taxi. I can't look at you right now."

"Lighten up Lou." Then she smiled. "You're only jealous."

13

NOW

"At least we can share a taxi home tonight." Donna sips her wine. "Now that we're practically neighbours."

"This is true." What she means is that she'll get in the taxi I'm paying for. She doesn't even attempt to get her purse out anymore. I suppose it's my fault. I allowed this when we were younger. Anything to shut up her claims that I was *born with a silver spoon in my gob.*

"Are you seeing Scott this weekend?" I'm certain something darkens in her face.

"Tomorrow. He's on a work's do tonight." I'd love to talk more about him to her, but it only winds her up.

"So *that's* why I've got you to come out with me." She nudges my arm and smiles. "Don't worry. I don't mind being second best. At least you've forgiven me for last weekend."

"Let's not go there." I'm still fuming every time I think about it.

"I really am sorry. Which is why tonight is on me." She whips her purse out and waves it in the air. "I'm so lucky to have you, and I never want you to forget that."

My eyes must widen. "Don't look so shocked. I've been paid, so I'm flush for a weekend."

"Sorry. I didn't mean..."

We sit in silence for a few moments. I fiddle with a beer mat. She watches the bar. Hunting for her prey, no doubt.

"We've been friends for a long time, haven't we?" She nudges me again.

"That means we must be doing something right, I suppose." I smile at her now, softening for the first time in a while. As well as I know her faults, I also know her good side. In fact, we know each other inside out.

"Cheers." She raises her glass. "To us. Me and you. I hope you'll always be my friend."

"Of course." I clink glasses with her. It's as though she's somehow sensed my distance towards her lately. But after the bullying I suffered throughout my schooldays, I do value the friends I have now, even Donna. We've weathered so much together over the years. Without her, I'd have fallen to bits at times. Like the time Darren disappeared at Christmas when Charlie was a toddler. Then there was the time he left me for good. Donna was a rock to me on both occasions. And many others besides.

"Don't tell me. You're sisters." A man plonks himself on the seat facing us. It's on the tip of my tongue to tell him that we're just having a quiet night, but she'd probably kill me.

"What if we are?" Donna looks delighted at this sudden appearance at our table. I suppose it should flatter me at being 'accused' of looking like her. But sisters? Although she's recently had her hair cut to the same length as mine, *and* had it highlighted in the same way, at *my* hairdressers, no less. And we're wearing similar clothes tonight. Denim skirts and sleeveless blouses, although in different colours and slightly different styles. It's as though she knew what I'd laid out to wear on my bed in advance. I shuffle in my seat, feeling uncomfortable as I consider this. Imitation is supposed to be flattery, so they say. But I don't like it. And she doesn't need to imitate me. She's gorgeous enough just as she is.

"Who's the oldest then?" He continues, beckoning towards his friend who's watching us from the bar. The man now sitting opposite tilts his head to one side as he studies Donna. There's something about him I don't like. He's too cocky. Too sure of himself.

"Guess." She sits up straighter in her seat and smiles, evidently pleased at instigating this game.

"I wouldn't want to offend either of you." He sweeps his gaze from her back to me. "But if I were to guess who was the oldest, I'd say you." He points at me. He's rough and ready looking, but well spoken enough. Definitely Donna's type. And he seems to fancy her.

"Correct." She clasps her hands together. "Only just though."

"Cheers," I say. "Though I'm the one who's a mum. So if I look haggard, blame my teenager."

"You've got a teenager." His eyes widen in mock surprise. "Never." He slaps the palm of his hand on the table. They look like builder's hands. He must be a tradesman, but I'm not going to ask him what he does. I don't want to show too much interest. Besides, Donna clearly has her eye on him. I only hope his mate doesn't get any ideas about me.

"It's too late now," I force a laugh. "You can't undo how hurt you've made me feel. Saying I'm the oldest."

"Perhaps I can buy you both a drink?" He pulls a wad of notes from the top pocket of his shirt. "To say I'm sorry." He's definitely dodgy. Who carries a wad of notes these days?

"Mine's a red wine." Donna nudges her glass towards him. "And she's on white."

"Back in a moment." He rises from the chair and strides towards his mate at the bar.

"Tonight's looking up after all." Donna drains the last of her wine. "But why did you have to tell them you've got a kid? Much as I love Charlie, that is."

"Because I have. My daughter's not some secret I hide from people."

"It's not exactly a great chat up line though, is it? *If I look haggard, blame my teenager.*"

"I'm not trying to chat anyone up though, am I? I've got Scott." His face creeps into my mind. It would break my heart if he was out there tonight, chatting someone up. I'm not sure how he'd feel about this situation here either.

"Can't you forget about Scott? Just for one night?" She frowns. "You've not been together for that long anyway. It's not as if you're serious."

"We're more *serious* than you think, actually. I really like him. We've even talked about buying somewhere together. Eventually."

"Really? You never said anything!"

"When we were away. He said he'd love to wake up with me every day." I smile at the memory.

"Great. I move in round the corner and you move away."

"We were only *talking* about it."

"Don't go mentioning Scott in front of these two. For my sake, if nothing else." She glances towards them.

"Why?"

"You'll put them off if they think only one of us is up for it." They *both* seem interested by the way they keep looking over.

"Up for what, exactly?"

"Oh Lou. Like I keep saying, you've got sooooo boring since you met Scott." She rolls her eyes again. "You need to loosen up a bit."

· · ·

"I'm Ash and this is Gavin." They sit facing us, Ash facing Donna, Gavin facing me. "And you are..?'

"Donna and Lou." She points from herself to me, beaming. "Good to meet you both."

"Cheers for the drinks." Personally, I'm not happy about accepting drinks from these men, but she would have killed me if I'd refused. In my experience, when they've bought you a drink, it's like you owe them something.

"So, what brings the two of you out tonight?" Gavin speaks for the first time as he looks around. "It's dead in here for a Friday, isn't it?"

"Do we need a reason?" I reply. "And we came in *because* it's quiet. We can actually hear each other speak." If that sounds hostile, I don't care.

"New house celebration," Donna says, nudging me.

"Together?" Ash arches an eyebrow, looking somewhere between curious and excited.

"No. Donna's moved around the corner from me." I glance up at the clock behind the bar, wondering how soon I'm going to bugger off from here.

"Whereabouts is that then?"

"Farndale. It's just off..."

"I know exactly where it is." Gavin laughs now. "A place where the cash machines only churn out twenties."

Ash laughs at this. "You must both have good jobs then." It sounds more like a question than a statement.

"We're both teachers." Donna takes a mouthful of wine.

"Really?" Ash pulls a face that shows he's impressed. "Well, you can put me in detention anytime." He winks at her.

"Easy!" Donna laughs as she strokes the stem of her wine glass up and down. It reminds me of the evening she turned up at mine for dinner when Scott was there and my hackles rise at the memory.

"I'm a foundation stage manager at a primary school," she continues.

Why is she lying? She's pretending she does my job. Why does she feel as though she needs to lie?

"What's one of those?" Gavin wipes his beer moustache away as he swigs from his pint. He's slightly overweight and looks as shifty as his sidekick. Mum's always told me to trust my hunches with men.

"Young ones. Nursery and reception class."

"Sounds like hard work to me. I've never understood anyone who works with kids or animals." Ash is watching her intently. "It's what my sister does too. I'll have to introduce you sometime."

"Sounds lovely." She beams at him. Blimey, they've only just met and they're talking about meeting family. Still, if he's talking about his sister being a teacher, maybe he isn't so suspect after all.

"Tell me the difference between kids and animals," he continues.

"I wouldn't know." She laughs. It's high-pitched, the laugh she always reserves for men.

"Do you enjoy it then?"

Bloody hell. If there's one thing I hate more than anything, it's small talk. I shuffle on the wooden stool. All I want to do is go home.

"Well, I must be good at what I do. Teachers from other schools come to watch me at work."

"And how about you?" He nods at me. "Are you at the same school, as well as the same street?"

"Erm no." I glance at her. There's nothing wrong with the job she does. I can't help but feel irked that she's passing off what I do for herself. After all, it took me years of study and training to get to where I am. She could do it if she really wanted to.

"And you're not married either." Ash is peering at her left hand.

"Free as a bird," she replies, beaming.

This is my chance to put them straight, despite Donna's warning.

"I'm divorced," I begin, even though no one has actually asked me. Men are always interested in Donna before me, not that I'm bothered. They only ever get interested in me when they take the time to talk to me. Not that many of them ever have done. "But I have a boyfriend now."

I sense her stiffen beside me. I don't care. She's got no right expecting me to lie about Scott. I won't ever tell him this. He wouldn't be very happy, and who could blame him?

"Ash is coming home with me." Donna sidles up beside me at the mirror.

"But you've only just met him."

"Stop acting like my mum." She plucks a lipstick from her clutch bag and looks happier than I've seen her in a long time. "I'm single. He's single. I've no responsibilities. Unlike you. Why shouldn't I have a bit of fun?"

"Is he *definitely* single though?"

"You heard him."

"I'd check that out before you go home with him. Find out his surname and have a look online. He could be married with three kids and a dog. No matter what he was saying."

"Like I said..." Donna smooths the lipstick onto her mouth. "You've got boring. His mate doesn't look too happy, does he? Since you blurted out about *having a boyfriend*."

"He looks fine to me."

"I can't believe you won't have a bit of fun. Just for one night. Let your hair down."

"I'm hoping Scott might be at mine when I get back. Charlie's on a sleepover at her friend's."

"Oh. Scott. I should have bloody known."

"What does he do anyway?" She always sulks when I mention Scott, so I'm changing the subject, even if I sound like my mother with the question I'm asking. "Ash?"

"He just said *this and that,* whatever that's supposed to mean."

"Sounds shifty to me. He looks shifty as well."

"Well, you'll get the chance to quiz him more thoroughly in the taxi, won't you? Perhaps he'll pay for it out of that massive wad of notes he's got on him."

"What are you doing Lou?" Scott calls down the stairs.

"Nothing. Just getting some water." I've drunk far more than I intended to, but at least the next week at school is an easy week. I've no more planning or assessments to do, just sorting and organising. Other than Christmas, the final week of the summer term is a time of year when we can *entertain* the kids, rather than *teaching* them.

My attention is drawn to my phone on the kitchen counter as it lights up. There are no prizes for guessing who could be texting me at nearly three in the morning. I need to check though, just in case it's Charlie.

"Bring me a glass up, will you?" Scott calls.

"Will do." I scroll through my messages, glad I had the foresight when I got this phone to disable the *message has been read* feature. Judging by the tone of these messages, Donna would be on the phone to me quicker than she accepted Ash's invitation to *see her home,* if she knew I was still awake. I could tell Scott wasn't happy when I told him I'd shared a taxi with her and Ash, but he'd have been even less happy if Ash hadn't parted company with his mate first.

> Are you up?

Then...

> I hope I haven't made a mistake. Ash has gone home. He said he had an early start.

> Oh Lou, what have I done? He says he'll ring me tomorrow, but what if he doesn't?

> Lou are you there? Text me back!

> Did Scott turn up? If not, can I come round?

If I was going to reply, which I'm not, I'd say, *no, you bloody can't. It's the middle of the night!*

"I might have known." Scott strides into the kitchen in his boxer shorts and his hair on end. "I take it you're looking at texts from Donna?"

I nod but push the phone away. He's got every right to have a face on.

He stands beside me at the breakfast bar. "Is everything alright?"

I nod. "Just man stuff. Again. I'll ring her tomorrow."

"You know we were talking about moving in together at some point?" He strokes his beard as he leans onto the kitchen counter.

"Yes?" I don't like the edge to his voice.

"I don't know if I could cope with your mate like *this* all the time. How do you put up with it?"

I stiffen. "Did you hear that? There's someone at the door."

He nods and sighs. "Don't tell me that's her. *At this time of night? Really?*"

"Flick the light off," I hiss. "Quick. If she thinks I'm up..."

He doesn't move. "Are you going to ignore it? Surely you're not going to hide in your own house."

"I'm not answering the door at this time of night." I stride over to the light switch.

"What if it's not her? What if it's..."

The garden gate creaks. "She's coming around the back." I dart towards him and grab at his arm. "Come on, let's go back upstairs. Quick!"

"I've a good mind to go out there and find out what she's playing at." Even in the faint light, Scott looks to be clenching his jaw.

"Dressed like that?" My gaze roams from his pecs down to his thighs. "Yeah. She'd love that. Come on." I tug at his arm harder as she appears on the patio, her face ghostly white in the security light which has flickered on. I dart to the door, back into the hallway, and luckily Scott follows me. Hopefully, the security light will have dazzled her enough that she won't have seen us hiding in the shadows of my kitchen.

14

THEN

"I'M JUST RINGING to say Happy Christmas."

I'd got to the phone before the second ring, praying with every fibre of my being that it would be Darren. It wasn't.

"It's anything but happy," I'd wept. "Darren hasn't been home all night. He went to the shop straight after dinner, saying he wouldn't be long, and that was the last I saw of him."

Donna fell silent for a moment. "Do you want me to come round?"

"No. It's alright. I'm fine. There's nothing you can do unless you've got a magic wand. I've tried all the local hospitals and the police." For the millionth time that day, I glanced toward the window. "I just hope he's not lying in a ditch somewhere. What other reason could there be for him to dump his wife and three-year-old on Christmas Day?"

"Oh Lou. You poor thing. Where's your mum?"

"I can't tell my bloody mum. She'll string him up. Her opinion of him is low enough as it is." At least Charlie was too young to know what was going on. I sat beside where she was sleeping on the sofa and ran my hand over her hair. She deserved better than this.

"You're lucky to have her, you know. My mum doesn't give a shit."

"Yeah, but she'd want to know why I haven't kept her in the picture all along. She's got no idea about the problems we've been having since Charlie was born."

"It's a good job you've got me to talk to," she said. "I'm always here for you."

Fresh tears swelled in my eyes. "Look. You get back to whatever you were doing. I'll be fine. Honestly."

"I'll be round shortly," she said.

"No Donna. It's OK. I don't want to spoil your day. Aren't you with your mum?" Though I guessed she couldn't have been, given what she'd just said about her.

"My day would be more spoiled by thinking of you and Charlie on your own, like this. I'll bring beer. My mum's just set off for a shift at the hospital anyway."

And she had brought beer. Lots of it. Then she'd taken care of Charlie when I fell into a drunken stupor on the sofa. She'd also dealt with Darren when he finally turned up later on that Christmas night. He'd been depressed, he'd apparently told her. He didn't want to come home to the atmosphere that had become the norm between me and him. It was the first Christmas after his dad had died and he wanted to spend it alone. To take stock of his life. Whilst he left his wife ringing around hospitals, worrying about him.

I was annoyed with Donna at first for not waking me. But I mellowed when she said my Christmas had been ruined enough without having a confrontation with Darren. Plus, it wouldn't be good for Charlie. Her heart had been in the right place.

15

NOW

"Why haven't you been replying to me?" Donna looks hurt as she faces me across my doorway. "I've been texting. I've been ringing. I even came round."

"And what time was that?" I fold my arms across my dressing gown, knowing perfectly well what time it had been. A vision of her ghostly face in the darkness fills my mind.

"Oh, it was late. But I thought it would be OK. After all, we're always there for each other, aren't we?"

"Scott stayed over."

"You never said for certain whether Scott would be here. Besides, when do we let a man get in the way of our friendship?"

"What was it that was so urgent you wanted me at *three in the morning?*" I widen the door to her, and she brushes past me.

"Oh. It's all sorted now." She peers into the lounge. "Is Scott here? Is he still in bed?" I don't like the eagerness in her voice. I don't like it one bit.

"He's gone home," I reply. "He had something to do... but he's coming back later." I add the last part quickly before she tries to make any arrangements with me. "We're going to play a game and get a takeaway with Charlie if she's up for it."

"A *game?*" Donna pulls a face. "I can't imagine that would be Charlie's cup of tea. Anyway, I thought she was going to her dad's tonight?"

"He's cancelled her staying over. Again." Fury rises in me once again as I remember our previous phone call. Where I could hear Liz chelping in the background. "He's just picking her up for a couple of hours and taking her out for dinner instead."

"He's *always* cancelling her staying at his house. What's up this time?"

"Tell me about it. I need to cheer her up. Stupid bloody man. He came out with some crap about Liz not being well. She sounded OK to me though, effing and jeffing behind him."

I glance at Charlie's school photo on the mantelpiece. She's the image of her dad, from the slant of her eyes to the blonde hair. "I don't really want her around that woman anyway. She's not daft and knows how jealous Liz is about her. And me." Donna follows me into the kitchen. "I'll put the kettle on. When I talk about the two of them, I get angry."

"I'd normally have taken Charlie for you," Donna begins. "She'd have loved a girly night in with me. It could have been the three of us if *Scott* wasn't coming here."

"I sense a *but* coming," I laugh. "I can see it in your face. Involving Ash, by any chance?" I might not be all that keen on him, but at least she seems happy.

"He rang me first thing." Donna says, as she passes the mugs.

"Right."

"He said he was sorry for rushing off after we'd, you know, but that he'd had some urgent business to take care of."

"At three in the morning? Did he say what it was?" I fill the kettle.

"No. I'm still none the wiser. But he's got wads of money, as you could see last night, and he's got a flat in Harrogate, so he must do alright for himself. And he doesn't *seem* married, or anything."

A picture of him emerges in my mind. The grin. The swagger. He was charming enough I suppose, but I can't get away from the hunch that there was something dubious about him. "Just be careful."

"When are you going to be happy for me? You always see the worst in things. In *people*." She pulls a chair from beneath the table and sinks onto it. She looks rough this morning. After they got back to her house, she probably carried on drinking. If I know her correctly.

"Your track record isn't exactly shining with happy results, is it? But I *am* happy for you. Of course I am." I spoon coffee into the cafetière. I always love the smell of fresh coffee. Especially at the weekend. "So long as he treats you well. I'm glad he's phoned you anyway. You must feel better."

"I'm glad too. I couldn't sleep after he left."

"Clearly." I think back to her face in the security light. It's an image that's imprinted on my mind.

"He's promised me he's single. And he's invited me for a meal at his flat tonight so at least I'll get to suss him out. He wouldn't have done that if he was married. Or widowed." She adds, and her eyes cloud over.

"He's invited you to his flat?" I turn from stirring the coffee to look at her.

She nods. "See. He can't be that dodgy, can he?"

"Look Donna, you'll shoot me down in flames for saying this, but I really think it's too soon for you to be going back to his flat. You hardly know the man."

She grins coyly and tucks a stray hair behind her ear. "I got to know him very well last night, actually."

"So it would seem. I take it you like him then?" I slide a cup of coffee towards her.

"Thanks. Of course I do. I was upset when he left in the night. I felt really used."

"I bet you did." I avoid her eyes. She hates it when I lecture her, as she perceives it. "That's why I keep telling you, you shouldn't play your best card this early on. You only met him last night."

"Oh, here we go. You're my friend, not my bloody mother Lou." A flash of anger crosses her face. "And saying all this doesn't explain why you ignored the door to me last night."

"I was asleep."

But she gives me a knowing look. If she knows I'm lying, she says nothing.

"Mum, will *you* try ringing my dad? He's not answering to me." Charlie sits in our bay window, she's not moved from there for the last fifty minutes. She's squeezed herself into the jeans Darren bought her a year ago and she's wearing a green t-shirt because it's his favourite colour.

Something sinks within me. He'd better not be standing her up. Again. This has gone on for years. It's me that has to watch as she waits for him, the despondency growing as the minutes tick by. Yet I feel guilty, as though I'm the one putting her through this time and time again. They make people fill out questionnaires and provide references to have a dog, yet anyone can become a parent.

I raise the phone to my ear, deliberating whether to speak to him in front of her or take the call into the garden. That's if he even answers. Just as I'm poised to leave a message, he does. There's a long pause before he speaks. Wherever he is, is in silence. I wonder if *she's* listening in. *Liz the lizard,* as Charlie calls her. She's not the woman he initially left me for, but she's still threatened by my very existence. Given half a chance, she'd probably rip my eyes out.

"Yes?" He says, irritating me with the sarcasm he loads into one mere word.

"What do you mean, *yes?* You were supposed to be here nearly an hour ago. Charlie's waiting for you."

"I've already told her. Liz isn't well."

"You were taking her out for tea. I heard her on the phone to you with my own ears. Nothing to do with *Liz.*" I can't help but load as much sarcasm as he does, into the word *Liz.*

"I'm sorry, but I actually can't drive right now."

"Why not?" Although I already know the answer. It's clear in the slur of his words.

"I've had a few pints, that's all. Me and Liz had a fallout."

"That figures. Because you were supposed to be seeing Charlie? Look Darren, what's her bloody problem?" I uncurl my legs from under me and jump to my feet as though I can oppose him better whilst standing. "I've had just about enough of it. Is she there? I want to speak to her."

"No! Mum!" I look at Charlie's stricken face. I shouldn't be having this conversation in front of her. I stride towards the door.

"You're not speaking to Liz," Darren replies. "No way. You'll just make things worse."

"For who? What could be worse than a thirteen-year-old girl staring out of the window for an hour, waiting for a dad who doesn't give a shit about her?" I'm at the patio doors, just about out of Charlie's earshot, I hope.

"I do give a shit. Of course I do. It's just... Look, I'm not getting into it all with you."

"You've afforded a few pints though. But you can't even stump up some maintenance for your daughter? You're an absolute waste of space."

"Don't start all that again. I've already told you that paying towards the roof over my head is my priority. I've got to look after *myself* first."

"According to Liz, you mean."

"Well, if you hadn't thrown me out... That was my house too..."

"How the hell have we got around to this? I'm ringing to ask you why you haven't arrived to collect your daughter like you promised!"

I suddenly get a sense I'm being watched. Helen from next door, is standing by her open window. She slams it shut as I wave. My voice was on the loud side, I suppose.

"Look, just tell her I'm sorry, will you?"

"*Sorry* isn't good enough." I rub at the side of my head. I feel so stressed with it all today. "You don't even have the decency to let her know yourself. I can't stand by and let you treat her like this."

"Look I will not sit here and listen whilst you tear me down some more. I've got enough on my plate right now." And with that, the line goes dead. For a moment, all rationality nearly goes out of the window, and I feel like hurling the phone against a wall. I hate it when people hang up on me. Especially my ex-husband.

But one of us has to be a parent out of the two of us. I gather myself together and head back to the lounge where Charlie's still slumped by the window.

"I'm really sorry love."

"Why isn't he coming? Is it because of *her* again?"

"Something like that." It's easier for her to blame her dad's wife, rather than *him*.

"Has she stopped him from coming? She doesn't have to have anything to do with me. I hate her, Mum. She's so nasty."

"I know. I know. *What goes around comes around love.*"

"What's that supposed to mean?"

"It means that if you mistreat people, one day it comes back to haunt you."

"Well, I hope I'm around to see it." Charlie brings her skinny knees in to her chest and rests her chin on them, a mournful expression on her face. It breaks my heart to see it.

"Look love, we'll have a lovely night, no matter what. Like we talked about before."

"But I don't want Scott to come round," she wails. "I want Donna to come instead."

"She's going out tonight." *Thank goodness.* If she hadn't been, and Charlie had contacted her, she'd have been around here like a shot. Scott or no Scott.

"No one cares about me." Charlie lets go of her legs, rises from her seat and stamps from the room.

I sigh, deliberating whether I should cancel Scott. But I don't want to. And Charlie will probably sulk in her room all night no matter what I do. Bloody Darren. He was crap when she was little and he's even worse now. I don't care what ultimatums and pressure Liz imposes – he should have more of a backbone. I can't understand why he'd even want to be with someone who's so opposed to his daughter. Let the woman have an issue with me if she wants, but not Charlie.

As I blow dry my hair to prepare for Scott's arrival, a photograph flashes up on my phone screen. As I go to pick it up, at first I'm puzzled at why anyone would send *me* a picture of *me.*

Except it's not.

Donna's wearing a dress *identical* to the one I bought last week. No wonder she asked me where I'd got it from. *But how the hell has she afforded it?* It was triple what I'd usually pay for a dress. And with her hair styled exactly the same as mine, it's little wonder those men in the pub thought we were sisters last night.

> How do I look?

Like me, I resist the urge to reply. But I will not comment on her appearance.

> Have a good night.

I say instead. I should use the word *fab* or ace, but I can't bring myself to. And deep down, I suspect Ash is going to be far from Donna's happy ever after – I can tell just by looking at him. And as always, she'll come running to me when it all falls apart. For now, I'll just make the most of the respite when she's with him.

16

THEN

"CAN I STAY WITH YOU?" I clutched Charlie's hand as we stood with our rucksacks on Donna's doorstep.

"Course you can. You'll have to bunk down in the lounge though."

"I've brought some sleeping bags," I said, before dissolving into tears in Donna's arms. I couldn't believe what things had finally come to.

"Come on. Let's get Charlie settled, then you can tell me everything. I'll put some cartoons on for her. You'd like that Charlie, wouldn't you?"

I ruffled her hair and watched as she bounded after Donna. Thankfully she seemed reasonably unscathed by the altercation that had taken place between me and her dad. She'd been hearing far too much of that. The neighbours probably had as well.

"I've given him a week to get out of the house. Along with his stuff." I tore a piece of kitchen roll as I watched Donna pluck a bottle of wine from the fridge. "But I shouldn't need to stay here that long. I think he knows I mean it this time."

"You can stay here as long as you need to." She plonked two glasses on the table from out of the cupboard. "I'm glad of the company too."

"Well, I can't go to Mum's, can I? She'd be round there, giving him what for. It would only make things worse." I dabbed at my eyes. "I'll tell her what's happened in my own time. When he's gone."

"What's actually happened?" She glanced through the window as though watching for someone.

"Oh everything. He won't hold a job down for five minutes. We're arguing all the time. He leaves everything to do with Charlie to me and..."

"What?"

"I think he's seeing someone." As I said it out loud for the first time, it suddenly became more real.

She glugged wine into the glasses. "What makes you think that?" Her voice was flat and calm. I was almost disappointed.

"Just the way he's acting. Distant. Cagey. And I found an earring that wasn't mine behind the bed the other day."

"You're joking!" Her voice rose then. "What did he say about it?"

"That it must have been there from before we moved in. It was wedged between the carpet and the skirting board, so I don't know what to think."

She pulled a face which seems to say, 'as if.' "I've said all along that you'd be better off without him. You'll never be on your own. You've always got me."

"I never wanted to be a single mum. And who else is going to want me with a three-year-old and enough baggage to sink a boat?"

"You won't have to look after her on your own. Remember who's her godmother."

She was right. I had her. And Mum.

"First things first. We have to get him out of your house."

I started to relax, a combination of the wine dulling my senses and the fact that I could finally talk about it all.

17

NOW

"Talk about doing the walk of shame." I laugh at Donna as she steps into the hallway. "I take it you lasted the whole night together this time?"

She grins. "Yeah. I left his place an hour ago. I thought I'd have a coffee with you before I go home and back to bed."

"You didn't get much sleep last night then?"

"Erm. Nope." She follows me into the lounge and flops onto the sofa. "He's gorgeous. I'm so happy." She hugs a cushion to her chest.

"I'm glad. It's nice to see. Just take it steady, yeah?"

"What do you mean?"

"You know what I mean. You have the tendency to steam in when you first meet someone. Just take your time. Enjoy it for what it is."

"Yeah. Yeah."

I pour us both a coffee and head back to the lounge, preparing myself to get chapter and verse of everything he's said to her and how she knows this time that this is the one. Being a mother, and a teacher, it's a good job I'm well practiced in feigning more interest than I'm actually feeling, and saying yes in all the right places.

I doubt she'll ask about how my evening went – she rarely does. I'm not sure if it's because she's not interested or whether she's just too wrapped up in her own stuff. I'd like to talk about the fact that I could barely coax Charlie out of her room last night after Darren let her down, but Mum's probably the best person to speak to about that.

"You haven't noticed something."

"What?" My gaze instinctively travels to her ring finger. *Surely not!*

"No, not that, ya daft sod." She tilts her head towards the window.

I glance at it, wondering what she could be talking about.

"Look outside."

"Where am I looking?" Then I see what she's getting at.

"What I want to know," I gesture towards the car parked behind mine, "is how the hell have you paid for that?"

"Finance." She grins, either not noticing or ignoring my abrupt tone. "Lovely, isn't it?"

"It's exactly the same as mine! Why on earth would you want to get a car the same as mine?" This copy-catting thing is making me uncomfortable. That's if it is that. Maybe I'm just being paranoid.

"Actually, my car's older than yours. I don't think it's got bluetooth in it either."

"But it's a Mini, for goodness' sake. And it's nearly the same colour." I stare at it. We're going to look like right idiots if we go somewhere and arrive separately in our cars. They look bad enough parked out on the street like they are now.

"It was such a good deal." She shrugs. "I couldn't say no. I didn't even think about it being the same colour as yours. Come and look at it anyway." She grabs the keys from the coffee table.

I trudge after her out of the house and up the driveway.

"Did you not have to put a deposit down?"

"Well, yes," she says slowly, and I know what's coming. "I've had to borrow from my rent money. When I get paid, I'll put it back. I needed a car. Mine was on its last legs. Well, wheels." She laughs.

I don't. "Donna. Have you forgotten I'm the guarantor for that house of yours?"

"Of course not. What's that got to do with anything?"

"Blimey, do I have to spell it out? If you don't pay the rent, they'll come after me! And I'll need to pass a credit search when the time comes for another mortgage with Scott."

"Why, what are you thinking of buying – Buckingham Palace? This house must be worth a packet. You don't need a mortgage. It's alright for you."

Donna's stock phrase. "It's not *alright for me* actually. I've got a daughter to look after and bills to pay like anyone else."

"You wouldn't know money problems if they bit you on the arse."

"You've made your own problems. I've done my best to help you."

Her face darkens. "So now you're throwing it in my face?"

"Of course not. I just don't need the hassle of you not paying your rent and the agency coming after me.

"Chill Lou. It's fine. No one's going to come after *you*."

I lower my voice as I realise Helen is on the other side of the wall, probably listening in. "I can't believe you've put a car before paying for the roof over your head."

"Here we go again." She scowls at me as she folds her arms. "You used to be fun. What the hell's happened to you?"

"I'm acting like a responsible adult. Unlike you."

"You're acting just like you used to when you were with Darren. Maybe being in a relationship isn't the best thing for you."

With that, she flounces off towards her new car. Helen is on her knees weeding or pretending to be weeding. She watches as Donna screeches off toward her new house and then raises an eyebrow at me. Normally, we might have a brief chat, but today I ignore her and stride back towards my front door.

~

"It's me."

I balance the phone in the crook of my neck as I slide Charlie's plate in front of her.

"Yes?" It's only an hour since Donna stormed off. Hopefully she's ringing to tell me she's sorted out the rent. Or got rid of her car. It's just one drama after another.

"I'm sorry. I hate it when we argue. It might look like I was copying your car, but honestly, I didn't even consider it. Ash told me about it being for sale, so I thought I should have a look."

"What's Ash got to do with buying a car?" She's literally known him for two days.

"His mate has a garage and had taken it as a part exchange. It was too good an offer for me to pass up."

"Oh look. I don't need to know the details." I turn my back to Charlie and march over to the sink. "Just tell me you'll sort the rent."

"I already have. That's the other reason I'm ringing you."

"I'm listening."

"Look, things have been really tight lately and there's loads of stuff I need, especially with the new house. So I've just been approved for a loan."

"You've what? But as you've said yourself, you're on a third of what I am! How are you going to manage?" I'm surprised anyone has approved her for one, given her history. But I don't say that.

"I'll manage. Alright? I've worked it all out. And I'm a grown woman."

"Can I remind you of how you came to me in the first place? *Wanting a guarantor!* So don't give it *I'm a grown woman* with me."

Charlie looks at me with wide eyes as I stamp from the sink to the fridge. I need a glass of wine.

"I'm sick of not being able to afford things. It's alright for you. With your job, and the money your dad left you, and your savings, and..."

"This isn't a competition. And you know I help you out as much as I can."

"Of course I do." Her voice softens. "Which is why I've booked a little treat for us. In fact, I've just paid the deposit."

"Oh Donna." It's difficult to stay mad at her for long. Her heart's in the right place. She'll have booked us a spa thing or afternoon tea, so the thought's there, even if I end up paying the balance. It's usually the case.

"I've booked it for after we've broken up for the holidays, and it's during the week, so it doesn't interfere with your precious time with Scott. I remember him saying he'd be working over the summer."

"Go on then, tell me what you've booked. Don't keep me in suspense."

Charlie's head jerks up. In the silence of the kitchen, she must be able to hear what Donna's saying.

"Well, it's actually for the three of us. Like we were talking about in your garden the other week. Me, you and Charlie."

"Put it on loudspeaker Mum." Charlie puts her fork down.

"Hi Charlie. I've got a surprise for you." Donna says in a sing-song voice.

I suppose afternoon tea or a spa *would* be nice. Especially after the busy-ness of the last half term. And Charlie would enjoy it. She deserves a treat after how Darren and Liz have treated her.

"What is it then?" Charlie's voice has an impatient edge. "Tell me."

"Do you know how you mentioned going to Antibes the other day?"

Charlie's eyes widen like saucers. "We're going to Antibes!" Her voice is a shriek. "Yessss." She jumps up from her chair and rushes over to her phone. "Wait until I tell Jess."

"Sit down Charlie." I press the speaker button and hold the phone back against my ear as I stride from the kitchen. Bloody hell. As if Donna has booked a holiday for us all without even checking with me first.

"*Have* you actually booked it?" I close the lounge door behind me.

"Like I said, I've paid the deposit? I didn't want anyone else to bag it."

"When is it for?" I try to keep the heaviness from my voice.

In contrast, Donna sounds off-the-scale excited. "The second Monday of the school holiday, so a week on Monday - for four nights. We fly from Stansted at eight in the morning."

"Stansted? Why Stansted? And a week on Monday? So when's the balance due?"

"By Thursday. Hopefully my loan will have come through by then. Look Lou, if I hadn't grabbed it, someone else would have done. The bloke who owns the apartment is a mate of Ash's."

"Another mate of Ash's? So there's the car, the holiday apartment. What next?"

"Ash is busy that week. He was the one who suggested that I might as well get myself gone. Apparently it's a last minute cancellation. And if Ash isn't around, I'll only be twiddling my thumbs."

"You've only been seeing him for five minutes. Look, I'm not saying I'm not grateful, but why didn't you check with me before booking things that involve me and Charlie?"

"I didn't have time to check. Besides you never answer your phone."

"Only when I'm at work," I reply. "And that's because I'm teaching." I roll my eyes. It's a good job she can't see me.

"I needed to slap the deposit down before someone else did. It's only because I'm Ash's girlfriend that I didn't have to pay in full at this short notice."

"Ash's girlfriend eh?" I smile, despite myself. She sounds happy, and it's good to hear. I only hope it lasts and that my hunches about Ash are wrong.

"And what if we can't go?" I search the corners of my mind for a reason I can't.

"Why wouldn't you? Come on Lou, you'd have told me if you had something else planned."

Can I survive four nights at Donna's beck and call? She *is* my best friend, but things have become so much more intense recently. I've started to feel really suffocated when I'm around her, and it's not just because I've got a new relationship. "I do have a life of my own, you know."

"I know you do. But Lou – it's for four nights, not the whole summer."

"Why do you want *me* to go anyway?" I wave at Helen as she leaves her garden and passes the front of my house, staring through the window as she goes. "You keep saying how boring I am since I met Scott."

"Of course I want to go with you. And Charlie. She'll love it. You heard her reaction. But we need to move on it."

She's right about Charlie. It would be difficult to let her down with this holiday now she knows about it. Part of me wonders if they cooked it up together.

"I thought you were all loved up with Ash now. Doesn't he want to go with you when he's *not* busy? It's his mate's place, after all?" I realise I'm trying to talk her into it. If I'm totally honest, this holiday in Antibes is not appealing to me at all. I need to have a think.

"It's still early days with Ash. You said yourself not to go rushing in. Besides, I've already put the deposit down, haven't I?"

"I don't know. It's very short notice."

"Is it heck. Come on, live a little. And I can't afford to lose the deposit – you've just been wittering on at me about money."

"I don't even know if our passports are in date."

"You're not the sort of person who lets their passport run out. I've known you for long enough – don't give me that!"

"I'll have to check."

"Rubbish. I've seen your filing system, don't forget. I've never known anyone as organised as you are."

"Just let me have a think about it."

"What's there to think about?" Her voice takes on a new height. "It's ages since we've done anything like this. In fact, it's been ages since I've been away. I need it. You need it."

"Look I'll ring you back in a few minutes."

"I can't believe I'm having to talk you into this. It's four nights in the South of France, for goodness' sake. The Louisa of old would have snapped my arm off."

"I said I'll ring you back."

"OK. But you've said yourself what a rough time Charlie's been having with her dad. I need to know *today*. We need to get it paid for before someone else takes it."

"You said we had until Thursday?" I hate it when she tries to pressure me. In fact, I hate it when anyone tries to pressure me.

"We do. But I don't really know the man, do I? What if he gets a better offer? We don't want to lose it." There's a definite desperation in her tone.

"I like this word *we*. I suppose you'd better text me the details of what needs paying and where."

"Does that mean it's a yes then?" Her voice lifts.

"It's a probably." I don't see how I can get out of it. Saying no to Donna risks an enormous fall out. With her *and* with Charlie.

"I wonder who that could possibly be." Mum steps through the patio doors, her long dress swishing around her legs. I hope I look as good as her when I reach her age.

I drop my phone onto the grass. It's the third time it's beeped in two minutes. "I'm going to have to give her an answer. It's been nearly three hours since I said I'd ring her back."

"It's a miracle she hasn't turned up on the doorstep."

"She must be with her new man."

"Let's see how long this one lasts." Mum flops onto the blanket beside me. "This sun cream took some finding."

"He's nice enough on the surface. But there's something about him I can't quite put my finger on." She always falls for the swagger. "And it's his mate who owns the apartment in Antibes, which makes me even more wary about the whole thing. I'd be happier if it was through a holiday company really."

"If you don't want to go, say no." Mum shields her eyes against the sunlight as she looks at me. "Oh, this is the life. Rub some on my shoulders, will you?" She passes me the bottle.

"You'd better keep your voice down Mum." I glance up at Charlie's open bedroom window as I blob cream into my palm. "I don't want to set her off again. She's got her heart set on this holiday. You should have heard her before you arrived. Talk about persuasion."

"Charlotte's thirteen years old." Mum lifts her hair out of the way. "You're the parent Louisa. And if you don't want to go away with Donna, maybe the three of us could go somewhere instead?"

Much as Charlie loves her grandma, she'd have a right tantrum if I were to book something with Mum instead of Donna. But I won't tell Mum that.

"Maybe we could do both." Bloody hell. From no holidays to two holidays in an afternoon. Plus, Scott's mentioned us doing something. Still, I shouldn't complain.

"So you're going to give in to Donna?" Mum holds her hand out. "Pass it here. I'll rub some on you."

"It's not *giving in*." I turn my back to her. "But I'll never hear the end of it if I dig my heels in. And besides, Antibes is supposed to be lovely."

"It *is* giving in. I often wonder what hold the woman has on you Louisa. Friends usually monopolise one another *less* as they grow older. But anyway, it's your life."

Her hands on my back remind me of when I was young. I'm so lucky to have her, as Donna often points out.

"Look, I think I'll have to say yes. But start having a look around for something. I'd love a few days away with you and Charlie too."

"Fabulous. There. Done. This weather's due to break soon. It's wall to wall rain next week."

I laugh. "You and your weather app."

18

THEN

"But you said earlier you were up for it." Donna stopped dead in the pub car park, fury etched across her face. She'd have probably stamped her feet if there weren't so many people around.

"I just can't be arsed tonight. And I've got an essay due in on Monday." I turned away and carried on walking.

"Lou. Stop. Look." She called after me. "Let's just jump in a taxi. We don't even have to stay that long. I might find someone I know in there and then you can go home."

I carried on walking. Within seconds, she was clip-clopping behind me on her heels.

"Please. For me. I don't want to go home this early!"

"I'm not forcing you to do anything. Just because I don't want to go clubbing doesn't mean you have to go home."

"Oh yeah." She grabbed me by the arm and swung me to face her. "I'm really going to rock up at the club on my own. Donna-no-mates or what?"

"Most of the time you dump me anyway." I shook my arm free of her grasp. "As soon as someone more interesting comes along."

"That's not true."

"It bloody well is. Anyway. I've told you. I'm going home. I've drunk more than enough tonight, and I'm knackered."

"Lou, you're nineteen, not ninety. What the hell's got into you?" Her voice rose into a shriek.

"Nothing's got into me. Look. I normally do what you want, but tonight I'm doing what I want."

"You let me down like this and I'll..."

"You'll what?" I set off walking again. As if she was resorting to threats.

She didn't reply – she evidently couldn't think of a fitting penalty fast enough. Instead, she ran after me again. Once beside me, she slowed, and we fell into step. For a moment, it seemed she had accepted my decision to go home.

"You're a boring bitch, do you know that?"

"And what a great friend you are, calling me names like that." I tried to tell myself it was the drink talking.

"It's true. Boring fucking bitch. I don't even know why I'm friends with you."

"You'll be texting in the morning, begging for forgiveness, telling me how drunk you were and how sorry you are."

"Will I hell." She stood in front of me, blocking my path as she shouted into my face. "You do my fucking head in, do you know that? I've had enough of you."

"But yet you want to go clubbing with me?" I laughed. "Just get out of my way."

For a second, I thought she was going to hit me, but she pushed me backwards. "You'll regret treating me like shit, you little bitch. After all I've done for you. I should have left you to get beaten up that day."

19

NOW

"What time's your flight?" Scott glances up from the takeaway menu.

"Quarter past eight." I sigh. "It's such a lot of travelling for only four nights."

"I can't understand why you're not staying longer."

"According to Donna, the last-minute cancellation was for fourteen nights. This mate of Ash's filled ten of them, which leaves the four she bagged."

"Ah, right." The lightness in his voice doesn't match his expression.

"And four nights is long enough in her company." I force a laugh as though I'm joking, but Scott probably realises that I'm not. He seems to have grasped how stretched mine and Donna's friendship is at the moment.

"It wouldn't be so bad if you were flying from here." He shakes his head. "Why on earth has she booked flights from Stansted when you live five minutes from Leeds Bradford airport?"

"She says it's three hundred quid cheaper to go from Stansted."

"Yeah but, the cost of petrol, not to mention the three hour drive each way. Me, I'd have paid the extra for the flights."

"Me too." I take the menu from him and try to scan it. I'm reading the words but not taking them in. I'm not even hungry.

"Didn't you have a say in it at all?"

"Not really. Donna seems to have taken control of this one. I've just sent her the money to cover me and Charlie."

"How's she affording a holiday at such short notice anyway? On a teaching assistant's wage? It's not that well paid as far as I know."

"She's actually a learning mentor, so no, it's not brilliant. Not when she's only got one wage coming in." I don't add, *as she so often reminds me.*

"So what's she done, won the lottery? There's the holiday, the car, the rent for the new house..."

"She's taken a loan out." The realisation that I'm the guarantor for her house slaps me around the face every time I think about it. But it's too late for worry or regret. What's done is done. I'd be lying if I said I wasn't concerned though. With her credit history, she'll be paying through the nose for a loan.

"Where is she tonight anyway?"

"Seeing Ash before we set off. She's cooking him a meal."

"I wondered why she hadn't been round here tonight."

"Why – would you have wanted her to be?" There's an edge of suspicion in my voice. He's told me about her flirting with him. Maybe he secretly enjoys it. With her blonde hair and green eyes, most men literally eat out of her hand. Until they discover how high maintenance she is. "Me and Charlie have to be round at hers for one o'clock." *One o'clock in the bloody morning.* We're going to be knackered.

"At least the motorway will be quiet whilst you're driving down."

"I'll have enough time with her over the next few days, won't I? Without her having come here tonight, I mean."

"You don't sound like you're looking forward to it."

"I'd rather be going away with you." I tuck my legs under myself and nestle into him. It might only be a few days, but I'm really going to miss him.

He pulls me closer. "Let's get something booked then."

"What about Charlie?"

"*And* Charlie. I'd rather have you all to myself, but if she wants to come, that's cool too. Do you want to find out if she wants something from the takeaway before I ring it through?"

"She's sleeping. Or at least she's supposed to be." I point towards the ceiling. "I've made some sandwiches for the journey. Although I'm hoping she'll sleep in the car. She's a grotty little mare when she's sleep deprived."

"She takes after her mum then." Scott laughs as he reaches for his phone.

"Hey!" I nudge him in the ribs with my elbow. "Until we live together, you can't say that."

"Let me know you've got to Stansted safely." Scott finally lets me go and I shiver in the midnight air. "Here." He peels his jumper off. "Stick that on."

"It'll be about half four when we get there, you know. You don't want me waking you."

"Of course I do." He smiles in the darkness. "I'll miss you."

"You too. I'll see you next weekend."

"Ugh. Pass me the sick bucket." Charlie drags her wheelie case through the hallway. "Come on Mum."

Scott blows me a kiss then heads towards his car. I turn to Charlie, my sense of misery evaporating when I see excitement shining in her eyes. It's worth going on a holiday I'm not entirely fired up about to make her happy.

"We're going on holiday," she shrieks as he drives away.

"Shush. You'll wake the street." I watch as his car disappears around the corner. "Come on then, let's get round to Donna's."

"Why are you wearing Scott's jumper?"

"Because I want to. And it's gone chilly."

We pass Ash on Donna's garden path.

"Have a good time girls," he calls without stopping to say a proper hello. To say I was there when they first met each other, I'm surprised at his lack of friendliness. He somehow looks even shiftier than the time in the pub. Perhaps I just didn't take as much notice of him that night, after all, I couldn't have known that him and his mate chatting us up would lead to Donna revolving her life around him.

"We will," I call after his retreating form. "Say thanks to your friend for letting us stay in his apartment."

"It's not exactly a favour. You're paying for it, aren't you?" With a flick of his hand, he dismisses me as he gets into his car. Some sporty thing, I've no idea what sort. I'll have to ask Donna – she takes much more notice of the car that a man drives than I do.

She appears in her doorway, illuminated in the hallway light behind her. "All set?" She claps her hands together. Hopefully hers and Charlie's enthusiasm will be infectious. All I want to do is run back and spend the next few days with Scott. I can't wait until the day comes when we can move in together.

"We sure are," Charlie replies. "How come we're going in your car Donna? I'd have thought you'd want Mum to pay for the petrol?" She's had many years, this daughter of mine, to notice how it's always me who pays for things where Donna's concerned, including petrol.

"I'm sure she'll contribute to the pot." Donna laughs as she drags her wheelie case over the doorstep. "I want to give it a run on the motorway with it being new." She shuts the door behind her. "Besides, I don't enjoy being a passenger, not on the motorway."

"I don't expect you to drive the whole way," I tell her. "We'll take it in turns."

"I don't mind driving. So long as you stay awake and keep me company. Besides, you'd only be insured third party – I'm not risking it."

I turn from her so she doesn't see as I roll my eyes once again at her. What she means is that she likes to be the one in control.

"How come you've got exactly the same car as my mum?" Charlie swings her case into the boot. "You're getting like twins!"

Donna shrugs. "There's no law against it, is there?"

My head jerks forwards as Donna nudges me. "You need to put your seatbelt back on Lou."

At least she's let me have a few minutes' peace at last. For the entire flight it's been Ash this, Ash that, house this, house that. She's barely let up since we left Farndale. First, she wouldn't let me sleep in the car on the journey down, insisting that I had to keep her company so she wouldn't get sleepy. And when I suggested *she* sleep and I drive, she reiterated the insurance thing, and then added that she's a safer driver than me on the motorway. *As if!*

Also, much to Charlie's disgust, we had *Donna's* choice of music and the air conditioning turned up full the entire time. Scott's jumper, which is now rolled up behind my head, didn't even keep me warm, with her constant conversation keeping Charlie awake too.

To nearly top it all, when we went for a wee at the airport, I was craving a few seconds to myself, and she was still wittering away in the next cubicle. I've never felt so irritated by anyone as much in my life and hope it's just because I'm tired. No way can

I spend the next four days in this frame of mind. I shouldn't have invited Scott round last night. I should have been sensible, like Mum suggested, and got a few hours of sleep. I'm absolutely exhausted.

We will shortly start the descent, a robotic voice sounds over the tannoy. *The expected local landing time will be 11:20am, and the temperature is currently twenty-nine degrees.*

"Oooh." Donna leans forwards to look past Charlie and out of the window. "I can't wait until we land."

"Me neither." Though Charlie looks as knackered as I feel.

"We're going to have to have a couple of hours when we get to the apartment." I tell Donna, nodding towards Charlie.

"What do you mean? A couple of hours *what?*"

"Sleep, of course." I try to straighten out the crick in my neck. "Look at the state of that one. You could put your shopping in the bags under her eyes."

"No Mum. I'm not *sleeping.*"

"I totally agree." Donna squeezes her arm. "You tell her Charlie. We're on bloody holiday." She shakes her head. "*Sleep!* Blimey Lou, don't you remember the holidays we used to have? How many hours sleep did we have that time we went to Dublin?"

I sigh and contemplate the fact that it might have to be energy drinks and sugar to get me through until this evening. Even Charlie will have to crash and burn at some point, and it's not as if we can go clubbing whilst she's with us. If I can just bat it out...

≈

"Are you sure this is the right place?" I look up and down the street as Donna rings the buzzer for the third time.

"Yes. Look." She thrusts her phone in front of my face. I'm so tired I can't even focus on it. Perhaps we can go down to the beach. If I can just implore her to leave me alone for an hour, and to stop talking at me, I'll have a power nap in the sun.

"I'll try ringing Ash." She brings the phone to her ear.

I lean against the wall. Charlie lays her case down and sits on it. "As if we can't get in. What if he doesn't come Mum? What will we do then?"

"Don't worry. We'll sort something out."

"Oh you have such little faith." Donna grins as she ends her call. "Ash is going to get in touch with him. He's got a different number."

I lay my case on its side too and join Charlie on the ground.

"Cheer up you two. We're on holiday." Donna sweeps her arms skyward. "It's going to be fabulous."

"How can you be so energetic?"

"She's in luuurve." Charlie laughs.

Donna laughs too. "Actually, I was sensible and got some sleep yesterday. I didn't get up until nine last night when Ash came round."

Ash this. Ash that.

"Oh look. He's texting me now." She waves her phone in the air, then looks at it. "The man, his mate, will be here in twenty minutes. He's been held up."

"Good of him to let us know." I slump against the wall. "Did he expect us to be telepathic?"

"We might as well go over there and watch out for him." She points to a bar which spills out onto the pavement.

For once, I agree with her. A glass of wine will either bring me back to life or finish me completely. At least once we're in our apartment, I'll be able to close my bedroom door on her incessant conversation.

20

THEN

WOULD the remaining two passengers please board flight 104 for Dublin? This is your third and final call.

"Shit! How did we miss the first two calls?" I giggled as I wiped my hands on the edge of the towel.

"It's a good job we came to the loo when we did." Donna checked herself in the mirror. "I certainly wasn't paying attention to the announcements out there."

"See what gin does to us?" I pushed her towards the door. "We'll have to act sober or they might not let us on."

"It's not my fault the flight was delayed." In our drunken haze, we nearly tripped over each other trying to get ourselves and our cases through the toilet door.

"Yeah but you're the one that's plied us both with doubles!" She broke into a run towards the departure gate. "Quick. Come on."

"It was happy hour," I said as I caught her up at the gate. "Though whoever heard of happy hour at half ten in the morning?"

"That's the good thing about holidays." She turned to me as

our passports were being checked. "We can drink whenever we want. In fact, we can do what we want, when we want."

"Young, free, single and twenty-one!" I nearly fell up the steps behind her. "Oh no." My face burned as the entire plane broke into applause at our arrival.

"Sorry. We're really sorry," we kept repeating as we attempted to remain upright in the aisle. Some passengers looked away in disgust, others looked amused. And, what seemed to be a stag party, looked particularly impressed when we took our seats in their midst.

"Excellent." Donna nudged me. "It's going to be fabulous. Dublin with my best friend."

"This is the life." I glanced beyond one of the stags out of the window. "We should do something like this every year, no matter what happens, or how old we get."

"I'll drink to that." She slapped me on the leg. "Well, I will once that steward turns up with the trolley."

21

NOW

"How come there's only one key to the place?" I frown as I glance around the apartment. My kitchen at home is bigger than the dining area, kitchenette and lounge space put together. Poor Charlie's on the sofa bed. I watch as she pulls it out and tucks her case underneath. She hasn't complained, so that's something. It's a good job she's only thirteen. I doubt it would be long enough for a fully grown person.

"Are our rooms through there?" I reach for my case and point towards a door. "You can always bunk in with me, if the bed's big enough."

"No, you're alright thanks, Mum."

Her expression tells me she'd rather poke her eyes out with a cocktail stick than share a sleeping space with me. I feel quite insulted.

"Me and you are sharing, actually." Donna points to the room at the end. "There's only one bedroom. Didn't I mention that?"

"You know full well you didn't." I'm struggling to keep the annoyance from my voice as I follow her in, expecting to see twin beds. "Nor did you mention that there's only one bed." I look from her amused face to the double bed. *Great. Bloody great.* There'll be no respite. None.

"It's a good job we're such good friends, isn't it?"

I throw my case to the side and dump myself on the bed. "I'm getting a migraine," I lie. "You'll have to leave me on my own whilst I get rid of it."

"Really?" She pulls a face. "You've not had one of them for years."

"It must be the heat." I rub at my head. "Charlie," I call, trying to muster up a weak, migrainy sort of voice. "I'd like you to have a nap for an hour or two as well. Then we'll go out."

"She can come with me." Donna rests her hand on her hip as she leans against the wall. "We'll come back for you in an hour."

"*I'm* Charlie's mother, not you." I lie down without looking at her. "She's having a nap. And we'll get ready to go out in *two* hours. In the meantime, *you* can do what you want."

"Fine then." She turns on her heel and stamps back into the kitchen area.

A few moments later, the door slams. When I peer out, I'm relieved to notice she's gone. Charlie looks to be falling asleep on the sofa bed. Thank goodness.

I rub my eyes as my phone beeps at the side of me.

> I'm in the Waka Bar on the seafront. I'm sitting outside. Don't be long.

I sigh as I haul myself to a seated position. Really, I'd like a shower after the journey, but she'll only moan at being left on her own if I don't get down there.

"Come on, Charlie." I shake her. "That's enough napping for us. We'd better meet Donna."

I stagger to the bathroom and splash water on my face. The shower's so tiny, I doubt I'll be able to stand up straight in there. Thank goodness we're only here for a few nights. Before agreeing to come here, I should have checked this place out. I guess Ash looks so minted; I assumed his mate who's rented this place to us must be too.

When we arrive, I expect Donna to be chatting with someone. Instead, she's staring pensively out to sea, cradling a glass of wine. She certainly looks ten times better than I do after the long journey here. But then, she always does, whatever the circumstances.

"About bloody time." She scowls as we approach her table. "Some holiday this is so far."

"We're here now, aren't we?"

"This one's on you then." She turns from me and beckons to the waiter. I don't really want to drink but if I were to order a coffee, I'd never hear the end of it. And I feel too groggy right now to put up an argument with her. Mum's right about our friendship – there's something very off. More and more as time goes on. I can't carry on like this.

"Can we get something to eat?" Charlie tugs the menu from its holder.

"Of course." I smile at her. "Go for it."

Donna smiles at the waiter as he lays a plate in front of her. "So - we've got some early starts this week." She plucks a knife and fork from the pot between us. "I hope you're good at getting up Charlie. I remember me and your mum when we were teenagers. We were dreadful."

"Speak for yourself. And what do you mean, *early starts?*" I thank the waiter as he sets a second glass of wine in front of us.

"Well, we've only got three full days here, so tomorrow we're going to Monaco. On Wednesday, we're going to Cagnes-sur-Mer, then on Thursday, I've booked Frejus." She tilts her head to one side, as though waiting for my reaction.

"What do you mean, *booked*... what have you booked exactly?"

"Bus tickets for all of them. I've kept all the receipts so you can settle up with me. And tickets for one or two things whilst we're in each place. One of us had to be organised."

"Maybe I don't want to be organised." I glare at her, though she probably can't see this because of my sunglasses. "You should know me well enough to know I like to go with the flow when I'm away, not have everything plotted out. Especially not *for me.*"

Charlie glances around as she chews her chicken, evidently to make sure no one has noticed my raised voice. "Don't you two be having a domestic."

"Did you not think," I continue, "to consult me before *booking* things? Is this not mine and Charlie's holiday too?"

Mum was right. I should have had more backbone. If I was away with Scott, or her, I'd be having a far better time.

"But I want to go to Monaco Mum. There's yachts there we can look at. I've seen pictures of them."

"You should thank me, not have a go at me." Donna scowls as she picks at her steak. "I go to all this trouble and then..."

"Why bus tickets anyway? Surely the train would be better? We wouldn't have to set off so early then. Don't you think we have enough early starts back at home?" Not that I plan to languish around in bed. Perhaps if I hadn't been forced to share with Donna, a lie in or three would have been good.

"Have you seen the prices of the train tickets?" She purses her lips in the same way Mum would have done at me when I was younger.

I exhale a long breath as I stare out at the scene beyond us.

The pure blueness of the sea makes me want to go for a paddle. It's the first time since I've sat down here that I've considered the beauty of what's around me. I just wish I was here with Scott instead of Donna. But I'm not and I've got to stop thinking that way.

∼

We squeeze into a gap between two seats and I grapple for a loop to hang onto. The bus sets off with a lurch and I lumber into two men opposite me. Charlie can only just reach a loop to hang onto one. We'll have aching arms by the time we get to Monaco if we have to travel like this for the entire journey.

I glance enviously at the passengers who've caught the bus at a stop early enough to get a seat. I don't know if I can stand like this for three quarters of an hour. It's only nine o'clock, and already the stench of communal body odour on this bus is threatening to knock me sideways. What's it going to be like when we catch the bus back later?

Donna must notice me wrinkling my face in disgust. She smiles. "I'm sure a seat will come up soon. I'll let you have it. Age before beauty."

"I'm only a year older than you." I can't keep my grumpiness out of my voice. "Which is hardly over the hill, is it?"

I pull out my phone with my spare hand. So much was my rush this morning that I didn't have time to text Scott and say good morning. I'll compose my text each time the bus stops at lights, or whatever. Whilst it's moving, I need to hang on for dear life.

"For God's sake Lou." Donna's smile turns to a glare. "Leave lover-boy alone. You're away with me and Charlie."

"Stop telling me what to do." A red mist descends. *Who does she think she is?* "In case you haven't noticed, I'm a grown woman. And you're getting on my bloody nerves."

"Sor-ree. It's just... do you see me texting Ash every five minutes?"

"Haven't you been in touch with him since we got here?"

"I've sent him a couple of texts, but he hasn't replied. Probably because he knows I'm away with *you*." She gives me a pointed expression. "And I prefer to be in the moment, spending my time with the people I'm actually with."

"Since when?" I laugh.

I stare at the bedroom ceiling, willing the next twenty-four hours to be over and done with. The three days that have elapsed of this holiday so far feel more like three weeks.

"Make us a coffee love," I call to Charlie. "Be a sweetheart."

"We'll have to pick one up on the way." Donna glances at her watch, then leaps out of bed. "We're running late. If you hadn't snored half the night, I might not have slept through my alarm."

"Precisely why we should have had our own rooms." I stretch my arms and legs out. One more night in this lumpy bed before I'm back in my own. I can't wait.

"You were that loud, they probably heard you in the next apartment."

"It's the wine that does it." I laugh. I feel like adding, *without wine, I wouldn't have survived this 'holiday' so far.*

"Just get a move on Lou. We've only got half an hour to get down to the bus stop."

"We can catch the next bus, surely? I'm going to jump in the shower. Charlie needs one as well." Again, I don't add that I want to drop Scott a text before I get sorted.

"No, *we can't catch the next bus.* You've seen how packed they get. Besides, I've pre-booked the tickets."

"I don't care. We'll buy some more. I want a shower. But before that, I'm getting a coffee." I look at her with what I hope is an expression that should dare her to argue back.

"But we might not get a place on the bus. We haven't got time for a coffee." I swear she'd stamp her foot at this moment if she could get away with it.

"Then we'll do something else instead. Maybe I'd like a chilled-out day today." I walk to where Charlie's clattering around in the kitchen. "A wander round the old town, the shops."

"Booooring." Charlie swings around, knocking a mug to the floor as she goes. "Whoops."

"Another one bites the dust." I laugh as I reach under the sink for the dustpan.

"That's the *third* thing you've smashed since we've been here Charlie." Donna marches into the kitchen and stands with her hands on her hips, whilst I sweep the crockery up. "You can bloody well pay for the damage you've caused."

"*The damage?*" I rise to my feet and face her. "We've *paid* to stay here, haven't we? Surely breakages are part and parcel of any stay in a holiday apartment. That's why there's a little thing called insurance."

"Don't go getting all sarky on me Lou. It doesn't suit you." She holds the flap of the bin open. "This place is Ash's friend's, remember? It doesn't look good if we break things and don't leave the money to replace them."

"Leave him some money then." I tip the broken pieces into the bin. "If it eases your conscience. Thanks love." I take the coffee Charlie's made for me. "But don't go telling my daughter what she should and shouldn't pay for."

"I'm off to get dressed." Donna turns on her heel. "Just hurry, will you?"

. . .

Frenemy

Donna paces up and down the lounge as I blow dry my hair. I'm purposefully taking my time to rile her. Our friendship has turned even more sour this week. I thought I knew her better than I know anyone, but what is it they say? *If you want to really get to know a person, go on holiday with them.*

"Why don't you just meet me at the beach?" I suggest, as I turn the hairdryer off. "I'm going to give Scott a ring, then I'll be half an hour behind you."

"Half a bloody hour," she snaps. "It'll be lunchtime before we get anywhere at this rate."

"Donna's right Mum," Charlie looks up from her phone. "You're on a right go-slow this morning. And it's boiling in here. I want to get out as well."

"Why don't you come with me?" Donna unhooks her bag from the back of the chair. "We'll leave your mum to do what she wants. Oh wait, there's only one key."

"Well, leave it here then. I'll lock up when I've done." I brush the sweat from my top lip. Charlie's right, it really is sweltering. Though I'd still rather be at home in overcast England. It's a shame really. Antibes is gorgeous and I haven't appreciated one bit of it this week.

"No! What if you lose it? It's the only one we've got." She plucks it from the back of the door, as if she's scared I'll get to it before she does.

"Why would I be any more likely to lose it than you?" I point my hairbrush at her as I speak. Surely she can't be serious?

"I'm not saying you would, it's just..."

"You like to be in control." I finish the sentence for her. "Listen to me Donna. I've run my own household for the last twenty years and have brought up a child to the age of thirteen - so far without incident. I think I can be trusted with a door key, don't you?"

She closes her fingers around the key. To say I'm baffled by her refusal to leave it with me is an understatement.

"Right, do you know what... Charlie sit down. You'll have to wait for me." I wag my finger towards her. "Donna, why don't *you* bugger off, and go to wherever it is you've got *planned?*" I wave my arms around as I rant. "You go your way, and today, let me go mine."

"But I want to go with Donna," Charlie whines.

"I said sit down." I point at the chair. "You're staying with me."

"Listen to her," Donna says through what sounds like gritted teeth. "You're treating her like she's five years old. If she wants to come with me, you can't stop her."

"I think you'll find I can. Charlie, you move one muscle without me, and I'll be confiscating your phone."

"It's not fair." She throws herself onto the sofa bed.

"Do you really mean this?" Donna glares at me. "You're just going to dump me on my own all day? Well thanks a bloody lot."

"We need some space from each other," I reply. "Otherwise, we're going to seriously fall out."

22

THEN

"Alright, alright. Bloody hell. Is there a fire or something?" I swung my legs over the side of the bed and tried to ignore the sudden spin of my head.

"So - you *are* in there?" Donna stood open-mouthed outside my room. "I've been looking everywhere for you, and I mean *everywhere.*"

"Did you not think to check in here?" I held the door wider, and she followed me back into the bedsit. My wicker chair creaked beneath her weight as she threw herself into it. "I'd have thought here would have been the most obvious place."

"I've been knocking. Three times, in fact." She gave me a funny look. "I didn't hear you come back last night. So where the hell have you been?"

"Here."

"Really?"

"The whole time! I was drunk, wasn't I? What time is it, anyway?"

She looked at her watch. "Nearly five o'clock."

"In the morning?" I glanced at the darkness through the crack in the curtains.

"No, the afternoon, ya daft sod. I've been worried sick about you." She stepped towards me, her bracelets rattling with the movement. "I thought I was going to be identifying your body."

She was always the drama queen. "You haven't been in touch with my mum, have you?"

"Of course I have. That's the first place I went looking."

"Great. She'll be having kittens. You shouldn't have involved her."

"She's having a drive around for the millionth time, looking for you."

"You're joking."

"Honestly, Lou, we've searched half of Yorkshire. She was on the verge of ringing the police."

"You daft bats." I reached for the glass of water I couldn't remember pouring myself. "I've been here the whole time."

"You must have been seriously drunk not to have heard me banging on your door. You shouldn't have locked it."

"Drunk enough, I suppose. I've been worse. What else do you expect on New Year's Eve? Besides, you went off with what's-his face?"

"I didn't go off anywhere. You shouldn't have left the club without me. Whatever happened to our code of conduct? We never leave each other with men we don't know. And we never leave a club alone. Anything could have happened..."

"Well look, there's no harm done, is there? I'm fine. You're fine. I'd better let my mother know though."

"She thinks you've been murdered. I thought you'd been murdered. Don't go doing that to me again!"

"What getting drunk on New Year's Eve and sleeping it off? Why ever not?"

"You're the best friend I've ever had." She stared at me with mournful eyes. "If anything ever happened to you..."

I laughed at that. "Gosh, you have been stressing. And if I'm such a good friend, put the kettle on while I ring my mum."

"I think we need something stronger than tea." She pulled my curtain back to reveal our stash. "Hair of the dog."

23

NOW

"I HOPE you're in a better mood than you were earlier?" Donna raises her eyes from her magazine.

"I'm off for a paddle. I'll leave you two to kiss and make up." Charlie kicks her shoes beside us and runs towards the sea, her hair billowing behind. I smile after her. She might be a teenager now, but there's still a little girl in there somewhere. It's been good, Charlie and me being able to spend the day together – just the two of us. Once she'd stopped sulking, that is. We don't get proper quality time like we've had today very often. Partly because of her age, and partly because of the busyness of our lives. Nor was she constantly looking around to check we didn't bump into anyone who might know her whilst out with me. After all, I'm the most embarrassing creature on two legs.

"I guess so." I flop onto the blanket beside her. "I'm sorry I was such an arse this morning. I suppose I needed some space. From time to time I get like that."

"Which is why I offered to take Charlie off." She folds her magazine in half.

"Charlie's my daughter." I watch as she tries to skim pebbles and a memory pops into my mind of Darren trying to teach her on the beach at Bridlington. It had been a sticking plaster sort of holiday, but one where he'd spent every spare moment sneaking off to use his phone. "It's a different sort of *space* that I'm talking about. One where every spare second doesn't have to be filled with conversation."

"I thought we were almost family – me and you." She points at me then gestures towards herself, looking hurt.

"We are." I rest my hand on her freckled shoulder, which is slimy from sun cream. "I'm tired, that's all. It's been such a busy half term in school, and I could have done with a bit of downtime this week, instead of a load of running around."

"It sounds as though we should have a holiday to get over the holiday." She twists her hair into a knot on the top of her head and wraps a band around it.

No chance. I think to myself. "Scott's going to organise something for us," I tell her, realising with a warm glow that I'll soon be back with him. I've taken to sleeping with his jumper pillowing my head. Behaviour which is unheard of for me. Being so far away from him this week has made me realise how much I think of him. I was hesitant when he first mentioned us buying a place together in the future, but I've quickly come around to the idea. I'd love a new start in a house where Darren's never lived. And now that Donna's moved in around the corner...

Her face clouds over at the mention of Scott's name, which can only mean Ash still hasn't been texting her back. For all the irritation she shows whilst I've texted him this week, she's ten times worse when she's got a phone in her hand. It's always been the same though. One rule for her and another for me.

"Have you and Ash still not been in touch?"

She shakes her head and her eyes mist. "He's gone back into his man cave, by the sounds of it. He warned me he's a bit of a loner." She brushes a tear away and stares out at Charlie who's in the sea up to her thighs. "His replies, when he actually bothers, are as though he's texting a mate. When he texted me back earlier, it was to say what film he was in the middle of watching. I'd sent him a really nice message as well."

"Well, if anyone can drag him out of his man cave when we get back home, you can."

"It's alright for you to say." She picks at the hem of her dress. "Why can't I find someone like Scott? Why do you get all the luck? With *everything.*"

Time to change the subject. She's spiralling. I reach across to my rucksack and tug out one of the bottles. "A peace offering," I say. "You look as though you could do with one."

"I've already had three," she replies. "That's how pissed off I've felt today."

"It sounds like I've got some catching up to do, then." I pass her one of the plastic cups. "It's a good job I've got reserves." I point to the other bottle sticking out of my rucksack.

She gasps. "Is that a magnum?" She holds out her cup and I pour.

"It sure is. Charlie," I call, "there's some lemonade here if you want it."

"Let's just sit here." Donna shuffles on the blanket and appears to brighten somewhat. "And we can put the world to rights."

"Whilst we get pleasantly pissed and watch the sun go down." For the first time this week, I feel almost like myself again.

"That sounds like a plan."

"It'll be just like the old days." I raise my cup towards her, glad that our earlier hostilities seem to have melted away. That she can get under my skin so easily shows how close I am to her. I was just the same with Mum when we lived together. Which is why I left home at nineteen.

"Mum, I'm hungry. And I'm bored." Charlie tosses her phone onto the blanket. "You both witter too much when you've been drinking wine. I ought to record you."

"Don't you dare! We'll just finish this bottle. Then we'll go back to the apartment."

"And you're slurring your words. *Mum*, are you drunk!" She shivers and drags her cardigan from my bag.

"Of course not."

Donna falls back onto the blanket, laughing. "There's a Maccies across the road." She points at the flashing sign. "As if we've come all the way here for that."

"Mum. Can we? I haven't had a Maccies in years."

"I suppose it saves cooking." Not that I'd be cooking in that kitchen. I haven't even thought about food. I've been so wired this week that my appetite's faded.

"And it might soak some of this wine up. Are you OK going on your own? If I watch you cross."

"I'm thirteen, not three." Even in the semi-darkness, I can see Charlie rolling her eyes.

"What your mum means is that she's had too much of this stuff to walk over there herself." Donna points at the quarter-full magnum bottle.

She's right.

"Says you," Charlie gets to her feet and brushes sand from her legs. They're skinny, like her dad's and go a lovely colour in the sun. Unlike mine, I just turn red and freckly. "You're slurring as well Donna."

"Just get some food." I reach for my rucksack and pull out my debit card.

"Oooh, you must be drunk." She holds the card against her chest. "I could go on a right shopping spree with this."

"Straight there. Straight back." I muster my mock-stern voice as I point over the road. "Burger and chips all round."

I swivel round to watch her as she walks to the edge of the beach and stands by the road, waiting to cross. It was on the tip of my tongue to remind her that cars come from the opposite direction than what she's used to, but she's already out of earshot by the time I've thought of it.

"She's fine." Donna pushes my shoulder playfully as she swivels around to join me. She knows me too well and can probably see the concern, which I'm sure is etched across my face. "You worry too much."

"When you've had a kid yourself, you'll understand." I realise I'm saying the wrong thing before I've even finished the sentence.

"Thanks a bunch Lou. You know I'd love to have a baby. But my biological clock's ticking so loudly, it's deafening."

"I know. I'm sorry."

Her mouth twists into a pout as she plucks fibres from the edge of the blanket. "You're always coming out with these sly digs at me, aren't you? Does it make you feel good?"

"No. of course not. I didn't mean to say something that would upset you." I reach out and lightly touch her arm. "Really." Oh no. Here we go again.

She tugs her arm away from me. "What you've got could have been mine. Maybe it should have been."

"What are you on about?" I turn to face her. "*What* should have been yours?"

"All of it."

Even in my drunken haze, I'm confused. "All of what?"

She pauses, as though deciding whether to proceed.

"Go on."

"You know I told you about Darren making a play for me after you'd split up?"

"Yes?" I turn my attention back to the fast-food restaurant.

Charlie's blonde head bobs amongst the others as she waits in line. She's all that matters to me, really. Donna's changed. Our friendship certainly isn't what it was anymore, and it's taken this holiday for me to realise that I've *got* to take action. Even if she does only live around the corner now.

"Well, I didn't quite tell you the whole truth about things."

"Which is?" I finish the warm prosecco in my cup and pour some more. It seems like I'm going to need it. I can't look at her.

"Me and Darren. We had history. Before the two of you met, I mean."

"*History?* In what way?" Oh God. What's she going to say?

She falls quiet, as though deliberating how much to tell me.

"Just tell me."

"We slept together."

Something coils in my stomach. "When?"

"The first time was before you and he met."

I swallow. "*The first time?* So I take it from that, you slept together *after* we'd met as well?"

"I've been wanting to tell you for years." She stares down at her hands.

"So why have you told me *now?* To hurt me, or to make yourself feel better?" I stare at her. She's so pretty, she could have her pick of any man. Yet here she is, admitting to having slept with my ex-husband, the father of my daughter. After all this time.

"Sometimes the guilt eats away at me, that's all."

Yeah right. This is from the person who wouldn't know guilt if it bit her on the arse. "When? How often? *Where?*"

"When you were expecting Charlie. Then when she was little, when you weren't getting on. And a few times after you broke up."

I gulp half of the prosecco in one hit. Perhaps it shouldn't matter now that she slept with my ex-husband whilst I was with him. After all, we've all moved on and I'm with Scott. I always knew Darren couldn't keep it in his trousers. But Donna? She's supposed to be my best friend. So, yes. It *matters*. And what also threatens me is that she's now shown more than a passing interest in Scott too.

"How many times?" My voice sounds strangled. *Do I even want to know?*

"I don't know. Only a couple of times when you were pregnant, but..."

"So you came and supported me whilst I was giving birth, whilst all the time, you were sleeping with my husband? I can't believe this. Why haven't you told me before? Why now?"

"I don't know. I've had a lot to drink, I guess. These things come out."

"No Donna. You're telling me because you want to hurt me. You want to bring me down to where you are." I jab my finger at her. "Just because Ash hasn't been in touch with you."

"That's not it at all." There's venom in her voice. Like she's got any right to snap after what she's just told me.

"My mother was right about you all along."

"What's that supposed to mean?" Her head jerks to one side. That's got her attention. She can't handle *anyone* thinking badly of her. She imagines it when it isn't there, and it drives her insane with insecurity when it is.

"That I shouldn't trust you. But I've always stuck up for you whenever she's said it. To the point of telling her that there's a line you wouldn't ever cross. Our so-called *code of conduct*. But it seems you've broken it. Again and again and again. Is it still going on now? Are you *still* having sex with Charlie's dad?"

"No! I finished it. Just after he left you."

"*After he left me!* You're saying not only were you going behind my back like that, but you're the bitch that totally broke my marriage up?" I feel sick as the enormity of it all sinks in. "The one he was sneaking away to have sex with?"

"Your marriage was already breaking up Lou."

"Don't you *Lou* me. He left me for *you*. No wonder he wouldn't tell me your name. So it was *you* I caught him on the phone to. I can't believe it."

"I'm not proud of what happened. Which is why I'm telling you."

"Once you got him, why did you *finish it?* Did the attraction wear off when he was suddenly single? After all, you like them *unobtainable*, don't you?" People along the beach can probably hear me shrieking at her, but I don't care anymore.

"That's not how it was." But there's a hint of a smirk playing on her lips as though she's enjoying this drama between us. She's certainly brought me down. "I felt bad, so I ended it."

I feel like slapping her. I need to get away. Now. Anywhere. "You need help. You think the world revolves around you, don't you Donna?"

"No I don't. That's your department. You think the universe revolves around *you*. Well it really doesn't."

24

THEN

"I wasn't sure whether to tell you." Donna twisted the volume control on the radio.

"Mummy I like that song," Charlie called from the back. "Put it back on."

"Tell me what?" I glanced sideways at her as we pulled up at the lights.

The pause was maddening. Donna held it as though she was announcing the Oscars.

"Tell me what?" I repeated.

"It's Darren."

"What about him?" I twisted round to look at Charlie. She was busy undressing her doll and didn't seem to be listening.

"We've been messaging."

"You and Darren?" The lights turned green, so I set off again. "And?"

"Look, I'm sorry Lou, there's no easy way to tell you this, but he's asked me out."

I pulled the car up at the side of the road and looked at her head on. "Like on a date?"

"Yes." She turned to look out of her window. I could tell she was smirking. She always did when she was nervous, or imparting 'big' news. It was like a nervous twitch of hers that she couldn't control.

"The bloody cheek of him. Who the hell does he think he is?"

Her eyes met mine, but she took too long to agree with me.

"You're surely not thinking of saying yes, are you?"

"No, but…"

"Oh my God. Do I need to remind you of our code of conduct? We. Do. Not. Go. Near. Each. Other's. Men. Ever." I glared at her. Clearly she was sounding me out. Hoping I'd say, *do what you want. Me and Darren are history.*

"Besides, he's single now," I added. "You prefer them married or engaged to be married, don't you?"

"I'll ignore that remark." She turned to me then. "You're obviously upset at what I've told you. And no, I wouldn't dream of going out with him. I just thought you had a right to know that he'd asked me. He's moved on, and so should you."

25

NOW

"AM I GLAD TO BE BACK." I absorb the familiarity of Mum's lounge. Photographs of me at every life stage smile down from each corner of the room. Pre-Donna photographs. Right now, I wish I'd never met her. Getting beaten up that day by those girls would have been preferable. They couldn't have hurt me as much as she has.

"Where's Charlie?" Mum pushes a mug in front of me on the coffee table. The sight of her is like balm on sore skin after the week I've had.

"At her friend's. I said I'd only be a couple of hours though."

"Isn't she seeing Darren this weekend?" Mum frowns as she glances at the photograph of the four of us at Charlie's christening. I wish she'd take it down, but she refuses, saying it's a memory of a special day, even if Darren is on it. Much as I'd like to erase the man from my life, I can't.

People say that buying a house together or getting engaged, or married is a big commitment, but it's having kids together that is. I'm bound to that man for the rest of my life. Because of Charlie, I'll always have him to contend with. Although the way

Liz is treating her is nearly grounds for stopping her from going there completely.

"Don't tell me he's let her down again."

"Don't talk to me about *bloody* Darren." Donna's face swims into my mind. The long eyelashes, the mock-apologetic tilt of her head. "Sorry. I've yet to have it all out with him. I've only heard *her* side of things so far."

"Why, what's happened?" Mum's got that look she would have reserved from when I came home upset from school as a kid. "What are you on about?"

"Darren and Donna." It feels weird, placing their names side by side. Even as her best friend, I've accepted she can be a pain in the arse but what she's done is on another level. There are few friends who could forgive something like this.

Mum sits beside me on the sofa and peers at me. "What do you mean? He's living with that Liz piece of work, isn't he?" Her voice hardens as she says *Liz's* name. After the trouble she's caused for Charlie over the last couple of years, Mum would love to tell her what she thinks of her.

"Since when has that ever stopped Donna going after what, or should I say *whoever* she wants? If a man's in a relationship, it's more of a turn on for her."

Mum looks uncomfortable, probably at me using such an expression in front of her. "You mean Donna *with* Darren?" Her face darkens as she emphasises the word *with*. "Surely not?"

I nod. "Friends with benefits. It's been going on for bloody years right under my nose and I didn't suspect a thing."

"You mean that even when you and him..." Her voice trails off. She looks too horrified to even say *I told you so.* "Oh, love."

I nod and fall into the softness of her jumper. "She was supposed to be my best friend. I thought I could trust her." She puts her arms around me as I sob onto her shoulder.

"No wonder you sounded so down when I phoned

yesterday." She strokes my hair. "Why didn't you say something?"

"I had Charlie sitting at the side of me." I raise my head. "I don't want her to know. Not yet anyway. I've got to get my head around it first. Sorry." I brush the mascara streak I've left on her arm.

"I just don't understand Louisa. When did it all start?"

"Before Darren and I even met apparently, from what she said."

She looks thoughtful. "Well, that's not so bad then. If you hadn't even met..."

"Then they started up again whilst I was pregnant. Then who knows how many times after that? She's the woman he left me for."

"But you went to stay with her, didn't you? When you first separated? So how can it have been?"

I nod, miserably. "She's always been a good liar. Back then, I didn't know what I would have done without her."

"Meanwhile, she was the person your husband was sleeping with behind your back." Mum shakes her head. "She broke up your marriage."

"All those nights she stayed up with me whilst I was in pieces." I suddenly recall the Christmas when Darren deserted us. She 'dealt' with him whilst I was comatose on the sofa. *I bet she did.*

"You should have come to me, love. I'd have looked after you and Charlotte."

"I hadn't wanted to worry you. So I laid it all on Donna. I don't know how she could even look me in the eye." When I think about it, I cringe. As best friends do, I laid my soul bare.

"Because she's an absolute bitch." Her face is white and pinched. I don't think I've ever heard her use that word. "Wait until I get my hands on her."

"No Mum. Let me work out first how I'm going to handle it

all." The financial entanglement I've allowed myself to get into with her keeps rearing up in my mind and giving me a good kicking. I'm not going to tell her about that just yet.

"I don't want you to get involved." And I really don't. Mum enjoys her life. She doesn't need the stress of becoming embroiled in mine. Her life would be far too routine for me – she has set days for doing set things like pilates, or lunch with a particular friend, but she's happy with things. "I need *you* to talk to, as a bolthole from things, not to get caught up in my toxic mess."

"When did you find out about them? Did she tell you?"

"The last night of the holiday. If it can be called a holiday." I shake my head at the thought. "We'd been on the verge of falling out most of the time we were there, but I thought we'd sorted things out on that last day." My mind fills with an image of us toasting our friendship with our plastic cups of wine before it all came out. "Then she got drunk, and I said something she didn't like about her not knowing what it's like to be over-protective as a mother. She seemed to use it as an excuse to suddenly unburden herself."

"But why now? It's been years since you and Darren parted company."

"That's what I asked her. She couldn't give me a straight answer." As she swings her foot, I study her pink toenails. "I think it's because I'm happy and my life's going well. I've got you, and Charlie, but then I'm also really lucky with a job I love, and my house, and now Scott." It's a good list to have and I'm sick of her trying to make me feel guilty for having it.

"What have you told him? Scott, I mean?"

"Just that Donna and me had a fall out on holiday. I've spared him the details so far."

"I've often seen in her eyes how jealous she is of you." Mum's eyes narrow.

"But she's no need to be jealous. It's crazy. And because of what she's told me, our friendship's over."

"I'm glad to hear it. Don't you dare go forgiving her. I don't care how long ago it all happened. Friends don't do what she's done to each other."

"I know Darren and I are no longer together, but I can't forgive her."

"Nor should you love." She lifts her mug from the table and wraps her hands around it. "I bet the journey home together wasn't much fun."

"It really wasn't." I recall Charlie's puzzled face, but something seemed to stop her from asking too many questions. "I kept my earphones plugged in the entire time and Charlie sat in between us on the plane. She knew we'd fallen out, but I let her think it was a continuation of the rest of the holiday." I sip my coffee. "She's barely speaking to me for falling out with precious Donna."

"She has her on rather too much of a pedestal, doesn't she?" Mum rolls her eyes. "Perhaps you should knock her off it. Tell Charlie the truth."

I sigh. "I can't. She's only thirteen. I know she's ahead of her years in lots of ways, but she's at a funny age. She's already fighting to keep Darren in her life, so it will really feel like an upheaval when her relationship with Donna is threatened too. I think I'll probably tell her eventually though."

"Fair enough. Did you still travel back up with Donna in the car?"

"Did I heck. The plane journey was bad enough. No. Charlie and I got on the train. We stayed in a hotel in Antibes on the last night as well." I think back to how I had to zone Charlie's protestations out about leaving Donna on her own. "I can't bear to be near her. It feels as though our entire friendship's been nothing but a lie."

"Come here love." Mum passes me a tissue and reaches out

for me again. "I know it feels awful, but you're honestly better off without her in your life. Hopefully, you're seeing her through the same eyes I always have."

"I am," I sniff. "It's only taken me twenty-odd years. But she won't leave me alone. I know how the men she meets feel now. Her texts and calls are relentless."

"Donna's here." Charlie pokes her head around my bedroom door with a panicked expression on her face. I'm busy packing away my holiday clothes. When I first unzipped my case, I felt like binning everything in there. Thank goodness that 'holiday' is over and done with.

"Tell her to go home," I reply, as I sit on the bed. I know that I'm being unfair to Charlie. She doesn't know the extent of what's going on, yet I'm expecting her to get rid of Donna for me. But I don't feel very rational at the moment.

"Mum." Charlie steps inside the room and lowers her voice. "She's got a massive black eye and blood all over her face." She points back towards the door. "And she's crying her eyes out. You've got to come."

Sighing deeply, I drag myself from the bed and head towards the door. I can hear Donna snivelling as soon as I step onto the landing. "Go to your room whilst I deal with this."

"But I want to see Donna. I haven't seen her since we got back."

"I said go to your room."

She stamps across the landing and slams her bedroom door.

"You've got no right turning up here unannounced." I glare at Donna as I descend the stairs.

"Please Lou. I need your help. Look at me."

"You gave up the right to come running to me when you

slept with my husband." I lower my voice as I deliver the last few words, almost hissing them at her.

"You don't know how sorry I am." Blood is splattered all over her jacket. Whoever has done this has given her a right pasting.

"What, sorry that you told me, you mean?"

"Please don't turn me away. I need you. *Please.*" She steps forward from the door.

"What's happened?" I'm glad Scott's not here tonight. Things are new and nice between us, and I don't want to spoil it. I don't want to give him the impression that my life's full of drama. At the moment, he's my oasis of calm, away from it all, and we get little enough time together as it is with his work. And mine, in term time.

My tone of voice and perhaps something in my expression must have altered whilst I've been thinking about Scott. Donna's shoulders appear to slump with relief, and she says, "Can I come through?"

"Just for a few minutes and I'm only letting you because I don't want Charlie listening in to your latest drama." I would probably be better stepping out of the front door and speaking to her on the driveway, but it's not dark yet and I don't want the neighbours nosy-ing, especially Helen from next door.

"Oh, thank you."

Her gratitude is almost sickening, but if I'm honest, there's a small part of me that's curious about what's happened to her. Perhaps she's told Darren about her confession to me, and he's lost it. He never hit me when we were together. Being a hemophobic, he possibly feared ever making me bleed. But he used to have a temper. There were a few holes he'd kicked in my walls that had to be re-plastered after his departure.

Or maybe Liz has found out about him and Donna. She's evidently no stranger to being handy either. I've had her physically threaten me in the past when I've taken her to task about Darren having contact with Charlie. I keep out of her way now, and the situation has been simmering rather than boiling over in the last few months. The older Charlie gets, hopefully, the easier it will all become. One day she'll have to make her own mind up.

But I get the sense that whatever relationship Darren and Donna had over the years is still going on. After all, he's with someone again, which makes him a far more attractive proposition to Donna. God help her if Liz ever finds out. I'm not even with Darren, and she hates me with every fibre of her being.

"I went to see Ash," Donna says in a small voice.

"Did he do this to you?" I suspected something was 'off' with him, but he didn't look like the violent sort. "So what happened?" I'm aware I'm keeping my distance. A week ago, I'd have been making a right fuss of the state she's in.

"I needed him." She slumps on a chair at the kitchen table and drops her head into her hands, dripping blood on the polished surface.

I tear off a piece of kitchen roll and pass it to her. "That's your problem. You *need* people."

"He even called me a stalker." She bursts into tears.

"Why? What on earth have you been doing?" I know deep down that nothing justifies him hitting her, but any sympathy I would normally feel is evading me. Without her confession from the other day, I'd have been on the phone to the police by now.

"I've been going to his flat over the weekend. I thought he wanted me there." Thinking back to before we went away, she was there nearly every night for the fortnight they'd been seeing each other. As soon as he was available in the evening, she'd jump in her car, and she was there.

"And?"

"I wanted to go tonight, but he'd told me to stay away. Said he had things to do. But I was bored at home, and decided to surprise him. I thought that as soon as he saw me, he'd change his mind."

"He hit you for *surprising* him?"

"I found him in the club where he plays snooker." She rakes her fingers through her matted hair. "He was with a woman. I was watching them for ages through the window first." At this memory, she breaks into fresh tears.

I'm itching to say *what goes around, comes around*, and the situation with her husband running off with their florist enters my mind. I put a lot of store in karma these days.

"What happened then? You should have just walked away."

"I know I should. But I was gutted." She dabs at her swollen top lip and stares at the floor. "To be honest, I caused a bit of a scene."

"I can imagine." But even bloodied and bruised, she still looks beautiful. However, she clings to people like her life depends on it and then wonders why they feel suffocated. She's done it with me. But despite everything, I can feel myself softening. I do feel sorry for her. She just needs help, not just with whatever has gone on tonight but with how she is in general. Maybe it's up to me to make sure she gets herself referred somewhere. "So what did you do - to cause a scene, I mean?"

"I poured a pint over the woman's head, then I went for Ash. A few of the others pulled me off him and dragged me out."

"Then they did that to you?" I point at her face.

"No. The woman he was with followed me to the car park. With her mate. If it had been one on one, I might have stood a chance. But they were both laying the boot in." She lifts her top to reveal her six-pack midriff. Bruises are emerging up the side of her ribs already.

"And where was Ash whilst this was happening?" Surely he would care about her enough to stop her being beaten up.

"Watching." Her voice cracks. "He just stood there. I thought he liked me, but he watched as they kicked me again and again and again." More tears pour down her cheeks. "He said if I come near him again, he'll finish me off himself."

"Well, I hope you've listened to him," I tell her. "If you do go near him again, you'd be an absolute fool."

"I know." She smears snot mingled with blood across the back of her hand.

I rip off another piece of kitchen roll. "Do you want a glass of wine?" I glance up at the clock. "Then I'll take you to get yourself checked out. Make sure nothing's broken."

She smiles through her tears. "That would be amazing. Thanks Lou."

26

THEN

"HE'S BACK AGAIN." Donna let the curtain fall back and raced towards the door.

"Is it definitely him?"

She opened the lounge door a crack and peered into the hallway.

"I can't say for certain. It's nearly dark out there. Plus, it's frosted glass." She turned the light off and opened the door wider. "It certainly looks like him. Same height, same build."

"Close the door, will you? Just ignore it. He'll go away."

"I know you're in there Lou." Darren thumped on the door with what sounded like his fist. "I just want five minutes. There are things I need to tell you."

"Well I've got nothing to say to you!" I yelled back. "So go away before you wake Charlie."

"You know as well as I do an atom bomb won't wake Charlie once she's asleep." His voice was muffled beyond the door.

What he was saying was true. Charlie was the most beautifully behaved baby. Which had been a good job since Darren had barely been around.

"Please Lou. I'll tell you everything, I promise. It's time we got everything out in the open."

"What shall I do?" I hissed at Donna. "Shall I see what he's got to say? I'd like to know who this woman is."

She frowned. "What good will that do?"

"I don't know." I shrugged. "Give me a sense of closure, I guess."

I jumped as the thumping moved around to the side window. "I only want to talk to you. Just give me five minutes. You know I love you Lou."

Donna suddenly darted forwards. She inserted the key chain and pulled the door as far as it would allow. "Piss off, will you? She doesn't want to speak to you."

"You! You! How dare you get involved in this? After everything you've done." He booted the door. "Let me in now. I've got every right to speak to my wife."

"You either do one now, or I'm calling the police."

"You wouldn't bloody dare." He booted the door again.

"Right. That's it."

"No Donna. It'll only make things worse." I watched as she pressed the button on her phone three times and raised it to her ear. "And what did he mean, after everything you've done?"

"The man's deranged. Making a complaint is the only way we're going to get rid of him. It's me and you now Lou. Police, please."

"I'll check on Charlie." I moved towards the foot of her stairs, trying to stem the tears that were pouring down my face. Was this really what it had all come to?

27

NOW

"Please change your mind. It's Friday. I'm dying to get dressed up and hit the town."

Donna's acting as though nothing ever happened. After what she told me last week, she expects me to go out with her like normal. What planet is she on? And with the bruises on her face, I'm surprised she's even considering going out.

"No. I'm meeting Scott in a couple of hours." Not that I should even be giving her a reason. In fact, even if I was desperate to go out, she'd be the last person I'd be spending time with after what she's done.

"Well, at least meet me first then. Like you did before. I'll pay this time. I know I've still got a lot of making up to do."

"You can't make up for what you've done."

"Don't be like this."

Though I hate myself for it, the desperation in her voice tugs at my conscience. And she really must be desperate if she's offering to pay. She's certainly splashing the cash since she took out her loan. But in all honesty, I just want to get ready and meet Scott tonight. Donna needs to accept that things have changed. I can't let her pull the same strings with me as before - besides I can see straight through her manipulation tactics.

I've decided to have it out with Darren tomorrow. He should know that I've found out about it all, even though she insists that it's been months since they've slept together. I'm also battling with whether I should let Liz know. If she was to suddenly be out of the picture, it might change things for Charlie. It could be my one chance to get rid of her. But I'll decide on that later. I'm going to intercept him when he comes to collect Charlie and take it from there. That's *if* he comes to collect her.

"It's only me." Mum's voice echoes from the hallway.

"I'm off Donna. My mum's here to look after Charlie." She starts to say something but I cut her pathetic, whiny voice off mid-sentence and drop the phone into my handbag. And it feels good.

If Mum had any inkling that I was on the phone to her, she'd have me assessed and sectioned. If they ever come face to face again, I dread to think what she'll say to her. Which is another reason I want to confront Darren. Before Mum does. After all, she knows all about that now.

I smile as I pull up outside my house. Scott told me last night that he loves me. And he's finally changed his Facebook status to *in a relationship*. I know I'm acting like a teenager but so what? He's the first man I've allowed myself to fall for since I split up with Darren. And that was years ago. Scott mentioned about living together *again* last night. He seems really keen and even pulled up a couple of houses he's come across on his phone. People might say it's early days for us to be living together, but you just know when you know. And we were friends for quite some time and got to know one another before getting together as a couple.

Things feel perfect when it's just me and Scott. When I stay at his house, I'm just Lou, the woman. Instead of Lou, the mother, the foundation stage manager and the other baggage, also known as my so-called best friend.

"Anyone in?" I call as I let myself into the sun-dappled hallway. I kick off last night's sandals and pad through to the kitchen in bare feet where Mum's left me a note.

Charlotte's ground me down. I've taken her into Leeds for new trainers and lunch.

I smile again. Mum's such a pushover where Charlie's concerned. I reach for my phone to tell her to have her back for two when Darren's supposed to be collecting her, but then decide not to. It's better if Mum and Charlie are well out of the way when he knocks for her. I'll text and tell them to be back for half-past two. Charlie might have forgotten about it anyway. I imagine she's more excited about the prospect of a new pair of trainers and whatever else she can wheedle out of her grandma.

My phone beeps.

> Remember I love you.

I can't grumble. OK, I've got this Darren and Donna situation to deal with, but the rest of my life is pretty good. Then it beeps again.

> I'm setting off now. Put the kettle on.

It's Georgia. I almost forgot about our arrangement. It's a good job I've come home when I have.

With only a couple of weeks left of the school holiday, we've arranged to do an overview of the first term back. We always do it together, so she has some input and knows exactly what she's doing once we get back into it. As a teaching assistant, she's amazing, and goes far beyond what she's paid to. Her love of the kids drives her, and I always make sure she gets an extra special present at Christmas and something at the end of the school year.

By the time Georgia taps softly on the door, I've lugged my planning file out of my 'teacher-box,' and have the long and medium-term plans spread across my kitchen table.

"Hello stranger." I hug her as she steps into the house. "It's good to see you." And it is. Her presence offers a sense of normality in my current chaotic life.

"How's your summer going?" She lets me go and kicks her sandals off. They land next to mine.

"Ah, you know. Eventful. Quick. How about yours?"

"Same." A look enters her eyes which I haven't seen before. Georgia is always so bright and cheerful. It's a prerequisite for working with four and five-year-olds. She's only just walked in, but something is definitely up with her.

"Is everything OK?"

"Just family stuff." She follows me towards the kitchen.

"Your brother again?" From the snippets she's told me over the time we've worked together, he's terrible news. Which has always surprised me, given how lovely she is. I've met her mum too, and she's the same.

"He's out on licence."

"Ah, right. Have you seen him?"

"He's pestering me to, but my parents will be really upset if I do. They've washed their hands of him." It's the most she's talked about her brother since she originally confided in me about the situation. He'd just been sentenced for affray and drug dealing, and she'd broken down at school. I had to drag the story from her, and she swore me to secrecy. She might be more open now we're out of the school environment. And despite the Donna and Darren saga, I've got more capacity to listen to her now, much more than when we're caught up with the end of school day tasks.

"I thought he got longer than two years?" I do mental calculations as I look at her. "That's how long he's been in prison, isn't it?"

"He had to serve so much time of his sentence inside, and the rest out on licence. He got out a month ago. Just as we were breaking up for the holidays."

"Some summer you've had then." I pass her a coffee. "You look like you could do with one of my extremely fattening cookies to go with that."

She smiles then, for the first time since she arrived. "Let's get on with this." She slides one of the planning sheets towards herself. "It'll do me good to get my brain into something else."

"Well, if you decide you want to talk about it." I reach across the table and squeeze her arm.

"Right loo break, methinks." Georgia rises from her chair with a yawn, her blonde hair cascading down her back as she stretches.

"I think we've earned a break." I stretch too. "We've done well in two hours. Literacy's sorted for the first week back, numeracy, all the areas of provision..."

"Outdoor provision," she adds. "Then we just need to plan the class layout and displays, and we're done, aren't we?"

"Will you still be OK to give me a hand for a few hours next week... just with moving things about in the classroom?"

"Depends which day."

"Any really. I'll probably be spending most of the week in school, getting prepped for our new little darlings."

"Yeah, that's fine. I'll let you know which day... anyway," she says with a pained expression. "I must get to the loo before there's a puddle all over your lovely kitchen."

I flick the kettle switch and reach into my box for the displays folder. As I spread the contents on the table, my attention is averted to Georgia's phone as it lights up. *Brad calling.* That's her brother. *Bradley.* She must have set his photograph on her contact list. That's the difference between being a teacher and a teaching assistant. She'll get time to do things like that. Eager to see what a recently-released prisoner convicted of affray and drug dealing looks like, I tilt the screen to have a closer look. I nearly fall off my chair as I stare into the face of none other than *Ash.*

"Was that my phone?" Georgia slides back into her chair. "Oooh, I'm glad you've put the kettle on again. I was just thinking about how I could murder another coffee."

"Yes, it was. *Brad.*" I glance at her from where I'm standing, hoping the shock I'm feeling isn't registering on my face. "Sorry, I didn't mean to be nosy, but I couldn't help but notice." I busy myself in making the coffee.

She sighs as she reaches for her phone. "I don't know what to say to him. Especially because he's up to all his old tricks again – I found out a couple of weeks ago."

"*Really?*" I need to stay casual here. Find out what I can. *Should I tell her about Donna?* I don't know what to do for the best. There's that saying, *it's a small world,* but this is ridiculous. "Why? What's he doing?"

"I don't know the ins and outs, but I know for certain that he's dealing again."

"Dealing what?" I might sound naïve here, but this is a world I've never encountered.

"Drugs. Class A ones. Heroin and coke as far as I can tell. It funds the lifestyle he's got used to. But he's into all kinds of other stuff too." She shakes her head. "I know enough about him that could land him back inside in a breath."

I stare at the kettle, trying to process this. "So why don't you? Report him, I mean?" I suppose it's easy for me to say, especially since I haven't got siblings. I don't know what that bond feels like. Maybe if I'd had a brother or sister, I wouldn't have put quite so much store in my friendship with Donna.

"How can I? He's a lot of things, but he's still my brother."

"But if it were to come out that you knew something all along, you could be in big trouble. Is he worth that?" Perhaps if I can persuade her to turn him in, that could be the problem solved. He gets sent back to prison and Donna would be none the wiser. If it comes to where I have to tell her what I know, it could get ugly. Especially if Ash were to find out. Or *Brad*, should I say. I don't want him coming after me. Especially if he's been convicted of *affray*.

"Nobody knows what I know." Poor Georgia, she looks as miserable as a dark December day. So will Donna if she finds out about this.

"But *I* know now." It's true. No matter what, I can't just un-hear what I've found out.

"You wouldn't say anything, would you? You're my friend. In fact, you're the only person I've talked to." There's a real desperation in her voice. I keep my back to her as I stir the coffee. She continues. "I didn't plan to say *anything* to *anyone* but to be honest, I've been going mad with it all."

"I'm not surprised. It's a hell of a situation to keep bottled up." I spin around and smile at her. "And you're too lovely to be related to someone like that."

"He was lovely too when we were kids. I mean, we had exactly the same upbringing." She lowers her gaze. "My parents have been gutted with it all. Especially since he was released."

"What changed for him?"

"The mates he found in his teens, I guess. Then he got greedy. He likes the good stuff and trafficking and supplying drugs to dealers is the easiest way to get it. *It beats working,* is what he's always said."

"How did you find out he's dealing again?"

"From a friend of his. Someone who's got himself straightened out – I've known him since we were kids. He's trying to keep away from Brad, and so am I."

"Right." I nod, still not sure where to take this next.

"You can't say anything Lou. To *anyone*. Brad knows some *very* dodgy people. He even threatened me once."

"*Threatened you?*"

She nods. "A few years ago, it was all about money." She says that as though it makes it all better. "There have been people who've crossed him who've been *taken out*, as he puts it."

"*Taken out?*" I swallow.

"From what I can gather, he's a *huge* fish in this world he's in."

That does it. "He's been seeing my friend," I tell her. "But he's going by the name of Ash."

Silence hangs between us for a moment.

"What?"

"It's true."

"You're joking." Georgia pales beneath her make-up. "Which one?"

"Donna."

"Shit. Donna, as in your best friend?"

"Yes. To be honest, I thought he looked a bit of a dubious character but..."

"*You've* met him as well?" Her voice rises a notch. "When? Where?"

"Just in the pub – about three weeks ago. Him and his mate chatted us up. He went home with her." I wonder if the man he was with, Gavin, is in the same league. If I hadn't have been with Scott, I might have...

"Tell her to stay away from him Lou. Well away. He can come across as nice enough on the surface, but then..."

"Oh, I can see that." I glance out of the window, trying to calm my thoughts by looking over the garden. One minute we're talking about what's going in the home corner and the water tray, the next we're discussing people taking other people 'out.'

"So now what?" Georgia looks at me as though I have all the answers. "Are you going to tell her who he really is?"

"I think I'll have to," I reply. "Although things have gone hugely wrong between them. *Hugely wrong.* It seems she's not the only woman he's been seeing."

"That figures." She stares into her coffee. "He's never been a one-woman sort of person."

"She caught him the other night and the woman he was with attacked her." Donna's battered face emerges in my mind. She might be a pain in the arse, but no one deserves that kind of treatment. "Well, her *and* another woman did."

"Oh my God." Georgia's hand flies to her throat. "Was she OK?"

"Yeah. Ash or Brad, or whatever his bloody name is, just stood there and watched as they kicked ten bells out of her."

"Bloody hell. Has she reported it?"

"I don't think so. She said she doesn't want all the hassle. And she reckons it's over between them, but you never know with Donna."

"She's *got* to stay away from him." Georgia rubs at her forehead.

"I know, but I don't see how I warn her to stay away from him without her knowing the full story. She'd be like a dog with a bone until I told her the truth."

"OK. I understand that." Her voice falls again, and she studies me with her pale blue eyes. Eyes that I now remember being the same as Ash's. They're quite striking. "Of course you can't *not* tell her. But when?"

"I'll do it later. She's still black and blue from the other night, so she won't be thinking of going back there in a hurry." *Can I really face Donna today?* I was in such a good mood before. "Come on, Let's get finished up here. Then I've got something else I need to deal with." I'm thinking of Darren's arrival at two o'clock. "Then I'll sort Donna."

Georgia shakes her head. "I just can't believe what a small world it is. Your friend and my brother."

"Why does he call himself Ash though?"

"If anyone was to do a Google search on his real name, they'd find out everything about him. He was in the news when he got sent down. The piece they did about him was scathing." Georgia's eyes fill with tears. "I couldn't hold my head up for ages afterwards."

"You've done nothing wrong." I reach for her hand.

"I know. But you know what some people can be like."

28

THEN

"I can't believe he's here with her." Donna turned away from me with tears in her eyes. "He knew we'd be in tonight."

"How could he have done?" It's been over a week since you split up.

"I messaged him."

"I told you it was best to leave things be." I turned to face her. "Chasing him isn't the way forward. He'd be more likely to come back if you just got on with your life and looked like you were enjoying yourself."

"How can I? It's rotten, what he's doing to me."

I tugged on her arm, trying to twist her to face in another direction. "Stop watching him then."

"I can't. He's flaunting his new girlfriend right in front of me. I thought he liked me. I thought he wanted me."

"Come on. Let's sit down." I led her through the club towards a table in the corner. With my massive pregnant belly, the crowd parted to make way for me. She'd begged me to go out, but really, the last place I wanted to be was in a club, watching her ex get off with someone else. Darren hadn't been happy about me going into a club at eight months pregnant, either.

"As if he dumped me for her." She pointed across the room. "Look at the state. Her skirt barely covers her arse."

"It's his loss, Donna. You'll find someone much better."

"It's alright for you to say." She looked me up and down as I lowered into my seat. "You're married with a baby on the way. I'm starting to think I'll never get what you've got."

"Never mind all that," I frowned at her. She always, always made it be about me. "If you want my advice, get on that dance floor and show him you don't give a toss."

"The last thing I feel like doing is dancing."

"You've dragged me out when I should have my feet up. The least you can do is try to enjoy yourself. Even just a bit." I gave her what I hoped was my most imploring expression.

"Will you come with me?" she sniffed.

"After I've been for a wee. This baby of mine is pressing right on my bladder. I don't think I'll be too energetic, mind."

"You're so lucky to be able to say that." She nodded towards my belly. "I hope it happens for me one day."

"Don't think we haven't noticed you." A voice echoed around the walls as I sat on the loo.

"Yeah," said a different voice, just as catty as the first. "Desperate or what? He's with me now. As I'm sure you can see."

"Do one, will you?" It was Donna. I thought she'd gone back into the club. I needed to hurry up.

"Look at him again and I'll..."

"You'll what? Come on then?"

I heard a click of a heel and knew I needed to get out there. But when you're in mid-flow at eight month's pregnant...

"I'm not going to fight you. Just stay away from him."

"Anyway," the other one laughed, or should I say, cackled. "You should hear what he says about you?"

"What?" As if she was asking.

"Limpet. Desperado. Charity case."

"And that's just for starters," said the other. "I could go on."

I yanked my tights up as quick as I could and flushed, just as one of them said, "I could wipe the floor with you."

Donna was squaring up to them as I pushed the cubicle door open with a bang. "You'll have to get past me first."

They both laughed like drains.

"Come on," I hooked her arm with mine. "They're not worth it. She'll find out in no time at all about his small, what shall we call it?" I waggled my little finger in the girl's face. "Let's go and dance."

29

NOW

"Mum, I've only just remembered about Dad." The town hall clock chimes three in the distance. Charlie must still be in Leeds. Her voice has an urgent edge. "I can't believe I forgot."

"Yeah, I thought you must have done." I'm glad now that it slipped my mind to text her. I've had the situation with Ash on my mind instead.

"Has he been and gone?" The urgency in her voice turns to hopefulness. I hope one day she stops idolising him. He doesn't deserve her. "He was picking me up at two."

"No love. I'd have let you know if he'd turned up. He must have forgotten too." I'm just glad she didn't cut her time short with her Grandma to rush back and have a fruitless wait for him. But I'll keep this thought to myself for now.

"He always forgets me." Her voice drops. "I've tried ringing him and his phone's off."

"It was off when I tried as well."

"Grandma says I've nothing to feel bad about," Charlie continues. "She says *I'm* the teenager. It's fine for *me* to forget, but Dad's the parent, and should do everything he can to spend time with me."

"Well, you haven't got as much of an argument against him not turning up today, really." *Though I have,* I think to myself. "You've both forgotten. You must be having a good time with your Grandma."

"I am. I've got trainers, new jeans, some headphones..."

"I hope you haven't been spending all her money." I laugh. She enjoys spoiling Charlie, but still...

"No. I had some of my own. Anyway, the other reason I'm ringing is because I want to stay at Jess's tonight. Especially now that I'm not going out for tea with Dad."

"Has she invited you to stay? Or should I say, has her mum?"

"Yes. Her mum's going out, but she'll be back later. That's why Jess wants me to keep her company. You can ring her mum and check."

"OK, I will do. If it's fine with her, then it's fine with me. Just come back here first and pick up what you need. Is Grandma OK?"

"I'm shattered," Mum calls out. Charlie must have me on speakerphone. "I'll be glad to get home and put my feet up."

I smile to myself. Scott's coming around later, so at least I'll have the house all to myself with him. He really will be my oasis of calm after I've been round to see Donna. The smile fades from my face. I'll have to tell her about Ash – I've got a responsibility to.

But first I'm going round to Darren's. Not only has he not arrived to collect Charlie, or even rung to cancel, *yet again,* he's also not paid for Charlie's maintenance. It's the third month in a row he's let me down with it. And since his phone is off, I've got every reason to turn up at his house. At least if he tries using Liz as an excuse for his own shortcomings, she'll be there to speak for herself. It's not going to be pretty, but it's time to do something. For Charlie's sake. I'm sick of shutting up and putting up.

I still haven't decided how to handle telling Darren that I know about him and Donna – I'm just going to go with the flow and if I come out with it, I come out with it. It might depend on whether Liz is there though. Perhaps I should keep things just about Charlie this time. It might be better if Liz isn't there when I confront him about Donna.

They live in a two up, two down end terrace three miles away from us. It's like the house me and Darren first lived in. A concrete front yard and washing pegged from house to house across the street.

Whilst I'm on route, I try to call him three times, hoping to deal with him by phone rather than in person. I felt more confident about the thought of confronting him when he was coming to my house, when it would have been just him and me. The prospect of butting heads with Liz isn't an attractive one.

"What do you want?" Liz opens the door and her face falls at the sight of me. Her heavy green eyeshadow matches the green of her t-shirt. Charlie would definitely call her Liz the Lizard if she could see her now.

"Charming. Hello to you too. I'm here to see Darren actually." My breath is coming in short bursts even though I've only walked to the door from where I've parked further along the street. This woman has always set my teeth on edge and made me anxious.

"What for?" She leans against the door frame.

"I need to speak to him about our daughter. Can you let him know I'm here please?"

"Couldn't you have rung first?" I swear her lip is curling in dislike of me from where she stands in her elevated position on the doorstep. I stare her in the eye. There's no way this woman has any right to look down at me.

"I've tried already to call him. So has Charlie. He was supposed to collect her at two."

"That's got nothing to do with me." She folds her arms.

"Can you let him know I'm here? Please."

Her eyes bulge from their sockets more than usual. The woman is infuriating. "He's not in."

"Where is he?"

"How should I know? I'm not his keeper." Her voice has the scratchy edge of a twenty a day smoker. I don't know what the hell Darren sees in her.

"Except you *are* his keeper, aren't you? Does it feel good coming between a dad and his daughter?" This is the first chance I've ever had to have it out with her. What I'm saying needs to be said at last.

"I'm not coming between *anyone*. Just because I want nothing to do with her."

I swallow the anger that immediately rises. "Why not Liz? Charlie's a nice kid. You knew Darren had a daughter when you married him. What's your bloody problem?"

"Look here. If I'd have wanted kids, I'd have had one myself. And I certainly don't see why I should have to pay for someone else's."

"I'm not asking *you* to pay. I'm asking Darren to. This is the third month he's not paid what he should for his daughter. It's not good enough."

"I'll tell you what's not good enough, shall I? It's you." she steps forward and points at me. "Miss High and Mighty, thinking you can turn up on my doorstep, calling the shots."

I take a deep breath. I'm going to get nowhere with this woman. She's as rough as a badger's arse. "When will Darren be back? I really need to discuss this with him."

"So you can harass him about money we haven't got? You don't need his bloody money – you've got enough of your own."

She points at me, infuriating me further. But I'm going to keep a lid on myself.

"We'll let the Child Support Agency decide that, shall we?" I smile my best mock-sweet smile at her. "I'm sure they'll agree with me. Darren brought Charlie into the world as much as I did. He should pay towards her upbringing."

"You wouldn't dare." She steps out onto the pavement and faces me, reality seemingly dawning on her. "You can't! The bloody CSA. They'll take him for all he's got."

"Good." I don't budge. "Because any man who treats his daughter like he's treated ours over the last couple of years deserves everything that's coming to him."

"He was right about you," she sneers. "Totally up your own arse, aren't you? What other words did he use, oh, yeah, frigid, boring..."

"Frigid." I laugh. "Funny you should say that." I step back from her. "That must be why he was sleeping with my best friend behind my back. She's *far* from frigid." I smile at her again. Here we go – killer punch. "And it turns out he still is."

"What did you say?" Her face falls and her fists curl at her sides. Any minute now, she's going to go for me. It's time to get out of here.

"You heard." I yank my keys from my pocket and start towards my car. "Too-da-loo."

It takes a moment to get my breath back once I jump back in my car. As I glance in my rear-view mirror, Liz is striding towards me. I hurriedly start the engine and drive off just as she thumps at the rear door. I wouldn't like to be in Darren's shoes when he gets home.

· · ·

As I pull up outside my house, I tug out my phone. The only message is from Mum.

> I've just dropped Charlie at Jess's. She took a change of clothes from my house. You know where I am if you fancy a glass of wine later.

> Thanks. But Scott's coming over. I'll bob round to see you tomorrow.

> OK doke. Have a nice evening.

I try Darren's phone and then Donna's. Both are switched off. They're probably together somewhere. Liz might be an absolute cow, but there's a slither of me that feels sorry for her. Darren often switches his phone off to avoid me, but it's very unusual for Donna, as she's normally glued to social media. I decide against leaving her a message. What I need to tell her about Ash needs doing face to face. I'll probably leave things until tomorrow now. Scott's due round in just over an hour and we get precious little time together as it is. And I need to get ready.

30

THEN

I STARED INTO THE SKY, and the gloom stared back at me. There's never a good day for a funeral, but the pouring rain was in keeping with the fact that the funeral was for Cameron who never even made it to the age of twenty-three. Luckily, he hadn't been with Donna at the time of his heart attack. She was in enough of a state as it was.

Before I could pull her back, Donna edged her way to the front of the mourners and helped herself to a fistful of earth. The woman who I'd since found out was Cameron's fiancée glared at her. In her shoes, I think I'd have done more than merely glare at her. An older woman embraced her, and she stepped back.

We walked behind a couple of men who I recognised as Cameron's friends from one night when Donna was getting off with Cameron in the club. He'd told her he was engaged and that his fiancée was away. That would put many women off, but knowing he was engaged seemed to only turbo charge Donna's desire. And before long, they were meeting up at least a couple of times a week.

Donna closed the gap and caught the arm of one of them. "Have they said what caused his heart attack yet?"

They paused and allowed us to fall into step with them. "Weed."

"It must have been strong stuff then."

"It was. But Cam apparently had a pre-existing heart condition. What happened would probably have happened anyway."

"I didn't expect you to be here," the other said, frowning at Donna. "She knows about you, you know — his fiancée." He pointed towards the brunette head bowed several feet ahead of us.

"I don't know how she found out," Donna said, looking towards her. "But at least it's all out in the open now."

"She'd have been better kept in the dark if you ask me," he replied. "Anyway, I hope you're not coming to the wake. I don't think you'd be very welcome."

Donna's eyes filled with tears and her lip was trembling, so I answered for her. She didn't look as though she'd be able to keep it together.

"No, we're not. Donna just came here to pay her respects. And I came to support her."

As we were about to leave the churchyard, a hand landed on her shoulder and spun her around.

"He was only having a bit of fun with you, you know?" Cameron's fiancée squared up to Donna as I watched on, wondering what to do.

"It was much more than that actually," Donna replied, jutting her chin out defiantly.

"Do you reckon?" She laughed. "Is that why he always came back to me?"

"If you were giving him what he wanted..." Donna's voice

rose as everyone watched on. "He wouldn't have needed to look elsewhere, would he?"

"That's enough." The woman who'd been comforting his fiancée at the graveside began marching towards us. "Have some respect. And women like you," she wagged a finger at Donna. "Going after other women's husbands. I hope someone really hurts you one day, so you know what it feels like."

31

NOW

"You and your blinking phone." Scott groans as I reach for it. "I'll clear the plates, shall I?" He rises from the table, a little too sharply.

"I'm sorry. I just need to see if it's Donna. I've been trying to get hold of her all day and her phone's always off."

"I thought the two of you had fallen out?" He pulls a face as he slides his plate onto mine.

"We did. But it's kind of sorted." I hope my tone of voice says *subject closed.* He'd think I was an idiot to be giving her the time of day after what she's admitted to, if he knew the full story. But I'm more worried about Mum finding out I've been speaking to her. She'd go ballistic, in fact she'd probably have a go at Donna directly. The whole thing's messed up enough as it is, and in the midst of it all, is Charlie.

"What did you *kind of* fall out about?"

"Hang on. Sorry. Just let me read this." I squint at the screen. "I'm sorry." I glance up at him. "I'll just be a couple of minutes. Then I'm all yours."

He raises his hand as if to say, *don't mind me,* and begins stacking the dishwasher. He doesn't look happy though. I don't suppose I would be if he was side-lining me for his phone. However, he doesn't know the full story yet.

> You've tried to ring me six times. What's so urgent?

Was it *six*? That's not like me – it shows how hard I've been trying to get hold of her today.

I type back quickly. I'll answer this, then I'll turn the thing off. If anything comes up with Charlie, she'll call Mum if she can't get hold of me. I don't want to spoil my evening with Scott, but I need to see Donna tomorrow. Perhaps I should have made sure I told her about Ash today, but after the row with Liz, I gave up with it. I couldn't face any more.

Are you around tomorrow?

> I don't know.

My curiosity is immediately piqued. It's not like her to give such curt replies and she normally puts an x at the end of her messages, or a smiley face. She *must* be with Darren. I still haven't heard from him either.

What do you mean? Where are you?

> I'm out at the moment.

Where?

> Just out, right?

Why are you being like this? It's me who should be off, not the other way round, after what you've done.

Yeah, well, you'll be pleased to know I'm back with Ash again, so I'll be staying well away from Darren in the future.

You're what? Are you mad?

What am I supposed to do? You wouldn't even give me an hour of your time last night.

So it's my fault that you want to hang around with nutters. Is that what you're saying?

He's not a nutter. It wasn't him that hit me, it was the women.

He IS a nutter. And you don't know the first thing about him.

Well with friends like you, it's no wonder I've had to go back to him. I was lonely.

You're pathetic.

The doorbell echoes through the house. Great. Now what?

"Next time." Scott wipes his hands on a towel. "We're going out for dinner. And you're leaving that bloody phone here."

"I'd better see who it is." And then I'll make it up to him, I tell myself as I stride to the door. He's every right to be pissed off at me. He'll be setting off home if I'm not careful.

"You're seven hours too late."

"What?" Just with one word, I can tell Darren's drunk. Very drunk.

"What the hell do *you* want at this time of night?"

"I want to talk to you." He barges past me into the hallway, drowning me in lager fumes. "What the hell have you been fucking saying to Liz?" He slams the door after him with his foot.

"And you are???" Scott steps out of the kitchen and looks from me to Darren.

"This is my ex-husband, Charlie's waste-of-space father."

"Don't you *ever* call me that." He steps towards me. He reeks. It's just like the good old days.

"You stay right where you are." Scott comes closer as well. "Lou, do you want me to throw him out?"

"In a minute," I reply. "I want to hear what he's got to say for himself first."

"Do you want me to leave you alone?"

"No." And I really don't. Perhaps Scott needs to know about my current dramas. He might be more understanding of why I've been preoccupied.

"I want to hear what you've been telling Liz." Darren jabs his finger towards me. "She's thrown me out because of you."

"No Darren. She's thrown you out because of *you*." I point back at him. "I just hope Donna's been worth you losing two relationships for. Though in hindsight, she did me a favour." I glance at Scott who's just standing there, watching us. He's worth ten of Darren.

"There's nothing going on. Not any more."

"According to Donna, you've been falling in and out of bed for the best part of twenty years. Even when I was pregnant!"

"So *that's* why you've fallen out with her." Scott leans against the hallway door and surveys Darren with a look of distaste. But I see a flicker of relief that he now knows what's going on. I guess in his eyes, I could have been distracted tonight for any number of reasons.

"I've only just found out. Whilst we were on holiday." I turn back to Darren.

"Why did she bloody tell you?" Darren's voice rises, full of drunken anguish. "And why didn't you come to me? Why did you have to tell bloody Liz?"

"I tried, but your phone was off and Liz was being a right bitch this afternoon," I reply. "Plus, no matter what I think of her, she's got a right to know. No woman deserves to be repeatedly cheated on. You're an utter bastard."

"Don't you talk to me like that. Not in front of..." He narrows his eyes as he turns towards Scott. "Who are you anyway?"

"Scott's my boyfriend. Not that it's any of your business."

"It's every bit of my business when he's in this house with *my* daughter." He jerks his neck towards the stairs. Now he's close up, I see the lines of age and the shadow of a beard.

"Well, that's a laugh." I'm so glad not to be married to him anymore. "*Your* daughter. The daughter you let down week after week after week. The daughter you can't even put your hand in your pocket for. You'd rather spend your money on booze."

"I can't give you what I haven't got, can I? And it's not as if she's short of anything. I'm fucking sick of all the grief from the lot of you. You. Liz. Donna." Spit sprays from his mouth as he rants. "You can all go to fucking hell."

I lower my gaze. I can't bear to look at him. "You'll be hearing from the CSA anyway. I'm sick of you not paying. She's your daughter as much as mine."

"Do your worst Lou. I'll just pack my job in. You can't get blood out of a stone."

"Have you heard this?" I turn to Scott. I've gone from not wanting Scott to know *anything,* to involving him smack bang in the middle of our altercation. "*Father of the year,* or what? I tell you what. Don't even turn up here for her again. Not until you can act like her dad. You don't deserve her."

"You can't stop me seeing my daughter. In fact, where is

she?" He pushes past me towards the bottom of the stairs and curls his head around the bannister. "Charlie?"

"She's not here. Not that I'd let you see her in the state you're in anyway."

"Who the fuck do you think you are?" He twists his head to look at me. "You can't stop me."

"I think you'll find I can."

His fists curl at his sides. "You think you can speak to me like I'm something you stepped in, and humiliate me in front of *him*." He steps towards me again, more quickly this time and he's so close that his spittle lands in my face as he points towards Scott then back at me. "You will *not* humiliate me. You're going to get what's coming to you."

"Right, that's enough." Scott rushes over and in one movement he twists Darren's arm up his back. "Out *now*. Turn up here again and we'll ring the police." He pushes him towards the door.

"Get the fuck off me." Darren's body stiffens.

"I said out." Scott pushes him over the threshold.

"You haven't heard the last of me." He wags his finger as he stands in the doorway. I dash over and slam it shut.

"I'll be back," he shouts through the letterbox. "When you haven't got loverboy to come to your rescue. You'd better watch your back."

"Is that your phone *again*?" Scott tenses as I curl into the side of him on the sofa.

I shake my head and leave it where it is. A glass of wine has calmed us both and we're back to being just *us* again. I'm relieved he was here tonight with Darren turning up in that mood. He only usually gets like that when he's had a skinful, though tonight he was different, more wired. He seemed capable of anything.

It rings for the second time. I sit up straight, unsure what to do.

"Do you really *have* to answer it?" Scott says. "I was hoping to take you to bed shortly."

I smile at him. "How can I refuse such an offer?" Then just as my finger hovers over the off switch, I get a message notification.

> Please. Please. Answer your phone Lou.

I wave the screen in front of Scott. "Look at this. I'm going to have to ring her back, aren't I?"

He sighs and shuffles away from me. It's a small move but speaks volumes. Damn Donna. I wish I could distance myself from her shit. I will. As soon as all this Ash situation is dealt with. I've got to.

"Thank God." She sounds hysterical. "He's broken my arm."

"Who? Ash? What happened?"

"He-he wanted me to go home... after he'd got what he wanted from me, that is." Her words pump out between sobs.

"Calm down Donna. I can hardly make out what you're saying."

"When I kicked up a stink he went for me. Owww." I have to hold the phone away from my ear. "It really hurts."

"Where exactly are you?" I glance at the clock. Nearly eleven. Bloody hell.

"Near his flat. On the edge of Harrogate. He threw me out. *He threw me out.* What am I going to do?" She breaks into fresh sobs.

Scott's shaking his head. "Tell her to ring a taxi."

She must overhear him. "I need to get this arm looked at Lou. And I've no bank card with me. Can you come over?

Please? I'm scared. What if he comes after me again? Or what if those women do?"

"You need to go to the police with this. It's no good me coming over. I can't fight him off any more than you can."

"I can't go to the police. He knows where I live, doesn't he?" I imagine her face, a sheen of snot and tears. "He's already warned me not to ring them."

"I really don't want to be mixed up in all this." *Especially with what I now know about him.*

"Please Lou. Help me. I'm scared. I can't drive with my wrist like this and I'm over the limit anyway."

"So am I! I've had three glasses of wine. Hang on a minute. Bloody Charlie's trying to get through. Hello?" Scott gets up and walks to the window. His face says it all.

"Mum, can you meet me?" She sounds upset but nothing like the hysteria I've just had from Donna. "I've fallen out with Jess."

"Oh no! You're still at her house, aren't you? You'd better not be trying to walk home on your own."

"I'm in her front garden. Her mum's not back and she said I can't go back inside. I just want to come home Mum."

"Why on earth have you fallen out? She's supposed to be your best friend." *Like that counts for anything,* I think miserably to myself. My phone's beeping again with Donna trying to get back through. This evening has turned into a right shambles.

Scott laughs, but it's a sarcastic laugh, one that seems to say *bring it on.*

"I'll tell you about it when you get here. Can you set off now Mum?"

"I'm on my way."

"I'll take you for Charlie, then I'll go for Donna." Scott glances at his watch. "I've only had a glass and a half all evening. Give me her phone number so I can find her."

"But she needs to go to A&E," I hold my hand over the mouthpiece of the phone. "It's Saturday night – it'll be packed."

"I'll drop her off there and leave her with cash for a taxi." He shrugs. "Take it or leave it. At least you'll know she's safe."

I nod. "Will you come back here?"

"Of course I will. You just sort your daughter out. Where is she?"

"Not far," I reply, wanting to kiss him. It's years since I had anyone other than Mum willing to put themselves out for me. "It'll only take fifteen minutes to drive there and back."

"I'll just get my wallet."

"Thanks for this." I rise from the sofa and stretch my arms towards him. "I don't know what I'd do without you."

32

THEN

"How do you feel?" Donna looked at me as I spread the contents of the envelope out on the table.

"Weird." I replied. "Kind of empty." I stared at the pages, waiting for a surge of misery, or elation, or something.

"We should go out and celebrate." She suddenly seemed excited.

"Celebrate what? That my marriage has fallen apart. That Charlie's father couldn't keep it in his pants."

She looked thoughtful for a moment. "We should celebrate your freedom. You can do whatever you want now. Be whatever you want."

"I could do and be whatever I wanted anyway. Darren would never have stopped me. But I got married for life." I stared down at the Decree Absolute. "I never wanted this. I don't think he did either, deep down."

"Whether you both wanted it or not, this is where you are. And you've got a lot to be thankful for." Donna rested a hand on my back.

"I know."

She let go and sat in the chair facing me, studying me with

serious eyes. "Do you remember what we said when we were teenagers?"

I shook my head. We'd confided in each other so much over the years that she could have been referring to anything.

"We said that men come and go, but friends will be there forever. Do you remember?"

I pictured us in my bedroom at home, swigging from the Lambrini bottle and trying on make-up. The memory brightened me slightly. I was still that girl, despite what had happened with Darren. "Of course I do."

"I'm always here for you Lou. Always. We're soulmates, me and you. Through thick and thin." She tilted her head to one side as though waiting for my response.

"It's not like you to be so sentimental without a drink inside you." I laughed as I squeezed her hand. "Thanks. It means a lot."

"Anytime." She rose from her chair and headed towards the fridge. "Now it may only be ten in the morning, but I think a glass of vino is in order. Don't you?"

The words *decree absolute* swam in front of my eyes as I stared at them. "I suppose so. After all, it's not every day you get divorced."

33

NOW

I SENSE Scott's weight beside me and rub my eyes as I glance at the clock. It's nearly four in the morning.

"Go back to sleep," he whispers in the semi-darkness as the loo in the main bathroom flushes.

"Who's that?" I push myself up to be seated. "Is Charlie awake? She'd better not be. It took ages to get her settled after that fall out with her friend."

"No. It's just Donna." He tugs his t-shirt off. "She said she didn't feel safe going home, so I didn't think you'd mind her in your spare room for tonight."

"No. Of course I don't. Is she OK?"

"Her arm's not broken. Just badly sprained. It took hours for her to get seen and x-rayed."

"I thought you were just going to drop her off?" I don't like how I'm feeling at the thought of them spending so much time alone, even in a hospital waiting room. It's been hours. I don't trust her anymore. And with good reason. But I should trust Scott. I *do* trust him.

"I couldn't just leave her there when it came to it. She looked utterly lost."

I wrestle with the compulsion to flick the lamp on so I can study his face properly. But maybe I won't like what I see. I'm fully awake now, and contemplating Donna being up to her usual tricks with *my* boyfriend. With her wide eyes and pouting lips, she'll have played the perfect helpless female. Men love rescuing a damsel in distress. And they've spent four hours in each other's company. Tears fill my eyes. What a night it turned out to be. I reach towards the bedside table for my water.

"Are you OK Lou?" The warmth of his hand on my shoulder is small comfort. "I thought I was doing a good thing, taking her in and waiting with her." He's still whispering. Probably just as well, since she's on the other side of the wall. It's a wonder she hasn't burst into my room. Now that my eyes have grown accustomed to the gloom, I can see the concern on his face. He's in a very different mood to the one he left here in. "I thought that's what you'd have wanted. What's up?"

"Nothing. I'm fine. Just tired. And fed up with the dramatics going on all around us." I haven't even told him about who Ash really is yet. Perhaps he wouldn't be so keen to be involved with any of it if he knew *everything*. That's a problem for tomorrow though. Or should I say *later today* now?

It's getting light. I honestly can't understand why Donna would have gone anywhere near Ash after what he allowed to happen to her the other night. I only hope this latest assault isn't going to fuel the blame she has towards me even more.

"Anyway, she's safe now." Scott peels off his jeans, revealing the muscly legs I've grown to love. But I don't feel like pursuing him, not with Donna in the next room. Plus, he looks knackered. "And she's not so bad once you get talking to her, is she?"

My heart misses a beat. "What do you mean?"

"Well, she clearly thinks the world of you. And Charlie. She told me she's desperately sorry for going anywhere near Darren."

They've obviously been having a very in-depth conversation. I should never have let Scott drive over. If it hadn't been for Charlie needing me... "Well she's hoodwinked you, hasn't she?"

"Let's get some sleep Lou." He stretches out beside me and yawns. "And like I said, next time, we're going out." Then he turns his back to me and within a couple of minutes, he's snoring softly. Meanwhile, I'm seething.

"Where's Scott?" Donna appears in the kitchen, wearing my dressing gown. Her hair's all over the place but somehow, she still looks fabulous. She might be jealous of my career and house, but I'm more than a little envious of her looks. Over the years, I've told her until I'm sick of saying it, how she doesn't need to be so desperate and needy whenever she meets someone. She should relax and let *them* chase *her*.

My hackles rise at the fact that Scott's whereabouts are the first thing she asks after. I've tossed and turned since he returned, mulling things over. I've almost made the decision that I'm going to put this house on the market. Whether he's ready to jump into living together soon, or not. I'm going to dig through my bills' file today, do some totting up – see what I can get on my own. I could sell this place, and well, I've got a good job.

Yes, Donna and I have been friends for well over twenty years, but our friendship has become claustrophobic to the point of being toxic. Her admission to sleeping with Darren is the final nail in the coffin.

"He's gone to the supermarket to get some bits in for breakfast," I glance at the clock, "well it'll be brunch now."

"Perfect." She strides across to the coffee maker. "I'm starving. I'll have to pour this with my good hand," she laughs then. "Thanks for last night, by the way. Bailing me out like that."

"Thank Scott, not me. He'd drunk much less wine than I had." I'd have plied him with a whole bottle if I'd have known they were going to use the waiting time to get to know one another. Intentional on Scott's part, or not.

"He's really nice. I can see why you like him." She winks at me.

I glare at her. "Don't even go there. Haven't you done enough damage in my relationships?" I stand from the table and snatch the cup from her hand before she has a chance to pour. "In fact, I think you should go home?"

Her eyes fill with tears. "I'm sorry. I really didn't mean... oh shit." She tugs her phone from the pocket of my dressing gown. "It's him."

"Who?" For a moment, I wonder if she means Scott. God help her if she does.

Her expression darkens as she blinks at the screen. Then I realise.

"Ash?"

She nods slowly as she lifts her gaze to meet mine. "He's outside my house."

"What. He's there right now?"

Her eyes are full of panic. "What do I do?" She looks back at the phone. "He wants to see me. I can't Lou. I can't go back there. What if he goes for me again? My face is still black and blue from three nights ago."

"Just ignore it." Then a cold dread creeps over me. "Does he know where I live?"

Hanging her head, she nods. "I pointed your house out to him when we were driving past."

"Bloody great." I think of Charlie upstairs as I close my eyes. I've not heard any movement from her room since last night. She was exhausted after her fall out with Jess. Protecting her is all that matters to me right now.

What to do. What to do. I can't expect Scott to confront Ash or get involved. Ash is in a different league than Darren. A whole different animal. Darren's a lot of things but he's harmless. Whereas Ash is dangerous with a capital D. Should I get in touch with Georgia? Bloody hell, what I am thinking? I need to just ring the police. Every instinct is screaming at me to do it. *Just ring the police!* The man's around the corner. But I need to tell Donna who he *really* is first. Then I'll ring them.

"What exactly happened last night? Leading up to him going for you, I mean?"

"It was awful Lou. He didn't leave a stone unturned. He told me it's no wonder I'm on my own with my sad eyes and whiny voice, and that my favourite topic of conversation is myself."

He's not wrong there.

"And judging from you not saying anything, you obviously agree with him."

"No. It's just..."

"He said I make him want to punch me. That I'm pathetic and desperate. Is that how you see me too?"

The doorbell echoes through the house. We stare at each other in horror.

"What if it's him? Lou. I'm scared."

"Stay there. I'll get rid of him. That's if it is him. Hopefully it's someone selling double glazing."

Sure enough, as I throw the door open, I get Ash's sneering face. "Where is she?"

I step out onto the path and pull the door behind me. "I'll talk to you out here," I say. "I've got my daughter inside."

He follows me to the garden wall, and I notice his car parked alongside it. I need to move myself where I can get a good look at the number plate. No doubt the neighbours will have noticed his car too. This is the one time when I hope

Helen is doing her nosy neighbour bit. Normally she just gets on my nerves. Not much goes unseen by her.

I step to the other side of him so I'm facing the front of his car. "What is it you want?"

"I want to speak to Donna." His eyes don't leave mine. They're as cold as steel.

"Why? Do you not think you've done enough damage? She was in A and E half the night because of you."

"I'll be doing a lot more besides if she's thinking of squealing to the police on me, like she's threatened." He hooks his thumbs into his belt loops. "I've had just about enough of her."

"So that's a threat as well, is it?" I hold his gaze. Donna might be scared of him, but I'm not. Or at least, I'm trying not to be.

"I just want her to leave me the hell alone." He jerks his head toward my house.

"So you nearly break her arm to make that happen?"

"I need to see her. *Now.* Like I said. I need to make sure this isn't going to go any further." Then his tone becomes more menacing. "You'd be as well doing yourself a favour and keeping out of things."

"I'm already involved, much as I'd prefer not to be. And now you're in my garden. Which makes me even more involved." I try to keep the shake from my voice, but I can't help it.

"I'm going nowhere until I've spoken to her." He widens his stance. He really looks like Georgia. Now I know they're brother and sister. Should I say something? Would it make any difference? Perhaps it will make things worse. I just need to get him to leave for now.

"My boyfriend will be back here any minute. I don't want any trouble. I just want you to go."

He laughs. "Am I supposed to be frightened?" Then his face

hardens. "Get Donna out here now, and then I'll be out of here."

"No chance. You've got ten seconds to leave, or I'll call the police myself. I glance at his registration. It's a private one, therefore easier to remember.

"You cross me and I'll..." His jaw hardens.

"You'll *what* Ash... or should I say, Brad?" I've said it before I meant to. Shit. I glance back at the house. Donna is peering through the gap in the blinds. I pray this man doesn't force his way in there. He could do a lot of damage in the time it might take the police to get here.

"What did you call me?"

"You heard. I know *all* about you." My phone is in my pocket. I'm going to have to see this through before I tell Donna if he pushes things any further. Ring the police. Tell them what I know. I'm thinking about a house move anyway. This will probably force my hand with that. But in the meantime, what I know is bargaining power. I must get him to stay away from Donna. Despite our recent differences, there's only me who'll step up and protect her. She hasn't got anyone else.

"What's that supposed to mean?"

"Whatever you want it to mean. You get away from my property, you stay away from Donna, otherwise, all it takes is one phone call and you're back inside."

"Who told you that?" He unhooks his thumbs from his jeans and instinctively I step back.

You're bluffing." He throws his head back as he laughs again. "You know fuck all about me. OK, so yeah, I'm called Brad. So what?"

"You're a drug dealing, swindling, violent scumbag." I step further away from him. "I might get you locked back up anyway. Before you do more damage to anyone else."

Shit. *Shit! What am I saying?*

As he grabs me by the scruff of the neck, there's a shriek of tyres. Scott's pulled up behind Ash's car at exactly the right moment. Or the wrong moment, from his perspective. "Get the hell off her," he roars as he rushes at him.

He lets me go. "You'll keep." He pretends to dust his hands down and jumps over the garden wall towards his car.

Scott stares after him, then back at me. "What the hell's going on? Who's he?"

"Like I said..." I try to keep my voice from shaking as Ash opens his car door. "All it takes is one phone call."

As he drives away, I've made a definite decision. I'm not just moving *house*, I'm moving *area*. After Scott and Donna have gone, I'm going to ring Georgia – things can't just be left like they are. I recall what she said to me yesterday, that even if Ash doesn't retaliate himself, he's got plenty of associates to do his dirty work for him. Which is why I feel too scared to call the police straightaway.

Surely Donna and I are small fry amongst the enemies his sort might have. But I can't take the chance. It's already gone too far. In the heat of the moment, I thought warning him off with what I know would work. But I've probably made things worse. Much worse. I need to speak to Georgia before I do anything.

And I've Charlie to consider. Mum would be beside herself if I were to tell her about the last twenty-four hours. First Liz, then Darren, now this.

34

THEN

"But everyone's got one." Charlie continued to whine even though I'd said a firm 'no' three times.

"Who's everyone?" Donna laughed. "You're very persistent – I'll give you that. I think you'd have ground me down by now if I was your mum."

"Jess, Amelia, Lucie, everyone. Can't you talk to her?" Charlie's voice lifted.

"You could always ask your grandma." Donna laughed again. "When Mum says no, ask Grandma."

I swung around from where I was making coffee. "Don't you even think of asking your Grandma, Charlie. She agrees with me anyway. Nine years old is far too young for a mobile phone."

"I disagree," Donna replied. "They've all got them nowadays."

I seethed silently. Donna was always doing this. It wouldn't be so bad if she offered her opinion when she was out of Charlie's earshot. "I've told her..." I looked from Donna to Charlie. "That she can have one when she starts high school."

"But it's not fair. That's nearly two years away."

"Let's see what Santa Claus brings you." Donna whispered to Charlie as I rinsed a cup.

"You wouldn't dare." I spoke through gritted teeth. "You buy her a phone and it will go in the bin."

"I'm her godmother Lou. Don't I get a say?"

"No, you do not."

"I hate you." Charlie leapt from her chair with such force it fell backwards. "I wish Donna was my mum."

35

NOW

I SHOULD HAVE PUT the radio on to drown them all out. The clank of cutlery against plates, and the sound of chewing and slurping is grating on every single one of my already frazzled nerves. Conversation has been thin on the ground over the last few minutes. It's as though no one knows what to say with all that's going on. Normally I'm comfortable if the silence is companionable, but the silence around this table is loaded with something.

But what is grating even more on my nerves is the fact that Donna is sitting at the table *still* wearing my dressing gown even though I asked her to put some clothes on. It doesn't look as though she's wearing anything under it either.

I can't help but watch Scott to see if he's checking her out, especially now they've 'connected' with each other in the hospital waiting room. Her bandaged wrist and bruised face appear to have awakened his protective instinct. It didn't go unnoticed that he poured her coffee and pulled her chair out before we sat down. I didn't get that treatment. I'll have to get her to go home after this. After we've spoken about Ash. I can't say anything in front of Charlie, but enough is enough.

Charlie's voice eventually slices into the atmosphere, which I'm grateful for. "Jess rang me before," she says. "She's really sorry about last night."

"So she should be. I'll be having words with her mother."

"No Mum – please." She pulls a face. "How embarrassing."

"I agree," Donna pipes up. "You can't do that to her."

I ignore her and keep my attention on Charlie. "So you've forgiven her – even after she literally threw you out of the house?"

"That's what friends do." Donna squirts sauce onto her plate. "Forgive."

I feel as though that's somehow directed at me. I want to tell her how lucky she should consider herself, to still be sitting in my kitchen, eating brunch after confessing to jumping into bed with Darren for years on end. If it wasn't for Charlie being here...

"It was my fault," Charlie shrugs. "I went off on one because she's off to a festival with some other friends. I felt really left out."

"And? That means you deserved to be thrown out into the dark at eleven o'clock at night?"

"I said some horrible things to her." Charlie stares at her plate through the beautiful eyelashes which she clearly didn't inherit from me. "I felt jealous, as I wasn't invited. But now I have been. Jess texted me this morning. Someone's had to drop out, so I'm taking their place." She raises her eyes to me – they radiate uncertainty mixed with hope.

"Which festival? When?" I don't like the sound of this. If it's a day thing and really local, I might consider it. But *only* then.

"The Leeds one. It's next weekend."

I snort. "You're *not* going to Leeds festival at the age of thirteen. No chance."

"It's only for *one night* Mum. I've already said I'll buy the ticket from the girl who's dropped out."

"With what? Brass buttons." I sound like my mum. She always used to warn me I'd understand once I had kids of my own.

"I've offered to lend her the money actually." Donna stabs at a hash brown, avoiding my gaze.

"You've done *what?*" I stare at her. At first I think I'm hearing things.

"Charlie asked me earlier. Lighten up Lou. She's a teenager. Teenagers go to festivals. End of."

"Thirteen is far too young. There's all sorts of drugs there."

"So you're accusing me of being a druggie now?" Charlie slams her fork down.

"More coffee, anyone?" Scott pushes his plate away and rises from the table. I don't blame him for trying to separate himself from our evolving drama. I wasn't expecting this. As if there hasn't been enough going on.

"No, of course I'm not love. But it's not safe for you at a festival. If I was there, it might be different."

"An older sister of one of the girls will be with us."

"I said no." I give her the look and tone of voice, which she'll know means business. "Don't even ask me again until you're sixteen."

"But I've already told Jess I can go. Donna's sending me the money this afternoon, aren't you?"

She nods but avoids my eye this time. This is the last straw. My friendship with her is so over. Her dressing gown, or should I say, *my* dressing gown has slipped somewhat. She's practically got her tits out, in my kitchen, in front of my boyfriend. I hate her at this moment.

"You had no right agreeing to this without my say-so." I glare at her.

"I don't know what your problem is. Charlie's a sensible lass. You've got to let her go sometime."

"It's not her I don't trust. It's other people. Look, this isn't even up for discussion." I wag my finger in Charlie's direction. "You're too young to go to Leeds festival and that's the end of it."

"What am I supposed to tell Jess?" She looks to be on the verge of tears. "You're making me look stupid. If she falls out with me again, it'll be all *your* fault." She points back at me.

I shrug. "I can live with that."

"I hate you." Charlie flings her knife and fork onto the table. "You never let me do anything."

"Go to your room and simmer down."

She throws her chair back and glares at me as she rises.

"Now."

"I really, really hate you," she yells again as she stamps towards the door. "I wish Donna was my mum, not you!" Then the door slams so hard that I'm sure I feel the house shake.

I look at Donna. I could be mistaken, but she looks pleased at what Charlie's just come out with. I've known her for so long that I can read every one of her expressions and can tell what she's thinking by her tone of voice. It's good in some ways, in others not so.

"I'm so glad I don't have kids." Scott sits back with us at the table.

"Thanks a bunch for all this Donna." I push my plate away. "Every problem I ever have seems to have you at the bottom of it."

"*As if you're blaming me?* Well, that's just great. I try to be a godmum and this..."

"She's *my* daughter. I've had just about enough of..."

"Right, enough." Scott slaps his palm onto the table. "Donna, would you mind waiting in the lounge for a few minutes? You both need to calm down."

"Don't go anywhere near Charlie's room," I shout after her. "And fasten that dressing gown up."

. . .

"Give Charlie a few minutes before you speak to her." Scott reaches for my hand. It feels good and I'm grateful for it. He's been noticeably distant towards me since last night. I'm getting as bad as Donna, fishing for crumbs of affection.

"Did you hear what Charlie said?"

"She doesn't mean it. She just sees Donna as the cool, more fun presence in her life, whereas you're the person in her eyes, that makes the rules and puts the dampener on her having fun."

"And is that how you see us too?" I drop my head into my hands. "Donna, cool and fun, and me... what did you say? A *dampener*? Cheers Scott."

"No, that's not what I meant."

"I'm off to speak to her." As I rise from my chair, I cannot look at him. I could do with getting rid of both of them. And I need to ring Georgia. I can't just leave things as they are. I'm worried Ash might come back. But first – Charlie. What a bloody weekend.

I tap on her door and stare at the shine of its surface. "Can I come in love?"

"No," comes the muffled reply. "Go away."

"Look Charlie." My voice echoes around the landing. "I know I've said no this time, but things will be different in two or three years."

"But I really, really want to go Mum." She's crying. "Please!"

I push the door open then and sit beside her on the bed. "Look love. Thirteen really is far too young to go to a festival. Grandma would have a fit." I smile.

Charlie doesn't. She raises her tear-streaked face to look at me. "That's because Grandma's old and boring. And anyway, I'm nearly fourteen."

"Do you know something? She'd be heartbroken to hear you say that." It's true. Mum adores her with every fibre of her being.

I stare around at her posters and my gaze lands on the makeup on her dresser. *Where did my little girl go?*

"I don't care."

"If you're going to say unkind things about your grandma, perhaps those trainers she bought should go back to the shop." I glance around the room for them. It's difficult to see much on this floor other than a carpet of discarded clothing.

"They can't go back. I wore them to Jess's last night, actually." She looks at me as though she's won the argument. She's turned into a right little madam.

"That doesn't mean I can't confiscate them."

Her shoulders slump and we fall quiet for a few moments. Without her audience, her previous anger seems to have died away as quickly as it flared.

"Even Donna thinks you're being mean." Her eyes fill with fresh tears, and she reaches for her phone. "I've told you that Amelia's big sister is going. Look I'll show you the group we've set up."

"I don't care what group you've set up – there's absolutely no way you're going. I can't believe you even said you could without asking me first."

"I really thought you'd say yes. Donna did too. That's why she said she'd lend me the money."

Donna, Donna, bloody Donna.

"Look at me Charlie."

"No." She keeps her gaze fixed firmly on her phone.

"Put the phone down. You're being rude." I try to keep my voice steady.

"You're the one who's rude. You don't even trust me, do you?"

"Of course I do. But I will *not* change my mind. You'll understand when you're older." I'm sounding like Mum again.

"Can you leave me alone, please?"

I sigh as I rise from her bed. At least she said please! I'll have to keep a close eye on her on Friday. Make sure she doesn't try sneaking off. As I make my way to the bathroom, I'm startled by the sudden beat of deafening music from her room, if it can be described as music. I nearly march back to make her turn it down but then think better of it. If that's how she needs to release her frustration, I'll leave her. For ten minutes anyway. If she thinks I'm upset by the music, she'll do it all the more.

Scott's no longer in the kitchen. Something flips inside me as I contemplate how he might have gone home after all the drama he's witnessed here over the last day. I wouldn't blame him if he had. I pad, barefoot, back into the hallway. The shape of his car is visible through the frosted glass. I haven't heard Donna come upstairs to get dressed, so she can't have gone home either. So unless they're out in the garden, they're sitting together in the lounge. And she's still wearing my dressing gown.

I step towards the lounge door and try to listen above the boom, boom, boom coming from Charlie's room. Nothing. I head back through the kitchen towards the patio doors, hoping against all hope they'll be out there. It's a nice enough day. A feeling of dread pools in my stomach when they're not. I try to dismiss it as I turn back towards the lounge. They're probably just glued to something on the TV.

I pause outside the door. There's several seconds gap between the tracks Charlie's playing. Then an unmistakable sound. My hand flies to my mouth.

Scott, when he's about to come.

I throw the door open. He turns to me, slack-jawed and glassy eyed, making no attempt to stop what's going on.

"You fucking pair of bastards. How could you do this to me?"

Donna's knelt between his legs, my dressing gown flapping open around her. She gasps at the sound of my voice and leaps to her feet. For a split second, I thought I was going to have to drag her off him.

Scott tries to hide his erection back in his joggers.

"Get out of my fucking house, both of you." I stare from one to the other.

I've not even been upstairs for twenty minutes dealing with my daughter, and the slag is on the floor, in my house, giving my boyfriend a blow job. Neither of them move.

"I said get out. I never want to see either of you again. I'll wait in the other room until you've gone."

I lurch towards the kitchen and slump onto a chair, trying to get my breath. I can't believe it. Or maybe I can. They're lucky I'm not tearing them limb from limb. But that's not my style. I don't know how I'm going to handle it, but two things are for certain. Donna will never, ever be welcome in my life again and it's over for me and Scott too. I hope his blow job was worth losing me over.

I choke back a sob as I hear them clattering around upstairs amidst the music, no doubt getting their stuff together. They're probably going to go around the corner to her house now. Finish what they started. A few minutes later, the door bangs. Neither of them has even tried to talk to me. But then, what could they possibly say? They can hardly say *it's not what it looked like.*

I really thought I could trust Scott. But he's just the same as all the others. I drop my head into my hands and sob like I've never sobbed before.

"What's going on Mum? What's up?"

"Nothing love. Just go back to your room."

"Where have Donna and Scott gone?"

"I don't want to talk about it. I just want to be on my own for a few minutes."

"But what's happened?"

"Nothing. Look Charlie. Please!"

"Is it my fault? Is it because of what I said before? I'm sorry, really I am."

"No, it's not your fault. Look, I'll come and see you in a minute. Just let me get my head together."

"Why won't you tell me what's up?"

"I will. Just leave me be for a little while."

I don't know how long I sit with my head in my hands. But there's a pool of tears on the placemat under me. I try to blink away my imaginings of what Donna and Scott will be doing right now in her house. The house I've acted as a guarantor for. One of my first jobs is to somehow relinquish myself from that. And when I get back to school, I'll have to swap my planning day, so I don't have to be anywhere near Scott. But even that won't be good enough. I don't know how I can ever face him again after what he's just done to me.

I get to my feet and head towards the cupboard where I have a bottle of vodka stashed. This is a vodka sort of day. I pour what's probably a triple, fill the glass with coke from the fridge and yank my laptop from my teacher box. As I start it up, I feel heavy at the recollection that the last time I used it, this time yesterday with Georgia, my world was still as it should be.

If I could only turn the clock back, my phone would have been firmly switched off last night. I would have left Donna to rot where she was. That way, I wouldn't have had Ash on my doorstep, issuing his threats, either.

I head for my social media accounts, blocking Donna and

201

Scott on every single one. A sob catches in my chest as I notice the *in a relationship with Louisa Rhodes* on Scott's status. I was so excited when he changed it. Then I block them on my phone and delete their numbers. I will not waver. I can not waver. What they've done to me...

I type *Bradley Harris* into Google. He must have the same real surname as Georgia. The search returns a string of irrelevant results. I re-type *Bradley Harris, drugs, Yorkshire* and there it is.

A Leeds man has been jailed for four years for his part in a serious assault in the city.

Leeds CID has welcomed the sentencing of Bradley Harris at Leeds Crown Court on April 1 for his part in a disorder in which a victim was repeatedly assaulted whilst on the ground.

The offence took place in the early hours of March 1, on the Main Street, when two men were assaulted by a group of males, resulting in one being seriously injured.

Harris (31) of Bentham Street was sentenced to four years and 3 months for unlawful wounding, affray, possession of a bladed article and possession with intent to supply Class A drugs. Harris pleaded guilty to the offences.

Detective Inspector Phillip Coates of Leeds CID, said: "We welcome the sentencing of this man for what was a disgraceful display of violence in Leeds city centre.

"One of the two victims continued to be attacked even as he lay on the floor, and it is extremely fortunate he was not more seriously injured, given the ferocity of the attack on him.

Harris was identified and swiftly arrested following the incident and I hope the conviction of the main perpetrator brings some comfort to the victims in this case. Enquires are ongoing into the identities of the three other assailants.

Something tells me that what I'm reading here is barely scratching the surface of Ash's wrongdoings, but it's enough to fuel me for what I'm going to do next. And I need to do it before

I change my mind. If nothing else, I'll be releasing Georgia from some of her current burden.

"Yes. I'd like to report some information about a man recently released from Leeds prison."

That's where Georgia said he was. "Handy for visiting," I'd replied when she told me, my voice loaded with irony.

36

THEN

"I'm never going to meet anyone," Donna wailed. "All the decent men are married or gay at our age."

"Not that you ever let that stop you." I gave her shoulder a playful push.

"It's alright for you," she went on. "You've got your career and Charlie, and..."

"But I'm happy on my own," I replied, trying to raise my voice above the noise. "Especially after how Darren treated me. No man's going to get the chance to do that to me again."

"So you're going to stay on your own *forever*?" I could see the disbelief on her face.

"Who knows? But it'll take someone pretty spectacular for me to get involved again."

"You're not even looking." She swept her gaze around the packed bar. "So how will you ever find someone?"

"If someone's going to come along, they'll come along. Now drink your wine and enjoy being out with me. You knew as well as I did that this latest one would never work out."

"Why can't I be as laid back as you are?"

"Because we're different people." I laughed. "Just do yourself a favour and stop trying so hard."

"But I can't stand being on my own. It's so lonely. I'm not cut out to be on my own. I need to be with someone."

"And there's your problem. Until you're happy on your own, you're going to struggle. Trust me."

"You're hardly the expert on all this with your failed marriage and your newfound singledom."

"I'm happy. So I'm the expert on that." And I was. Yes, a new relationship would have given life some shine, but the wrong one would have turned everything upside down again. After Darren, any other man was going to have to do far more than just sing for his supper.

She stared at me for a few moments. "That's it then. I'm going to be more like you. I'm going to have whatever it is that you've got."

37

NOW

I TIP my drink down the sink. Getting drunk won't do me any favours. Getting out of this house will.

"Charlie," I call up the stairs. "I'm going out for a couple of hours. Will you be OK?"

"Are you sure I'm old enough to be left on my own?" She replies, her voice echoey. She must be in the bathroom. "Since I'm not old enough to go to a festival." Her earlier concern for me seems to have evaporated.

"See you soon. Don't answer the door to *anyone.*"

I gulp in the fresh air as I leave the house. I'll drive the opposite way out of the street. If Scott's car is parked outside Donna's house, I don't know what I'll do. I certainly don't want to see it.

Walking usually calms me. But today I'm veering between despair and fury. One thing that slows me down as I stamp my way around the park is my curiosity with the benches – there's at least a hundred dotted around, all dedicated to the memory of someone. I've always found them an eerie sight. Every bench represents a dead person. I read the plaque behind me. Mother, Wife. Friend. I fight back the tears again as I wonder who'd spend time on a bench dedicated to *me*?

Mum feels like my only ally now. And Georgia. Though who knows how she'll react when she finds out I've turned her brother in to the police. I didn't have concrete evidence, of course, but at least he should be well and truly back on their radar. And hopefully I won't have to fear him landing back on my doorstep again.

I stare over the lake and observe the normality of everything going on around me. Families, couples, people just taking time out. I need to get a grip. Breathe in. Breathe out. But after what's happened, I'm a million miles from normality. An anger I've never known is snaking up and down my spine. Someone is going to pay. I yank my phone from my bag. There's a barrage of messages.

> I'm off round to Jess's. I need to tell her I can't go. I'm sorry for what I said before. I didn't mean it. I hope you're alright.

She's a decent kid is Charlie. All that matters to me is her. Now that I'm thinking more clearly, I should have brought her with me. What if Ash was to come back? Anyway, it's fine now. She's going to Jess's and she's accepted what I've said. And there's Mum, of course. The next message is from her.

> The glass of wine offer's still open love. If you've got time this afty?

I'm not sure I can face her right now. My first instinct was to run to her, but I'm best working it all out myself first.

> I hope you're pleased with yourself. We broke up years ago, but you're still fucking my life up.

You do a pretty good job of that all by yourself.

I type back to Darren.

Friend or foe, I think to myself as I scroll down to the next one – it's a number I don't know.

Can you tell your kid to return the key that Darren gave her to my house? She's no need to have it anymore.

I'll pass your message on.

I picture Liz on her doorstep, looking at me as though I was diseased when I was there yesterday. The silver lining in her cloud is that she won't have to put up with *a kid that's not even hers* anymore.

I'm surprised I haven't heard from Donna but then remember that I've blocked her number.

I reach into my bag for some water. A few sips of vodka and crying have dehydrated me. The sunshine couldn't be more at odds with how I feel today. Somehow, I'll have to pick myself up and start again.

My thoughts are broken into by my phone ringing. As I snatch it up from the bench beside me, part of me hopes it's Scott ringing to beg for forgiveness, but then I remember I blocked him as well. Not that I could ever forgive him. It's Georgia. I should have probably rung her before now.

"Lou. You were the only other person I told about Brad. He's being questioned by the police." She doesn't even say hello. "Was it you?"

I breathe deeply, hoping she won't be able to sense that I'm crying. "He turned up at my house this morning Georgia – he was threatening me."

"Threatening you. But why?"

"He beat Donna up last night. Then as I say, he turned up at my house this morning and grabbed me by the neck. I had to do something."

"If he finds out it was me who told you, he'll…"

"He'll be locked back up before he gets a chance. And he deserves all he's got coming to him." I sink further into the bench.

"But I warned you how dangerous he is."

"He doesn't scare me. He's got little man syndrome, if you ask me. Besides, he doesn't know it was *me* who rang them."

"I can't imagine it being that hard for him to find out."

"The police aren't going to tell him anything, are they?"

"He's got friends in low places, and some police officers don't behave like they're supposed to either. Believe me, we've found that out the hard way over the years."

My brain's going round and round like a spinning top. In the last twenty-four hours, my life has changed beyond all recognition. I haven't even told anyone what I walked in on this morning yet. I think I'm still in shock.

"Can I ring you back when I get home Georgia? I could do with talking about something else?"

"Are you OK?"

"Yes. No. Look, I'm having a walk, trying to straighten my head out. I just need some time, and then I'll call you."

"I'll be here."

"What a day. What a bloody day." I sink to the patio chair with a glass of wine, and stare into the darkening sky. I'm drinking far too much lately. Even Charlie's commented on it, but she's fast asleep now so I can do what I want. Even at the age of thirteen, she'd probably understand my need for wine if I were to tell her what happened this morning. Looking back, it's a good job she had her music on, or else she'd have heard everything. She even made me a cup of tea before she went to bed and told me again that she didn't mean it when she'd said she wished Donna was her mum. I wanted to tell her never to use that name in our house again, but she's too young to know about all this shit at the moment.

I haven't told Mum yet either. Today, I've needed to wallow in self-pity and get my head around things. I'll go round tomorrow – I could do with her shoulder to cry on. Georgia offered to sleep here tonight when I told her what I'd walked in on. I couldn't stop crying when I rang her back earlier, and she thought I shouldn't be on my own with all that's happened. And she doesn't even know of the hostilities I've had with Darren and Liz. But she's got enough on without having to babysit me.

This time last night I was curled up on the sofa with Scott. Other than the row with Darren, everything was fine. I'm on the verge of blocking him too, and Liz. It's more difficult to cut ties with those two completely because of Charlie. They've both sent me several shitty messages today. Both have definitely been drinking. Warnings, name calling - Darren, in one message, said he was going to prove I'm an unfit mother and get custody of Charlie. I read them to start with but eventually got to deleting them without reading. I can't take any more. Though perhaps I should save them as evidence.

It's my final week of the school holidays and to be honest I'll be glad to get back there. Scott shouldn't be too difficult to avoid once a month. I also hope things won't be strained between me and Georgia after what's gone on with her brother. I haven't heard any more about it, so they must be still questioning him. Part of me regrets ringing the police now – just in case he finds out it was me.

· · ·

I stiffen at the creak of the gate across my driveway. Perhaps it's next door's – Helen's always sniffing about, at all hours of the day and night. I'm certainly not expecting anyone.

I hold my breath at the sound of the doorbell. No way am I answering it. I've had more than enough for one day. I can't imagine it's going to be anything pleasant at this time of night. Thank goodness Charlie's a heavy sleeper. So far, I've kept the details of my horrendous weekend away from her.

A loud knock at the door makes me jump. It can't be the police, not this late, though the knock has a certain amount of authority within it. I can't face the police, if it *is* them. I take a big swig of my wine. My heart is hammering. Maybe it's Scott. He's the last person I want to see. So, I'm staying right here. Given the earlier row in my garden with Ash, perhaps I should be safely locked inside the house. I've had fair warning from Georgia of what he's capable of. And the sort of people he knows.

The letterbox snaps shut. *Who the hell would be looking through my letterbox?* Then I realise that whoever my late-night caller is, they're coming up the drive. Their footsteps become louder. I hold my breath. The lever on the gate is depressed. Then its familiar squeak. I jump to my feet.

I'm not sure what I notice first, the vacant stare, the glint of a hammer, or the fist curled around it. "What-what are you doing?" I raise my eyes from the hammer. "Look. We can sort this out, surely? Please. Just put it down."

My assailant steps towards me. I step back. It takes another moment for me to fully realise the danger I'm in. Do I run, or do I fight back here? This is serious shit. OK, so I might have ruffled a few feathers lately, but not enough to deserve being threatened with a hammer.

"Look. Come on. There's no need for this."

The hammer now held aloft tells a different story. This is no time to talk my way out of it. In a daze, I rush back towards the house, but then buckle as the hammer lands between my shoulder blades. "No! Stop!" Agony rips through me.

I yowl as the second blow connects with the hand I raise to protect myself as I turn around. My shoulder cracks under the force of the third one and I fall to the ground.

"No!" My scream is carried into the dusk as the hammer blows rain onto my head. "No. Please."

My brain is going to explode. I'm going to die with the echo of the sickening cracks of my skull resounding in my ears, and blood curdling in my mouth.

A vision of Charlie sleeping upstairs seeps into my mind. I try to get back up. But I can't see. I can't open my eyes. If I just keep still enough...

PART II
DONNA

38

NOW

"You need to get here. You need to get here right now." Scott's voice sounds strangled – it takes a moment or two to work out who it is on the phone.

"Where? What's happened?"

"I'm at Lou's. Just get here."

As I slide my feet into sandals, I wonder what he's doing back there. After the morning we spent, I was hoping *I'd* be more than enough for him now. But he regretted it afterwards, *really* regretted it, just like they all do. It's the story of my life. Of course, I haven't heard from him since he left my house beneath his cloud. And for the rest of the day, he's ignored all my calls and texts, again, like they all do. I've had enough of being treated like shit. I feel utterly used. He's taken what he wanted and discarded me. Then gone running back to Lou by the looks of it. She seems to have blocked me too. She's disappeared from social media and her phone doesn't even ring out when I try it. As the night has gone on, my intensifying anger has felt like huge spiders crawling around inside me – I haven't known what to do with myself.

. . .

The wail of sirens half deafens me as I run up the street toward her house. Scott's at the gate, pacing back and forth. He rushes towards me. For all the wrong reasons. "She's dead." He rakes his fingers through his hair. The same hair I had *my* fingers tangled in this morning. "Lou's bloody dead."

Everything's in slow motion. I stare at him for a moment. "*What?* Where?"

He points along the driveway.

"How?"

He doesn't answer, so I break into a run.

He catches the edge of my jacket as I pass him. "No, don't Donna. You honestly don't want to see her in the..." His voice fades into the darkness as I reach the gate into the back garden. Like he gives a shit about *me*.

The security light flicks on as I creep towards her. Nothing moves apart from a few wisps of her hair that aren't matted with blood. I glance towards the patio door. Blood is splattered everywhere, culminating in a large pool of it on the patio. From there, several drag marks point to where she's finished up at the side of the shed.

"Oh my God. Oh my God." I stare at the battered head of the woman who's been my best friend for over twenty years. "Lou. Lou, No!" I grapple around for her pulse beneath the sleeve of her dressing gown. Just in case. She's gone. She's definitely gone. Oh. My. God. Bile rises inside me. There's blood *everywhere*. It's like something out of a horror movie. She didn't stand a chance against the hammer in the centre of the lawn.

"Get back. Right now!" A pair of firm hands grab my shoulders, wrenching me back to my feet. "You shouldn't be here. This is a crime scene."

"But, but, she's my best friend." I'm steered backwards. I glance at Charlie's curtained window. Lou always joked she could sleep through an atom bomb. "Her daughter's up there," I cry out. "My goddaughter." I can't let her see this if she wakes up.

"We need a tent," one officer shouts to another. "Quickly. How old's the daughter?"

"Thirteen," I reply. By now, the neighbours from both sides are out. Helen's literally hanging over her fence. *Nosy bitch,* I feel like saying to her.

One of the officers notices them. "Return to your houses," he orders. "We'll be along to see you shortly."

"But I didn't see what happened," the lady on the left replies, not taking her eyes off Lou. "The poor love."

"Neither did I," adds Helen. "Is she...?

"Please just return inside. Now. An officer will be with you soon."

"What *has* happened?" asks the man on the left. "I just heard a load of screaming. Then it went quiet. I thought it was cats to be honest."

"I didn't hear a thing," says Helen. "I might have been having a shower when..." Her voice trails off.

"We'll be along to take a statement as soon as we can." He looks from side to side then back towards the gate. "In the meantime, please let us get on with our job."

As more officers pour along the drive, I'm ushered back towards Scott. Momentarily I turn and watch from the gate as they place a white tent over Lou - the friend who's been the closest thing I had to family for over twenty years. Before it all went so badly wrong between us. I stare back at the house, the blue lights swirling in time to my thoughts.

Who the hell's going to tell Charlie? It's probably going to be better coming from me. I'll be there for her. Darren's a complete waste of space as her father and her grandmother's not getting any younger. It'll be best if I take charge.

Scott's sitting on the garden wall, with his head in his

hands. This morning he was in bed with me. Now he's putting on a show about the woman he cheated on. I bet he wouldn't give a toss if it was my head stoved in with a hammer back there. My earlier anger returns. How fucking dare he treat me like this? I feel like...

"Is there somewhere you can both go?" A stern-looking policewoman marches towards us. "This is a crime scene now. We need to keep the risk of cross-contamination to a minimum."

"I'm Lou's boyfriend," Scott tells her, pointing towards the drive. "I'm going nowhere."

His use of the word *boyfriend* makes me feel sick and even more angry. Perhaps it should be him laid in the back garden. He's completely used me.

"Nobody will be allowed back in there until we've conducted our investigations. Which could take a couple of days."

"We can go to my house," I tell her. "I only live around the corner."

She pulls a notebook from her top pocket. "Address please? We'll have a couple of officers round to speak to you both shortly."

"Her daughter's still in there. We need to get her out." The panic in my voice surprises me as I'm reminded of Charlie. She's all that matters now. Somehow I'll get her through this.

From the look on the policewoman's face, Charlie being upstairs is news to her. "How old is she?"

"Thirteen. I've already told someone but nothing's been done."

"How well do you know her?"

"Lou is... was my best friend. I'm her daughter's godmother."

"And she's asleep in there?" The policewoman points towards the front door. "Through all this?"

"She must be. She'd have been out here by now if she'd woken up."

"Bloody hell." Scott makes me jump as he cries out, his voice full of anguish. Yeah, he's alright being upset now. If Lou had meant that much to him, he wouldn't have ended up in my bed this morning.

"Thank God she slept through it then," the policewoman says, her voice softer now. I guess a kid being involved changes things. Her life will never be the same after this. It's my job to protect her. The anger drains from me. I have to focus on Charlie.

"We need to get her out of there," Scott says. "Before she sees anything. Seeing Lou like that will be imprinted on my brain forever, so who knows what it would do to Charlie?"

"Just give me a moment whilst I speak to someone more senior. I'll see what's being done."

The woman strides purposefully back towards the side of the house. Scott and I look at one another. His eyes are dry. And he looks wracked with guilt. Probably after what happened between us this morning.

Me, well, I'm just numb. Anaesthetically numb. I don't know what to think or feel. Then I think of Carole. One of us is going to have to let her know what's happened. Perhaps that should be left to the police. They're trained to break news like this. I don't think she'd take it all that well from me. She's never really liked me. Not from the moment we met. It was like I wasn't good enough for her precious daughter. Her only child. I'm not good enough for *anyone.* Though Darren's told me in the past that he got the same treatment from Carole too.

The sky is awash with swirling blue lights. The whole street is out, rubbernecking. With the level of activity around here, it could be two pm on a summer's afternoon instead of half past eleven on a Sunday night. Everyone will ask *what's going on?*

What's happened? The nosy cow next door will be in her element.

Lou's lived here for years. It was the house she and Darren bought together. Scott slumps onto the garden wall as the officer strides back towards us. She glances towards another officer who's stretching crime scene tape across the entrance to the driveway.

"Just hold off with that for a few minutes," she tells him. "We're just going to get the daughter out first."

"Do you want to come up?" She nods at me. "I've been authorised to accompany you upstairs and to get her out as quickly as possible. Are you alright taking her to your house for now?"

I rise from the wall. "Of course I am."

"Does she have any other family?" She nods towards Scott. "Are you Dad?" She asks with so much uncertainty that she must be able to tell he's not. He's nothing really – especially now.

He shakes his head. "Someone should let Darren know what's happened though. And Lou's mother too." His shoulders sag further. "I'd hate to be the one to tell her. She's going to be in pieces."

"Leave that to us," the officer replies. "We'll get all the details from you shortly. Let's just get, what did you say her name is?"

"Charlotte," I reply. "But we call her Charlie."

"Let's just get Charlie out of here. Her bedroom curtains are closed, so we'll just wake her and accompany you back to your house."

"Then what? Can we tell her anything yet?" Scott's voice wobbles.

"Yes, but get her away from this scene before breaking the news to her. We'll have to tell her as soon as possible. She may well have heard or seen something."

I shake my head. "She'd be down here if she had."

"She could be too frightened. Anyway, let's get inside and we'll take it from there."

"OK." The poor thing. God knows how she'll take this. I don't even know if she and Lou made things up after the row they had this morning. Charlie told me when I poked my head into her room this morning that she was off to live with her grandma.

I pause for a moment, staring into the face of my god-daughter, watching her sleep. As soon as I wake her, things will never be the same for her again. However, I promised Lou from the time she was pregnant and asked me to be her godmother, that if ever anything happened to her, I'd always be here for Charlie. And the time has come to keep that promise.

"Charlie," I rest my hand on her shoulder and gently shake her. "Charlie. Wake up."

"Humph." Eventually she opens half an eye. "What's up?"

"You need to get up. We're going to my house."

"Why? It can't be morning yet."

"I'll tell you everything when we get there. Come on."

"Who's *she*?" Charlie sits bolt upright and points at the policewoman silhouetted in the landing light.

"I'm DI Susan Macron," she tells her. "We'll tell you what's going on in a few minutes."

"What's happened? Where's Mum?" She swings her legs over the side of her bed. "Tell me *now*."

"Just sit there for a moment." I unhook her dressing gown from the back of the door and pass her slippers, which I spot on the shoe rack. I've spent enough time here to know where she keeps her things, so I grab joggers and a t-shirt from her cupboard.

"Why are we going to your house? What are those things on

your feet?" She points at the plastic overshoes they gave me to come back into the house. She doesn't seem to have noticed the gloves.

"Quick as you can," says DI Macron.

"What's going on?" Charlie's voice is more urgent now. "Tell me where my mum is, Donna. Is it something to do with her being upset earlier?"

I bend down in front of her and take one of her hands. "Please just trust me. Get your dressing gown and slippers on. We need to get out of here."

Her face is full of fear as she slides her arms into the dressing gown.

"Right," says DI Macron as we join her on the landing. "Charlie, I want you to head down the stairs with Donna, out of the front door and straight up the drive."

"But why?" I'm suddenly reminded of when she was three and *why* was her favourite word. The *tiresome three-year-old,* Lou called her.

"Myself and my colleague who's waiting downstairs are going to walk with you round to Donna's house."

"But what's going on?"

"Come on." I head down the stairs and look back to check she's following. I nod at the officer waiting at the door as I stand beside him. As Charlie reaches the bottom of the stairs, she glances along the hallway and for a moment, she jerks as though she's going to dart towards the kitchen in search of Lou. I stretch my arm towards her. "Come on sweetheart. This way."

"You haven't called me that for *years.*" Terror crosses her face. "What's happened? I want my mum."

I want my mum. She hasn't said that for years either. It's been me she's sought out. And Darren who she's had on a pedestal. I hook my arm into hers and frogmarch her up the drive towards Scott. The officer is waiting with his tape, and as we reach him, Charlie glances back. Breaking free from my grip, she hurtles down the drive, only to be caught in flight by one of the police officers.

"My mum," she cries. "Where's my mum? Let me go! Get off me!"

I stare beyond where the police officer holds her. The back garden looks to be floodlit now and thank God, they've covered Lou's body with the tent. *Lou's body.* The two words are at odds with everything. *Lou's body.* How could my best friend have been so vibrant and full of life one minute, and so *dead* the next? The enormity of it all hasn't sunk in with me yet. But despite the feelings I'm wrestling with, I'm glad I'm here. Glad I can do the right thing by Charlie. I might have let Lou down in life, but in death, I can be everything she expected of me.

39

NOW

"No. Nooo. She can't be. I only spoke to her before I went to sleep." Tears stream from Charlie's eyes. Eyes that are exactly the same as Darren's. "She came to say goodnight."

"I'm so sorry sweetheart." DI Macron sits beside her in my poky lounge and rests a hand on her arm. "Really, I am."

"I wish everyone would stop calling me that," Charlie shouts as she jumps to her feet. "*Sweetheart*. And I don't believe you. My mum is *not* dead." She rushes towards the door. "I'm going to find her."

Scott leaps to his feet and rushes after her. "Come and sit back down please. We're telling you the truth. I've seen her myself."

"What happened? Was it *you*?" Her face is sheet white as she shouts into his face. "Did *you* kill my mum?"

"Of course not." He's fighting back tears as he presses his back against the door. "You can't go out there. Not until they find out what's happened."

"It *was* you, wasn't it? It was you?" Charlie flies at Scott and beats her fist against his chest. "I hate you. I've always hated you."

"Charlie. No." He holds onto her arms in what could either be a restraint, or an attempt to hug her.

"Come and sit down." Di Macron pats the space on the sofa next to her. "Scott, could you perhaps get her something to drink?"

"I don't want anything to drink." She wipes furiously at the tears cascading down her cheeks. "What good is that going to do?"

"I do." I jerk my head towards the kitchen. "Scott. Do you want to get something to drink for us? I'll stay with Charlie."

"I want my Mum. And my grandma. Where's my grandma? I want my grandma."

Something inside me plummets. I should have known this was coming. Once Carole gets here, she'll take charge, and I'm certain that's not what Lou would have wanted. She'd prefer someone who can step into her shoes. And that someone is me. Although to be honest, I feel completely out of my depth right now.

"One of our other officers is going to break the news to her at some point. I'm not sure when." DI Macron looks at Scott, still standing by the door. "You left her address with my colleague, didn't you?"

He nods and closes his eyes. "She's going to take it really, really badly. Lou was her world."

"Can you take me to her house?" Charlie breaks into fresh sobs. "I want to be with my grandma."

"You stay here with *me* for now." I shuffle up to her and draw her into my shoulder. "Let your grandma get her head around it first." I'll be the one who looks after her, not Carole. It'll be *me* that will ensure Charlie enjoys being a teenager. I know from several years ago when I witnessed Lou's will, that the mortgage will be paid off and that there's ample insurance to take care of her. Lou wouldn't have imagined in a million years that it would ever be needed.

"We could ask your grandma if she'd like to come here?" DI Macron's voice rises as she looks at me. "Will that be alright?"

"Of course." Though I suspect *here*, at *my* house, will be the last place she'll want to be.

"Someone will have to tell my dad. I won't have to live with him and Liz, will I Donna?" Charlie sounds panic stricken. "Please say I won't have to live with them. Liz *hates* me."

"You listen to me." I sit on the other side of her, taking her hand in mine. "You're thirteen Charlie. You'll be given a say in *everything*."

Scott watches on, his back still against the door. "Don't you think it's a bit soon to be talking about all that?" He peers at me from beneath his heavy-set eyebrows as though I'm diseased. I rarely regret jumping into bed with people, but in his case, I definitely do. I've never regretted anything more.

"I thought you were sorting some drinks out?"

His lip curls in what looks like disgust. "Your so-called best friend is dead, and all you can think about is drinks."

"She *was* my best friend and for your information, I just need something to take the edge off."

Charlie shivers violently next to me. I reach behind and tug a blanket from the back of the sofa. Wrapping it around her shoulders, I pull her closer. "Everything's going to be alright. I've got you."

"But it's not, is it?" Her voice cracks. She's crying again. "Nothing's ever going to be alright, ever again."

"You let it all out," I say. "Bottling it up makes things much worse."

"They can't be any worse," she sobs. "My mum's dead. *Why? How did it happen?*"

"That's exactly what we'll be finding out," DI Macron replies.

Scott holds the door ajar for the influx of three officers that appear in the doorway to my lounge. My house seems even smaller with all these people in it. I wish Scott would leave – I can't bear how he's looking at me.

DI Macron gets to her feet. "I'll be back in a moment." She walks towards them.

"I'll sort the drinks," Scott mutters as he turns on his heel and follows her out, closing the door.

"Why isn't he crying?" Charlie wipes at her eyes with her dressing gown sleeve. "I thought Mum and Scott loved each other. And why aren't *you* crying Donna? Don't you both *care?*"

"I guess we're in shock." I smooth my hand over her hair, again the same colour as Darren's. I've always seen him in her. "Everyone reacts in different ways when someone dies. There's no right or wrong."

"Right, here's what's happening." DI Macron reappears in the lounge doorway with the other officers behind her. "My colleagues DI Fletcher and DC Mason here are going to speak to you Scott," she nods towards him, "at the station, if that's alright?"

"You're arresting me?" There's almost a squeak to his voice.

Charlie sits up poker straight. "I knew it."

"Not at all," DI Macron replies quickly, her bobbed hair swaying in time to the shake of her head. "At this stage, being that you're the one who made the initial three nines call, you're merely helping us with our enquiries. We need to get everything on record."

"What about me?" I bring Charlie closer in, catching a whiff of the strawberry-scented shampoo on her hair. "I need to stay here with Charlie. You've no plans to ask *me* to go down to the station, have you?"

"We will need to take a statement from you Donna. Myself and..." She glances towards the door, "Sergeant Robin Wilson."

The officer she's gesturing to has a look of Tom Cruise. He

steps further into the room. In different circumstances, I'd be chatting him up and Lou would be rolling her eyes at me.

"But in the first instance, we can take that statement from you here." Her eyes flit from me to Charlie. "Will you be up to speaking to us as well?"

"But I know *nothing*. I was asleep. My mum was OK when I went to bed. She was still alive." Her voice fades as she gets to the end of her sentence. "I can't believe I'm never going to see her again."

"We just need to ask you a few questions. It won't take long." DI Macron's words are gentle but still ooze authority. I expect they'll have special training to deal with situations like these. She has hard eyes though, and I wouldn't want to be on the other side of her.

"But I've no idea what happened to her." Charlie sniffs. Her dressing gown is far too big for her and tonight, she looks far younger than her thirteen years. I feel a rush of protectiveness.

"Anything you can tell us might be helpful." She glances at Sergeant Wilson.

"We really need to catch whoever did this to your mum." He displays a flash of wedding ring as he plucks a notepad from his top pocket. Despite the circumstances, I feel a stab of disappointment.

"Can Donna stay with me?" She brushes the tears away and DI Macron passes a tissue from the box on the coffee table.

"Of course." She nods. "In any police procedure, even when taking a statement, an appropriate adult has to be present."

Lou would have laughed at the idea of me being referred to as *appropriate*. Especially now. But I'm pleased that Charlie's asked if I can stay.

I sip from the huge measure of brandy Scott poured me and relax slightly. At least I'm getting to stay here. Unlike Scott. The thought of Charlie facing this without me isn't a good one. She leans into me. Together, we'll get each other through it all. One day, everything that's happened will be like a bad dream.

"Right Charlie. I'm alright to call you *Charlie,* aren't I?" DI Macron flicks a notepad open. I try to read what she's already written upside down, but I've never been any good at that. It looks like she's made a note of some questions she wants to ask.

She nods. "Has anyone told my grandma what's happened yet?"

DI Macron looks inquisitively at Sergeant Wilson who's sitting in the armchair facing her. My insides sag at the thought of how Carole will react. It will not be pretty. Yet I can't help but compare her with my own mother, who probably wouldn't shed a tear if I died.

He clears his throat. "I'm not sure at the moment. I think most of the officers are going house-to-house amongst the neighbours. Whilst everything is recent."

"Would it not be better left until morning?" Here in my scruffy joggers and hair all over the place, I must look a right sight. There's a smear of Lou's blood on my sleeve. Suddenly, I feel sick and reach for my brandy to swallow it down. I can't get the image of her with the life smashed out of her head from my head. I'm trying not to imagine what must have been going through her mind as she was trying to drag herself from the spot where she first landed to where she ended up. But if the police are going house to house already, they must be confident that one of the neighbours has heard or seen something. Even late at night.

"I'm not sure whether they'll go tonight to break the news to her, or leave it until first thing," he replies.

I glance up at the clock. It's nearly one already. If I was Carole, I'd want to be left in ignorant bliss for as long as possible. It might be the last full night of sleep she gets for a while.

Sergeant Wilson rests a clipboard on his knee and unclips a pen from the side of it. Upside down, I see the words *Witness Statement.*

"Right, I'm going to start by asking you a few basic questions Charlie, and then DI Macron will take over and I'll write everything down." He clicks the pen. "Firstly, what's your full name?"

"Charlotte Ann Rhodes." Her eyes fill with tears. "Ann's my mum's and my grandma's middle name too."

"And how old are you?"

"Thirteen. Nearly fourteen." Her voice breaks with fresh anguish. "My mum's not even going to be with me for my birthday."

DI Macron looks back at her with eyes full of sympathy. "I'm sorry we've got to do this now, but as soon as we're done, you can get some sleep."

"I don't want to sleep. I only want my mum."

"If you need us to stop at any time," adds Sergeant Wilson, "Just say the word."

DI Macron gives him a look which seems to say, *why did you have to come out with that?* She probably wants to get through all the statements and interviews as quickly as possible so she can wrap the whole thing up in a bow and can go home to her nice warm bed with her husband. A quick check of her ring finger tells me she's married too.

Everyone's married, apart from me. I bet even Lou and Scott would have ended up married. I guess it was me who put a stop to that.

40

NOW

"RIGHT." Sergeant Wilson stifles a yawn. "I'm going to read your statement back to you, before I ask you to sign it."

"OK." I glance at the clock. It's going on for three am. They must be leaving it until the morning before letting Carole know. She'd have been round here if anyone had told her, and I've stopped Charlie from contacting her so far. At least I can get my head down for a couple of hours soon. For the last few hours, I've been running on adrenaline, but seem to have hit a wall now.

"I am Donna Meers and I live at the address given above. I make this statement about the death of Louisa Ann Rhodes on Sunday 23rd August.

Louisa and I became close friends when we were around sixteen. I am the godmother to her daughter, Charlotte Ann Rhodes. They live together at 7 Millfield Road, Farndale, Leeds, and have lived alone since the breakdown of her marriage, ten years ago, to Darren Rhodes.

I would describe Louisa and Darren as having a civil relationship since their divorce, but there have been some difficulties with his new wife, who I only know as 'Liz.' These difficulties are in relation to Darren's access arrangements and maintenance payments for Charlotte.

Louisa is in a new relationship with Scott and has been for around five months. He is the person who first notified me that an attack had taken place against Louisa.

I received a call from him on Sunday 23rd August at around eleven pm, when he told me to 'get round to Lou's house straightaway.' As I only live around the corner, I was there within a few minutes.

I arrived to find Scott in an agitated state, pacing up and down Louisa's driveway, saying he had found her in the back garden and that she was dead. I would describe him as being in shock.

Emergency services were not on the scene at that time, so I ran to the back garden to investigate. I thought he must be mistaken and was sure there would be something I could do to help her.

I found Louisa lying next to her garden shed, in a pool of what I believed to be her own blood, and it was clear she had sustained serious head injuries. The first thing I did after finding her was to check her pulse, but I was too late to save her. She was already dead.

I noticed a hammer in the centre of her garden on the lawn, about two feet away from her body. There was more blood near to the patio doors, some splattering and drag marks which made me think she had not died straightaway."

I brush away the tears rolling down my cheeks. I know statements must be factual, but this sounds so clinical, so cold, and to relive it out loud makes it all-the-more real.

"I then became aware of her daughter, Charlotte, who I know as Charlie, asleep upstairs. My priority became to get her out of the house without seeing her mother's body.

I cannot think who would have done this to Louisa. To my knowledge, she had no enemies. Therefore, I think it must have been a break in."

"Have you checked to see if anything's missing from the

house?" I turn to DI Macron. "Or are you looking for fingerprints?"

"The forensic team is carrying out a thorough investigation," she replies. "I can't tell you any more than that at this stage." She nods at Sergeant Wilson. "Do you want to continue?"

"The last time I saw Louisa was at around midday, some eleven hours before the attack took place. I had stayed at her house, in the guest room, the previous evening and had eaten breakfast with Louisa, Charlotte and Scott, late the following morning. She had not confided in me of any concerns for her safety and to my knowledge, she was usually security conscious." He passes me the form. "If you could just sign there, and there."

"Does it look like anyone's broken in?" I should mention Ash here, but something's stopping me.

"We really don't know at this stage."

"I'm sorry I couldn't tell you a great deal more than I did." Our fingers brush as I take the pen from him. "I honestly think it's a robbery that's gone wrong, but if she was sitting in the garden like she often liked to do in the evening, they could have sneaked in around the back."

"Can I also ask since it hasn't come up in your statement?" DI Macron leans forward.

"What?"

"I've noticed your facial injuries and the bruising on your arm."

"It's nothing."

"What happened?"

"Honestly it was nothing. I had a scuffle with a woman in a club – there was a man at the centre like there always is – but honestly, it was nothing."

"What man?"

"Just someone I've been out with a couple of times."

"What's his name?"

"Ash. I don't know his surname. Look, this has nothing to do with what happened to Lou, you know. This was in Harrogate." I just want the situation with Ash to go away now. After everything that's happened. I need some peace. I really daren't say anything about him. The last thing I need is him turning up at my door again. It was *me* he had a grievance with, not Lou. Not really.

"We'll be in touch." DI Macron rises from the chair, looking unconvinced. "If you think of anything relating to the investigation in the meantime, call us." She slides a card from the pocket of her jacket and passes it to me.

"What about Scott?" I rise too. "Will he have been interviewed yet?"

"I really can't say," she replies. "But I'm sure he'll let you know directly."

As I see them out, I hope beyond hope Scott hasn't mentioned what happened between us yesterday. It makes us look terrible, and I'd be mortified if Carole and Charlie were to find out. *Or* Darren. I can't imagine Scott will have been shouting it from the rooftops though - what happened between us won't be *his* finest hour either.

It was the most bizarre sex I've ever had. Scott kept his eyes scrunched shut the whole time and grabbed a fistful of my hair at the back of my head as he came. The entire thing felt quite rough, and I wondered if he was the same in bed with Lou. Then, after he'd got what he wanted, he completely stonewalled me.

All I want to do now is close my eyes on this dreadful day and escape into sleep for a few hours. Things, as they say, can only get better.

"Donna." I'm woken by a tapping on the door followed by a weight landing on the bed beside me. "Donna. Will you wake up?" I blink at the outline of Charlie in the emerging dawn, wondering for a moment what she's doing here. Then the reality of what happened last night rolls over me like a bus. I had a few seconds of forgetting about it all.

"I can't sleep anymore." She leans forward, dropping her head into her hands. "All I want is my mum."

"I know." Sitting up, I reach for her shoulder, which shakes with the force of her sobs. "I know. It won't always feel this bad, I promise."

"Grandma's just texted. She wanted to know which one was your house so she can come and get me."

There's no point in me fighting this. I'll have to stand back and let Carole take her, just for now. Of course, they need to be together at the moment. But as things start to settle, Carole will probably realise that someone with more energy is better suited to the demands of a teenager.

But at the moment, I need space to get my head around it all. The more I think about it, the more I'm really not sure if I should have mentioned Ash turning up yesterday. Maybe Scott will say something about him and then I'll be in trouble. It was *me* Ash wanted though. If he'd been hanging about last night, it would have been *my* house he'd have turned up at, not Lou's. And I just want to forget that I ever knew him.

"Did *you* tell your grandma about your mum?" I rub at my eyes. "Or did she already know?" I feel slightly hungover, even though, at the time of drinking them, the two huge glasses of brandy didn't seem to touch the sides. It's probably all the anxiety and lack of sleep that's making me feel this rough.

"She already knew. And she's on her way."

"The police must have told her what happened then." I take a deep breath, steeling myself for Carole's arrival. She'll be in a right state. I just hope I've got it in me to deal with her grief.

There's so much turmoil churning around inside me it feels almost impossible to deal with someone else's.

"I can't believe it. I just can't believe it Donna." She rocks backwards and forwards on the bed as though trying to comfort herself. An image floods my mind of Lou rocking her back and forth as a baby, and I blink it away. Poor Lou. Poor Charlie. She looks more child-like and yet more grown up all at once, if that's possible. In an instant she's been left mother-less, but at the same time, she must grow up fast if she's to cope with the aftermath. Except she won't be completely mother-less. That's where I come in.

"I know you can't believe it right now, but things *will* get better. I promise." As I say the words, I'm not even sure if I believe them myself.

"I just want to know who did it to her. And why didn't they get me too? I was right there in the house." She looks at me with frightened eyes. "What if they come back for me?"

"Over my dead body." I reply, then realise what I've said. I've always been the same. *Words first, thought later.* "Sorry, that sounded really crass. What I mean is they'll have to get past me first." I hold her gaze, well as much as I can in the faint light. "I'll do everything I can to protect you."

"That's what Mum was supposed to be doing." She bows her head. "And look what happened to her."

"I know. It's dreadful."

"I don't even know where I'm going to live. Or who's going to look after me?"

"Look, one step at a time." I reach for her hand. "We've just got to take things as they come for now. And I'll be there for you the whole time." I swing my legs around the side of the bed. It's time I got moving. Who knows what fresh hell today will bring?

"Will Mum still be lying there? In our garden, I mean?"

Tears wobble in her voice. "Or will they have taken her somewhere?"

"I really don't know." I reach for my dressing gown and am reminded of twenty-four hours ago when I borrowed Lou's.

"Can I see her?"

"I don't know the answer to that either. But I really think your mum would want you to remember her as she was, not as she is after what's happened."

Lou's matted hair and what looked like a hole in her head emerge in my mind again. I expect they'll take steps to disguise it and make Lou look better. So on that basis, maybe Charlie *should* see her. From what I've heard, seeing a body can help with the grieving process. Especially when the death has come as such a shock. I doubt it will be my decision though. I can only make my own mind up and have already decided I don't want to see Lou again. Last night was quite enough. I've never felt this numb in my life. I can't cry. I don't feel hungry. I don't know what I feel. I don't know what to do with myself.

"You don't think Scott killed her, do you?" Her words are slow and her voice is hesitant. She looks down at her slippers as she speaks. "I want to know why they took him away."

"Gosh, I really can't answer all these questions. They just wanted to ask him some things, with him being the person who first found her. And they've got all the equipment at the station to record what he says more easily."

We lapse into silence for a moment as I ponder whether to have another brandy instead of my usual morning coffee. After all, things couldn't be further from *usual*. Life, as I've known it for the last twenty-two years, will never be the same.

"Will they lock him in one of those cells?" She's wide eyed. "Like they have on the telly. If they do, that *must* mean it's him. And Mum was crying yesterday. I've only just remembered. Maybe I should have told that to the police."

"No. No," I blurt. "That was something else completely. But

we're just going to have to wait to find out." I really hope she doesn't continue with this line of questioning. What happened between me and Scott can never come out.

We both jump as the doorbell goes, sounding louder in the quiet of the early morning. At least our conversation has been stopped in its tracks.

"That'll be Grandma." She jumps to her feet. Though it almost pains me to say it, she's definitely the best person for Charlie to be around right now. I'm a mess. And I need her to forget about Lou being upset yesterday.

Here we go.

"Come here sweetheart."

I watch as they cling together, sobbing in shared heartbreak in my open doorway. Charlie really looks like a little girl, as she holds onto her grandmother, rather than the sassy teenager I know.

"I don't know what happened to her. I don't know what to do." It breaks my heart to hear the anguish in Charlie's words. And there's the guilt that's threatening to swallow me whole right now. Darren. Scott. Ash.

"I know. I know." Carole looks over Charlie's shoulder at me. "What have they said to you?" Her voice becomes noticeably colder. Even at a time like this.

"Nothing really. They're still investigating, aren't they?" I turn towards the kitchen. "You and Charlie will probably be the first to know when there are any developments. I'll make some tea, shall I?"

"Tea!" Her voice is a shriek as the kitchen door falls closed behind me. "What bloody good is tea going to do?"

"I hope you don't mind me calling round." Darren twists to look behind himself as he stands on my doorstep. He seems to be checking whether he's being watched.

"Do you want to come in?" I widen the door.

He nods, looking around again. "The police told me you've got Charlie." He steps onto the threshold, pushing his hair from his eyes.

"She was here before, but Carole insisted on taking her back with her." I stand facing him in the hallway. He looks as rough as I feel. "I let her go. I had to. For now, anyway."

"I might have known." He drags his fingers through his fringe. "That's why I came straight round. I was hoping to beat Carole to it."

"Come through." I gesture to the kitchen door. "Tea, coffee, or something stronger?" This is no time for past hostilities. No matter what's gone on before, it's a time to pull together. He might be my only ally. I certainly haven't got one in Scott or Carole. I'm on my own now.

"I think something stronger is in order." He tugs a chair from beneath the table. "If Carole thinks she's keeping Charlie, she can think again."

There's a calm to his voice which makes me wonder whether he *seriously* wants to step up to the plate as Charlie's surviving parent. I'm surprised but strangely pleased if he does. What Lou would make of it is anyone's guess though. "I agree. She loves her grandma but kicks off every time she's made to go round there."

"I didn't know that. How come?"

"Who'd want some old woman looking after them? Anyway, I always promised Lou that *I'd* take care of Charlie if it was ever needed." I tap the off switch on the washer as the spin cycle tries to drown out our conversation.

"I'm her father. And that *was* my house. I walked away once. I certainly won't be walking away again."

"You mean, you'd move back in there? But what about Liz?" I rinse two glasses, then turn to look at him. "She *hates* Charlie. And Lou would spin in her grave at the thought of Liz living in her house."

"It's *my* house," he repeats. "I *let* them stay there whilst I walked away. As you very well remember. Anyway, Charlie's the most important thing now, isn't she?" His jaw is set in a firm line. "Especially since Lou spilled everything to Liz on Saturday. I think our relationship is well and truly dust."

"What do you mean?" I slop the rest of the brandy into two glasses and chuck the empty bottle into recycling. I'll have to get another one, as no doubt I'll be needing plenty more of the stuff over the coming days. "Lou spilled *what?*"

"She went round to see Liz on Saturday." He rubs at the bridge of his nose. With crumpled clothes and what could be several days of beard growth, he looks knackered.

"Actually, it was me she came to have a go at, but I wasn't there."

"Lou said nothing to me about *that*." Shit. Shit. Shit. If Liz knows, details of mine and Darren's relationship might end up getting back to Charlie. That's the last thing I want. I should have kept my big mouth shut.

"I was supposed to pick Charlie up on Saturday, but Liz and I had been rowing, so I went and got pissed instead."

"There's a surprise." I sniff as I slide a glass in front of him.

"You've room to talk, Saint Donna." His voice hardens. "How many times have we slept together over the years?" He curls his fingers around the glass. "What I don't understand though, is why you came clean about it suddenly. It's not as if we were even seeing each other anymore. You don't know how much trouble you've caused."

He's right of course. And I've been asking myself the same thing since my stupid drunken confession when we were on holiday. I ruined everything. In the cold light of day, I'm unsure whether I was trying to unburden myself from the guilt I've often felt, or whether I was trying to hurt Lou. A bit of both, I think. I was gutted by Ash's lack of contact that week whilst we were away, and I was sorely jealous at the texts and calls she was getting from Scott.

"I was drunk, wasn't I? It seemed like the right thing in the moment."

"How can telling her about us *ever* have been the right thing? I've been living in my car for the last two nights and Liz, as you might imagine, is... well I can't even think of a word that would cover it. If she was to see you right now, I wouldn't like to be in your shoes. Put it that way."

"So... if you've been living in your car, how can the police have been round to see you?"

"They were knocking on my car window at six this morning," he replies. I was parked in front of the house. "I tried getting in there in the early hours, but Liz was having none of it. Anyway, she had to let me back in when the police turned up."

"Then what?"

"Did the police already know about me and you?" There's something in the way he's looking at me that's making me very uncomfortable.

I shake my head. "I didn't tell them anything. The last thing we want is Charlie finding out. I don't think she'd understand, to be honest."

"What about Carole? Does she know?"

I shrug. "If she does, she hasn't let on yet. And I'm sure she would have done. Anyway, she's bigger things to worry about right now, hasn't she? Her daughter's just been found dead, for God's sake."

"Scott must have told them about us then."

"He must have told *the police*?" I take a gulp of the brandy, which burns to my empty stomach. I can't remember when I last ate. Although, right now, I couldn't eat a thing. I think I'd be sick. "They know about me and you? Great."

"And they seemed pretty interested, if I'm honest," he continues, rubbing at the bristles on his chin as he speaks. "Then they asked where I was between ten o'clock and eleven thirty last night."

"They're suspecting *you?*"

"They asked Liz the same question too. When they first came to the house. So I don't know. They're probably asking everyone."

"What did you tell them?"

"Liz said she was at home, and I told them I was drunk in my car. Hardly very solid alibis, but they're the best we had."

It occurs to me that all Darren's talked about since he arrived is himself and his own predicament. "You haven't even asked how Charlie's coping yet," I say. In part, Lou's been right about Darren. *Snivelling, self-centred, drunken.* But he's incredibly good in bed, which has always lured me back.

"She's with Carole, isn't she?" His voice breaks into my inappropriate thoughts. God, my best friend is dead and I... "She'll be fine," he continues. "Until I get her back."

"So that's definitely your plan, is it?"

"I don't know what my plan is yet. But, like I said, it looks like me and Liz are dead and buried. And I'll be needing somewhere to live."

I should have known his agenda would be based on personal circumstances rather than in Charlie's best interests. Maybe it will come down to the court to decide. *Me, Carole or Darren.* From what I know, they would probably ask Charlie what she would prefer. Which is worrying with the misguided pedestal she's always had her father on. She'd be better off with me. But the court would probably favour her dad. Unless... There really could be an easy way forward here.

"Earth to Donna. What's up?" Clasping his hands behind his head, Darren leans back in the chair. "Are you OK?"

"Erm, I suppose so. Up and down. What else did the police say?"

His eyes cloud over and he looks away. "They were asking about the argument me and Lou had on Saturday night."

"What argument?" She never told me about that either. Not that I gave her a chance to. Guilt needles at me again. It's an unfamiliar and very unwelcome visitor. I don't do guilt usually. I never have.

"I was kicking off with her when I was drunk. I went round."

"What do you mean *kicking off*? Enough for her to report it to the police? Why else would they have come round to see *you*?" My voice echoes round the kitchen. There's no blind up yet and boxes are still stacked on the worktops. I haven't even unpacked properly. I hope the landlord doesn't change his mind about me renting this place. Lou was my guarantor.

I'm at it again. Selfish thoughts. Though maybe soon, I'll have somewhere permanent to live. A place where there'll be no extortionate rent to pay and I can do what the hell I want. I really have to box clever now. I'm literally fighting for survival.

"Scott must have told them about the argument I had with her, as well as the 'relationship' between me and you. To be honest, it sounds as though he's been trying to pin what's happened to Lou on me."

"Really?"

"Like I'm really capable of stoving my ex-wife's head in with a hammer. There's my phobia of blood, for starters."

Another image of Lou's battered head floods my mind. "You're blowing this out of proportion. If they really thought it was you who'd killed her, they'd have arrested you, surely?"

"They took us to the station," he says. "Me and Liz. That's where I was before here."

My hand flies to my mouth. "They arrested you? Why didn't you say? I thought they'd just gone to your house? What happened?"

"They didn't actually arrest us. And I waited in an interview room to be seen, rather than a cell. I'm *helping them with their enquires.*"

"That's what they said to Scott. I was here when they took him in."

"They'll be getting their evidence together," he replies. "But it wasn't me." He drains his glass. "You believe me, don't you?"

I stare from his face into my glass, feeling a surge of power. It matters that he cares what I think. "And they questioned Liz as well? At the station, I mean."

"Yup. They drove us there in separate cars. Anyway, they let her go before me. She's probably at home, changing the locks as we speak."

"And now what?"

"Well, they've asked me to stay *close by,* whatever that's supposed to mean. Their words, not mine. I'm actually wondering whether I should get a solicitor on standby. Like I said, I was round there rowing with Lou on Saturday night, then the next day she's dead. It's not as if I've got a solid alibi, is it?"

I close my eyes for a moment. Maybe... A scenario is formulating in my mind.

"What are you thinking?" He clasps his hands together on my kitchen table and watches me.

"If I'd have known, I could've given you an alibi." Time to *make sure* I have him on side. Joining forces with Darren could be a major gain against Carole. Perhaps I might need an alibi for myself anyway, but so far, no one's even asked *me* where I was.

He looks taken aback. "You'd do that for me? *Really?*"

"I guess. Well, it's too late now anyway."

We sit in silence for a moment.

"I know we haven't planned any of this," I say. "But you and me go back a long way, don't we?"

He nods slowly. "What are you trying to say?"

"Look don't get me wrong here." I'm trying to choose my words carefully. "Obviously, I love Lou to pieces. She was my best friend. However, I'm just going to come out and say what I've got to say."

"Go on."

"Lou's gone." I'm aware the word *gone* sounds insignificant in the scheme of things. "And Liz has thrown you out, hasn't she?"

"Ye-ah?"

"So, there's now me... and you." I point from myself to him. "Clearly, we've got *something* between us to have kept hooking up all these years. Even before you and Lou met."

He frowns, without replying.

"So there's Charlie. Your daughter. My god-daughter. And she needs looking after."

"Are you saying what you seem to be saying?"

He doesn't look completely against what I'm mooting here, which is a bonus.

I nod. "The courts would probably say that Charlie would be far better off staying in her own home, being in familiar surroundings. Near her friends. Near her school."

"I agree. But we'd have Carole to fight."

He's using the word *we*. This is good. "There's no court in the land that could reject a *father's* request for custody of his daughter. Not without really good reason."

He laughs. "I'm sure Carole could think of a few."

"The bottom line," I continue, "is that it'll boil down to what Charlie wants. I already know that living with me and Darren would be what she'd want. And it negates the possibility of her choosing Darren over me.

"But I know what you're like Donna. You're only interested in me when I'm attached to someone else. Lou... or Liz. You'd be off like a shot if we tried to go for it together. Legitimately, I mean."

"Try me," I reply.

41

NOW

"Right, I've spoken to Charlie." Darren stretches his arms above his head as he strides into the bedroom.

"What, just now? Whilst I was in the shower?" I stand from the stool and my towel unravels.

He nods. "She wants to go back home, as soon as the police will let us in, that is."

"I knew she would." Noticing his eyes appreciatively on my body, I wrap the towel around myself and perch on the edge of the bed, staring at my legs, which need a shave. My mind's not really been on sex these last few days. Just enough to keep him interested, but really, I've been faking it. "Surely they must be nearly finished in there. We need to make sure that the back garden has been cleaned up. Before Charlie sees it."

"When I drove past before it looked like they were wrapping up. The police tape's been taken away."

"That's a step forward. Anyway, what's Carole said about Charlie wanting to be at home? I can't imagine she's very happy."

"I'm not sure." He sits beside me on the bed. "Apparently she's barely stopped crying for the last three days. That's no good for the kid to be around. It sounds as though she's supporting her grandmother, rather than the other way around."

"I knew she would take it really badly."

"As if Charlie hasn't got enough to deal with. Which is why she's better off with me. With *us*."

"So, how have you left things with her?" I shiver. Even in the late August heat, it feels as though someone has walked over my grave, as the saying goes.

"I've told her to tell her grandma what she wants whilst I find out what's happening with the house."

"She can always stay here until it's sorted." I wave my arms around, letting my towel go in the process.

"We can always go back to bed." He looks at me with the appreciative look I've come to know well.

I pluck a pair of knickers from the drawer beside my bed and quickly tug them on. "Not now. We've got too much to get sorted."

"Spoilsport. Anyway, I thought the whole idea of us getting her is so she can be back in her familiar surroundings.

It's obvious that Darren just wants to be back in the house. But I can't blame him. It's looking like it will be *our* house too.

"That's the best thing for Charlie," I say. "But what if Carole wants to be the person who stays at the house with her?"

"I've already spoken to Charlie. And she wants to be with *me*." Darren leans back on the bed, resting on his elbows whilst looking pleased with himself. "Reading between the lines, I think she's struggling to cope with her grandma."

"I'm not surprised. Anyone would." I fasten the clasp on my bra.

"You don't *have* to do this." He doesn't take his eyes away from me as he speaks. "It's a big commitment, taking on me and Charlie, I mean."

"I want to."

"OK. Right, you get yourself sorted. I'll go downstairs and make some calls."

I pad barefoot into the kitchen, blinking as the bright sunlight hits the back of my eyes. I recall coffees out on Lou's patio on days like this, often with a hangover after we'd been out the night before. Now I'm facing the task of making sure it's clean of her blood.

"Here." He holds out a coffee to me. "I've been busy whilst you've been getting ready."

"You have?" I take the cup from him and sit at the kitchen table.

"I've spoken to the police, Carole *and* the hire centre."

"The hire centre? What hire centre?"

"According to DI Macron, the whole garden needs cleaning."

"I was expecting *something*, but don't the police sort the worst of it?"

"Nope. Anyway, I've put a deposit on a pressure washer. It'll be quicker to clean up with one of those." He sits facing me. "All you've got to do is take some ID when you pick it up."

"Why me?"

"I'm not dealing with blood. You know what I'm like. Besides, I'm off to pick Charlie up."

"Carole agreed to it?"

"She says she can't face setting foot in Lou's house. Not yet."

"Really?"

"But she's made it clear that it's a temporary thing." Darren frowns. "Once we know what's going on and the funeral's over with, she wants it all reviewing."

Something inside me sinks. "*The funeral.* Just the sound of that word makes it even more real." How I'm going to get through that day, I don't know. Lou and I used to discuss our funerals. Who might turn up, the music we'd play...

"I know what you mean. Oh, and Liz has been texting me too."

"Saying what?" I feel a stab of jealousy. I hope he's not going to go back to her. Not after the last few days we've spent together. He married her, so he's going to feel *something* for her. I'll have to make sure he forgets that, and quickly. Maybe I shouldn't have shunned his earlier advances.

He holds his phone towards me. I inhale a sharp breath and start scrolling.

> I know where you're staying. And you're going to get it. Both of you.

I actually feel relieved. At least she's not begging him to go back home.

> Any more of this shit and I'll block you.

> If you think you're getting any of your stuff out of this house.

> You can't stop me.

> Get that bitch Donna to buy you some new clothes.

"How does she know?" I look up from the phone at Darren.

"She'll have been watching. That's what she does. Especially after what Lou told her."

I still can't understand why Lou spilled the beans to Liz. And she went to see her *before* what happened between me and Scott, so it wasn't like a revenge thing. She was acting like she'd forgiven me about Darren. Things were going back to normal. Before I did what I did with Scott. And thinking of Scott, I'm not going to tell Darren about the texts we've been sending to each other whilst I was upstairs.

"I'm off for a shower," he says. "Then I'll go for Charlie."

"Take her out for a bit before you bring her back," I tell him. "I need time to pick up that washer thing and to get that garden sorted."

He pauses in the doorway. "There'll probably be fingerprint dust all over the place too. Can you have a look? Have you got a key?"

I nod. "Carole left the spare with me when she took Charlie."

"Thanks for sorting this. I know it'll be really hard, going back in there for the first time."

As I hear Darren's footsteps on the stairs, I reach into my bag for my phone. I'll have one more read of these messages before I hit delete.

> Are you OK?

I'd messaged Scott on Monday.

> I'm thinking of you.

> What the hell are you texting me for?

> You gave me your number. I'm just making sure you're alright.

> That was before. I never want to hear from you again.

> Why not? Look. We can support each other through all this.

> You've got to be joking. If it wasn't for you, Lou would probably still be alive.

> What's that supposed to mean?

> I should never have picked you up that night.

> But you did, and I was grateful.

> What happened between us was the biggest mistake I've ever made. I'll never forgive myself.

I imagine his face, twisted with misery. That's the thing with messaging. You can't hear the words or see the expressions.

> Look, what's done is done. I was only checking to make sure you're OK.

> I haven't told anyone what happened between us, if that's the real reason for you getting in touch. I've never been more ashamed of anything in my life.

I resisted the urge to make a sarcastic comeback.

> I've said nothing and I've no plans to. I don't want anyone finding out either. I won't bother you again.

I'm thinking of Charlie here but also now, of Darren. It's looking like finally, we might end up making a go of it. Once things have settled, we can live together in that house – become a family, of sorts. The life I've always yearned for will be mine.

I select all the messages and hit delete.

42

NOW

I'VE PULLED up outside this house more times than I could ever count. Next door's blinds move as I slam the car door and walk around to the boot. The pressure washer's smaller than I thought but will hopefully do the job.

"Is there any news yet?" Helen from next door leans over her gate. She must have seen me pull up and from her breathlessness, she seems to have come racing straight out. "I see they've finished in there."

"I suppose you'll have been watching them. You're good at that, aren't you?"

"What's that supposed to mean?"

"Look I haven't got time for gossiping. I'll leave that to you."

"There's no need to be funny with me." She actually looks hurt.

I rest the washer at my feet. "Sorry. I've got this to face, that's all."

"You mean the garden? *You're* cleaning it? On your own?"

"Yep." I squint at her in the bright sunshine, noticing the sweat moustache on her lip. This is a day for sunbathing, not for rinsing dried blood from patio slabs. "Unless you're offering to help."

"Well. I can if you want..."

"I was joking." She'd love that. If I invited her in, she'd get herself a ton of gossip fodder.

"At least I won't have to keep looking at it all."

"Close your curtains then."

"It's a terrible carry on." Helen visibly shudders, causing her jowls to wobble from side to side. "I was only talking to her a few days before. About the key that I gave to you."

We stand, just staring at one another for a moment or two. If she's digging for dirt, she won't get any from me.

"Anyway..." I pick the washer up. "I'd better get on with it. Charlie will be here soon."

"She's coming home? Here? After what's happened? But who's going to look after her?"

"Bloody hell. I feel like I'm on question time. Me and her dad, alright?"

"*Together?*" She looks puzzled. "You and Darren? Really? You're moving in?" She jerks her head towards the house

"It's for Charlie's sake."

"Oh... right." Her voice rises. "But he's leaving you to clean all that lot on your own?"

"He's got a phobia. Blood. Hemo-whatever-you-call-it."

"He got treated for that. He had CBT." She throws her head back and laughs. "He's spinning you a yarn."

"How would you know?" I deposit the washer back down again and rest my hands on my hips.

"I know his wife."

"Since when?"

"We were at school together." Her face darkens. "We weren't always friends, but anyway..."

"Lou never said anything."

"She probably wouldn't have known."

"Liz is Darren's ex now anyway. She threw him out. So, how much do you see each other?"

"Me and Liz? Oh, we bump into each other from time to time. A bit more so, recently."

"Why's that?"

"I don't know. Coincidence, I guess."

"Small world." I shuffle away from her, wondering what Lou would have made of her next door neighbour and Liz being 'friends.'

It feels eerie to be letting myself into Lou's house. The last time was when she went away for the weekend. It's a miracle Carole let me have the key back really.

As Darren suggested, there's fingerprint dust all over the place. That's the least of my worries though. The blood's the priority. But I'll be asking him about supposedly getting over his phobia. I could have done with some support with this.

Dust particles dance in the sun-drenched hallway as I carry the washer through to the kitchen. Much seems to be as Lou would have left it. Her *teacher box*, as she called it, is on the table. They'll probably have some sort of service for her at the school she worked at. I'd like to go to that. I'll probably take Charlie. There's an open bottle of wine on the side and her sandals are kicked off on the mat in front of the patio doors. I stride towards them and twist the key, which she always leaves in the back of the door. The fresh air is welcome as it blasts through the heat of the closed-up house.

What's not welcome is the scene which greets me in the garden. I can't believe the police haven't employed someone to deal with this instead of leaving it to us. The blood didn't look as bad in the darkness several nights ago, but now, in the light of day, it's horrendous. Dark brown, congealed pools. Thicker in some places than others. Thickest in the spot where she finished up. The vision of her slumped beside the shed spins into my mind, and I recall her wrist, limp within my fingers as I felt for the pulse I knew I would never find. I close my eyes against the memory.

I plug the washer hose onto the outside tap. When Lou first moved in, I helped wash the patio. I'd been sitting with a glass of wine, watching her do it, and had thought the process looked strangely therapeutic. I'd offered to wash a patch and had ended up doing the lot.

The force of the water makes the hose jolt in my hands as I hold the nozzle over the blood stains nearest the patio doors. The same blood that was running through the veins of my friend only days ago. Now in her house, I keep expecting to see her. It's as though I can feel her here, watching me. Nothing's changed, except she's no longer here. And for the first time since Sunday, the reality is clobbering me.

Bile rises in my throat as I wash away the drag marks around the sides of the biggest stain first. Dropping the hose, I dash into the kitchen and lean over the sink, gulping in air. I hate being sick and will go to great lengths to avoid it. I'm probably as phobic about being sick as Darren is, *or was*, about the sight of blood. I cup my hands under the cold tap and throw water into my face. Then take a few swallows. The water is cool and cleansing, and within a few minutes, my breathing has slowed and I feel slightly better.

I've got to do this. There's no choice in the matter. I reach for the bottle of wine Lou started and take a glass from the cupboard. A glug of wine will definitely make the job easier. "Cheers Lou." I hold the glass in the air, my voice sounding strange in the silence. She should be here, drinking this with me. It smells of her in here. It's so achingly familiar that the breath catches in my throat.

I psych myself up to go back outside. Before Darren turns up with Charlie, I have to get this done. I should have picked her up from her grandma's and taken her out, whilst *he* sorted this. Though really, I want as little to do with Carole as possible now that Lou's not here. If she was awful to me, I don't think I could take it right now.

Charlie would be hysterical if she saw her mother's blood all over the place. That thought is enough to force me back into the garden and continue what I've started. *Mind over matter. Mind over matter.*

The pressure washer certainly does the job. I squint through half-open eyes as I wash the hardened stains towards the drain in the centre of the patio. I try to imagine it's paint rather than my best friend's blood as she lay dying. I then raise the nozzle and direct it at the splatters on the wall of the house and up the legs of the patio table. It's all over the place.

I stop what I'm doing and look around. Someone is watching me. I can feel it. I try to carry on until suddenly, I can't stand it. I glance up and meet the eyes of Helen, next door. She waves from beneath her net curtain. I'm cleaning blood, and she's waving at me. Weirdo.

I shake my head and prepare to begin work on the spot at which Lou finished up. As I move towards it, my gaze rests on the patch of flattened grass where the hammer lay. They'll have bagged that up as evidence.

I wind the wire up on the washer and look over the sodden garden. The blood has vanished. And I need a shower more than I've ever needed one in my life. I'm feeling decidedly queasy and need to pull myself together.

I catch sight of myself in the hallway mirror. At first glance, I could be Lou, even with the green tinge to my face. People have always said we have a look of each other, more so since I started using the same hairdresser as her.

I tiptoe upstairs. I'll have to move my stuff over from my

house shortly. I'm certain it's what she would have wanted. When I've showered, I'm going to go through her paperwork to firm things up. Things need sorting as soon as possible, which is probably the main reason Carole let me have the key. It sounds as if she's too busy crying.

Being a single parent, and being *Lou,* she had everything in place. Charlie will be very well provided for, and so will whoever looks after her. It's looking increasingly likely it will be me and Darren. And once Charlie's living back here, it will be harder for Carole to contest anything.

I'll look after the home Lou's built up over the years and the daughter who meant so much to her. I'll make sure everything's just as she would have wanted it. And I'll be a better best friend than she could ever have imagined. After all, I've got *a lot* of making up to do.

43

NOW

I'VE ALWAYS WANTED AN EN-SUITE. *And* a walk-in wardrobe. Lou was slightly bigger than me, but I'll make sure her clothes don't go to waste.

When I slept at Owen's house a few weeks ago, *not that we did much sleeping*, I couldn't understand why his wife's belongings were still all over the place. She'd gone – so what was the point of prolonging the agony by keeping them around? But now, as I look at the pillow where Lou slept, her make-up littering the dressing table, and her clothes hanging in the wardrobe, I understand. I want to keep things just as they are too. It will be better for everyone if I just take over, without changing a thing.

I sit in front of her three-way mirror, looking at myself from all angles. The bruising on my face has completely faded now. Lou and I really do look like sisters. I *could* be her. I reach for her perfume, cradling the bottle in the palm of my hand before releasing a spray onto my wrist. Then my neck. When we were younger, we always wore each other's perfume. We enjoyed smelling the same.

As I towel dry my hair, I hear my phone ringing from where I left it in the garden. I tug one of her strappy summer dresses over my head and trot downstairs to answer it. I feel so much better after my shower and am definitely ready for another glass of wine. In the time I've been upstairs, the patio has nearly dried in the sunshine. If I get the machine back into my boot before Darren and Charlie get here, she'll know nothing about the garden ever being splattered with her mother's blood. And eventually, the visions will fade from my mind too.

I don't recognise the number. I'd better see who it is, though. It could be something to do with the investigation. I hit the call button to ring them back.

"Hello. This is Donna Meers. You rang me."

"It's Georgia Harris, I worked with Lou." There's not even a *hello.*

Georgia. We've only met a couple of times. Young, blonde and breezy. I was jealous that she spent day-in-day-out with my best friend. From working in a school myself, I know how close teachers and teaching assistants become. "Right. How did you get my number?"

"From Facebook."

I relax slightly. Maybe she's ringing to say how sorry she is, or to find out what I know. "So, you've heard? About Lou?" She must do since she talked about working with Lou in the past tense a moment ago.

"Of course I do. It's all over the news, isn't it?"

She doesn't sound very friendly... or sympathetic, to say I've just lost my best friend.

"We were supposed to be meeting this morning – me and Lou." Her voice cracks as she continues, and I can tell she's fighting tears. "We were getting the classroom ready."

"I was her best friend. How do you think I feel?"

"Some best friend."

"What did you say?"

"You heard."

I resist the urge to hang up. I haven't found out yet why she's even calling me. "What is it you want, what did you say your name was? *Georgia*?"

"My brother's been arrested."

"Eh? And what the hell has that got to do with me?" My voice rises. "Don't you think I've got enough on right now?"

"His name's Bradley. You know him as *Ash*."

"*Ash*? Why? What do you mean? Arrested? What's he done?" I run inside with the phone. This is probably not a call any of the neighbours should overhear. And Helen next door probably has her ear up to the fence. Since I've found out she knows Liz, I need to watch it. Things are enough of a mess.

"Did Lou not tell you anything about him?" Her voice is flat and cold.

"Tell me what?" *What now?*

"That *Ash*, as you know him, is not who he says he is. That he's got a ton of convictions for violence and drugs. That he's out of prison on licence, or he *was*, anyway."

"What did you say his real name is?" This really is news to me.

"Bradley. Bradley Harris. Do an internet search if you don't believe me."

Bradley. He looks nothing like a *Bradley.* "And you're saying Lou knew about this? So why didn't she tell me?"

"She only found out who he is the day before she died."

"Even after he turned up on Sunday, she didn't say anything. They were arguing in her garden." I don't add that I really didn't give her much chance to speak to me after that. I was too busy giving her boyfriend a blow job.

"She told me she was definitely going to tell you. Did he attack you, or something?"

"On Saturday night." I'd have thought there'd be a hint of apology within her voice, given that she knows her brother attacked me.

"Lou rang me on Sunday. She told me what had happened, and let me know that Bradley had turned up at her house, threatening her. And that she'd reported him."

"To the police?"

"Who do you think?"

"Alright. Look, I don't know why you're being so off. Especially after what your maniac brother's done to me."

"If I'm being *off*, as you say, it's because that's not all she told me."

I scrunch my eyes together as if that will stop me from hearing what she's going to come out with next.

"What you've done is disgusting." Her voice is as sharp as an axe.

"You mean with Scott?"

"I know all about it."

"She told you?"

"She had to talk to *someone*."

"I still don't understand why you've rung me, to be honest. If you're that *disgusted*."

"I might not like you or what you've done, but you've a right to protect yourself. It might be *you* next."

"What are you on about?"

"If Bradley gets bail after this, who knows what he'll do next."

"What do you mean?"

"What I mean, is that he's a nutter. I'm having to stay somewhere safe too."

"How come?"

"I made another call after I spoke to Lou on Sunday. To the police."

"What for?"

"I don't know whether I should go into detail. Not with you, anyway. You clearly can't be trusted"

"You said I had a right to protect myself. I need to know what you know."

"I only backed up what Lou had already reported. With a bit more detail. Enough to put me at risk as well though."

"Did you tell the police about what happened with me and Scott?"

"*What happened.*" She snorts. "From what I've heard about you..."

"Just shut up, will you? I'm asking you if the police know. Yes or no?"

"Why should that matter?" Her voice rises.

"Of course it bloody matters."

"Because you're suddenly bothered what everyone will think?"

"The thing is, nobody needs to know. Especially not now."

"I've said nothing about it... yet. I've only spoken to the police about my brother. Hopefully I've said enough to get him recalled to prison."

"But if you knew about what he was up to all along, why did you wait to do anything about it?"

"It was only when I found out what had happened to Lou, that I had to." Her voice dips. "I should have reported him earlier. But I'm as scared of him as everyone else is."

Perhaps I'm in the clear. She's only told the police about whatever it is Ash has been up to, and the threats he made to Lou. They're bound to be questioning him about her murder now. After all, it was only a matter of hours before her death that he was here.

No one can know about what happened between me and

Scott. The only other person who knows what happened is Scott himself, and he's already said that he wants to put the whole thing in the past.

"Look. I know what you must think of me," I need to get her on side. "But honestly, I've never regretted something so much in my life."

"It wasn't just Scott though, was it? Lou told me on Sunday about Darren too. Then with the threats from my brother on top of all that. She was in a terrible state. I hope you're happy with yourself."

"Who are you to judge me?"

"I was her friend. A proper friend."

"Look. I've had enough of all this. Just tell me, when was he arrested and I'll go."

"About an hour ago. He'll be waiting for his solicitor. Best case is he's recalled and remanded, if they've got enough on him, that is."

I end the call and sink onto a chair. Normally I'd go running to Lou with a revelation of this size. But there's no one for me to run to. I guess I can tell Darren about Ash, but that's it. That's after I've rooted out this news article Georgia mentioned. I knew he had a shady past but not to this extent.

OK, so it's as bad as she made it out to be. Gosh, I can pick them. But right now, thankfully, he's safely behind bars. Two hours have passed since Georgia's phone call, and I haven't heard a thing. Darren's just texted to check I've got the garden cleaned up. They're on their way back.

I jump as the front door bangs. It must be them. No one else has a key as far as I know. Then footsteps on the stairs. I dash from the kitchen to the hallway and heave out a long sigh of relief as Charlie heads straight for her room.

"Is she OK?" I look from Darren to the top of the stairs.

"She reckons she just wants to be on her own for a bit. I still haven't got my head around everything, so who knows what it must be like for her."

"I know. Poor thing. How was Carole?"

"As you'd expect. It's hit her like a truck. She looks as though she hasn't slept since it happened."

"But she was OK about you bringing Charlie back here and staying with her."

He frowns as he looks at me. "She was at great pains to remind me that this is only a temporary arrangement."

"Does she know I'm staying here?"

"You weren't even mentioned. To be honest, I was in and out of there. Charlie was waiting for me at the window, like she always does, and it was like Carole couldn't bear to look at me."

I know that face of Carole's well.

"I'll go up and talk to her shortly." It must be awful for her returning to her room, returning to this house. The last time she was here I was tugging her from her bed and turning her entire world upside down. But from now, everything's going to get easier.

"I'll have one of them if there's one going." He nods at my wine glass.

"I've just had the last dribble, but I know where Lou keeps reserves. Shit. Have you heard me, talking about her like she's still here?" As I head for the cupboard under the stairs, I almost expect her to jump out of it. I'm looking for her in every corner – still hardly able to believe she's gone.

"It's well weird being back here." He looks around as he steps into the kitchen. "Knowing she's dead." He takes the bottle from me and twists at the cap. "I can barely remember living here now. She's changed it completely since I did."

"She was painting you out." I laugh, though the sound is callous in Lou's kitchen. With her shoes, her fridge magnets and her kitchen signs. *Dinner is ready when the smoke alarm goes off,* says one. *This kitchen is for dancing,* says another. "At least, that's what she said." I'd helped her with the painting.

"You look to have done a good job out here. From what you said about how bad it was, I mean." Darren sweeps his gaze over the garden as he steps out onto the patio and sits at the table. "You'd never know anything so horrendous happened out here."

I follow him out. "Anyway, I've a bone to pick with you. You could have helped me."

"With what?"

"With the blood. You've had CBT to cure your phobia."

"Who told you that?"

I jerk my head to the right. "The woman next door. She's friends with Liz, from what she told me."

"Oh Helen. Yeah. I wouldn't say they're friends exactly. I think Liz was a bit of a bully at school."

"Not much has changed then?"

He laughs.

"They must be friends on some level for her to know something like that about *you.* Why didn't you tell me?"

"Look I'm much better, but not completely cured, if you know what I mean."

"I was well pissed off when I found out."

"I'm sorry. I couldn't have faced it."

"It wasn't much fun for me, you know, clearing that lot up. I was nearly sick."

"I'm sorry. I am."

"You said you were going to step up. Your words, not mine. Then you wriggle out of the first thing you could have helped with."

The only sound is the water fountain from the garden next door. "Changing the subject," Darren says after a few moments, "Liz still won't let me in to get any of my stuff - I'm going to have to go and buy some new clobber."

I haven't worked out how I feel about living next door to someone who knows Liz. She's nosy enough to be spying and reporting back. Still, we'll get beyond this eventually. I just have to keep my head down until we do.

"I've just found out someone's been arrested."

"For what? Lou's murder?" His voice rises.

"Shhhh." I raise my eyes toward Charlie's window. Thankfully, it's closed.

"Who? When?"

"You know that Ash, the scumbag that put me in casualty on Saturday?"

"Yeah."

"Well, he turned up here on Sunday morning, making his threats to Lou as well. He went to my house first, then came here."

"You never said anything about that before. What happened?"

"He was saying if I went to the police about what he'd done to me, I'd be looking over my shoulder. And Lou. And I've just found out he had more to lose than I ever knew."

"How did Lou get dragged into things? It sounds like *your* shit Donna."

"She went out there and started kicking off with him. I don't know what was said between them, as I stayed inside."

"*You stayed inside?*"

"Lou insisted. You know what she was like. She reckoned she could get rid of him. I was about to go out then Scott came." The mention of his name depresses me. And I really do feel shit now for allowing Lou to fight my battles. Rightly or wrongly, this is probably the main reason I've kept quiet about it.

"So how come this bloke's been arrested? Do the police know he had a go at Lou out *here*?" He gestures towards the front of the house.

"They do now."

"Why only now? Why didn't *you* say something before?"

"I didn't know who he really was. Or about his past. Now that I do, it changes things, doesn't it?"

"What did you find out? *How* did you find out?"

"I was speaking to his sister."

"Whose sister?"

"Ash's sister. She's called Georgia. And you won't believe this. She's actually Lou's teaching assistant. Here, read this."

I pull up the report I found about Bradley/Ash's sentencing and slide my phone across the table towards Darren.

"Bloody hell." He raises his eyes back to me after a few minutes. "He's got some history, hasn't he?"

"I'd never have gone near him if I'd known."

"I'm not sure I want me and Charlie caught up in anything that might involve someone like *him*."

Me and Charlie. What do I have to do to belong somewhere? When is someone going to care about *me*? Lou cared. She's probably the only person who ever really did.

"They've arrested him. So how can you be *caught up*?" I lower my voice. "That I got involved with a nutter that might be accused of taking his rage out on Lou can't be blamed on me. Don't you think I've been punished enough?"

"So Lou found out through his sister?"

"It sounds like it. I was too busy taking it all in to ask for the finer details. Georgia reckoned Lou hadn't known about Ash's convictions until the day before she died. He's been going by two different names."

"I can't understand why she wouldn't have told you as soon as she found out. I really can't."

"She was getting round to it, according to Georgia." I can hardly mention her throwing me and Scott from the house before she'd had a chance to tell me anything. I've just got to hope against all hope that she keeps that little nugget of information out of her statement.

At best, it looks terrible and will alienate Charlie and Darren. At worst, well... who knows?

44

NOW

GEORGIA'S NOT ANSWERING. My phone calls *or* texts. I want to know what's going on. I *need* to know what's going on. All that's in the local news so far is that they've arrested and questioned a thirty-one-year-old man from Harrogate in connection with the death of Louisa Rhodes. They'd have said if they'd released him or charged him. All I can do is wait.

And maybe I've been stewing over nothing. It shouldn't make any difference if Georgia tells DI Macron about what happened between me and Scott. OK, so it doesn't put me in a good light, but would a police officer even be allowed to tell anyone else about it? It's confidential, surely? No matter which way I look at it, what's done is done. I can't change a thing.

Despite the circumstances, the three of us had a reasonable evening yesterday. I coaxed Charlie from her room, and we watched a film with a takeaway. We let her choose both, so ended up with pizza and some teenage dross.

It was a strange night. Neither good, nor terrible. Just really, *really* different. But Charlie seemed relieved to be back home and spent much of the evening on her phone, texting. It sounds like her friends are looking after her, at least.

She looks terrible this morning though. I just passed her on her way to the bathroom whilst I was bringing coffees up for me and Darren.

"Do you need a hug?" I'd held my arms towards her but she just shot off into the bathroom. Even before all this, she'd become less affectionate with her mum, but I could usually manage to squeeze a hug out of her. Lou blamed it on her being a teenager.

It's weird the three of us, me, Darren and Charlie, being left together in the house like this, but I expect in time, we'll get used to our new normal. Everyone else will get used to it too. I wonder if Liz knows anything about our new arrangement here yet. She knew about Darren staying at my house, but not here. If she's still watching us, it's only a matter of time. Or Helen will tell her. Liz seems like a loose cannon and I don't trust her one bit. But it sounds as though it's well and truly over between her and Darren, thankfully.

We're nearly back at the weekend again, though the last few days are an absolute blur. Darren's bustling around in the kitchen, making brunch for us all. Not that I've got much of an appetite. I could never have predicted this scenario a week ago. It's awful to know that he'll be using the same hash browns Lou used on Sunday, eggs from the same box, and the tomatoes and beans which she bought.

It all feels wrong, yet somehow right at the same time. I'm sure this is how she would want it though. And I've never been a mother or a wife, so this is now my shot at it. *This* is what best friends do for each other.

He smiles at me as I sit at the kitchen table, watching him. We can make this work. I know we can. What we've got has stood the test of time, there's no doubt about that. And strangely, I'm glad Lou knew about us. My conscience is clearer for it.

I just need to close up that house around the corner. Hopefully before the end of the month, I'll be able to shift my stuff and tell my landlord that he can shove the word *guarantor* where the sun doesn't shine.

Music is booming from Charlie's bedroom, like the morning before Lou's death. The same music that prevented me from hearing Lou's descent on the stairs whilst I had Scott exactly where I wanted him. If the house had been silent, I'd have heard her. Would things have turned out any different if she hadn't have caught us in the act? Who knows? I still don't know how we got to that stage. I guess things had been bubbling between us the night before.

The music might be loud, but it doesn't prevent me from catching the shrill tone of the doorbell above it. Darren emerges from the kitchen at the same time as I reach the bottom of the stairs. The house lapses into silence and Charlie appears at the top of the stairs. We all look at each other as the doorbell sounds again.

Even through the frosted glass, it's obvious who it is. Two police officers. One man and one woman. I throw the door open to DI Macron and Sergeant Wilson. Perhaps they're here to let us know that they've actually charged Ash, Brad, or whatever he wants to call himself, with Lou's murder. Or let him go. When they do finally charge someone, we can set to work on finding our new normal and, between us all, make the arrangements for the funeral. I'm going to make sure my best friend gets the best send-off money can buy.

"Can we come in?" she says.

"Sure," I hold the door open as Charlie comes thundering down the stairs.

"What's going on?" she demands before they're even over the threshold. "Have you found out who killed my mum yet?"

"We're working flat out on it," Sergeant Wilson replies. "Which is why we're here."

Darren steps closer as well. We all face each other along the hallway. I'm standing with Darren and Charlie on either side of me. I scan the police officer's faces for a sign of why they're calling. Ash has been locked up for twenty-four hours, so they must have *something*. Or if not, they'll have let him go. He's got money to burn, even if I know where it comes from now. He'll have appointed the best solicitor possible.

"We've just been to your house Donna," DI Macron begins. "Obviously you weren't there, so we thought we'd try you here."

It's strange how they're singling *me* out. If they've anything to report, they should direct it at all of us.

"The forensics finished everything they needed to do," Darren adds. "So we've brought Charlie home. We're going to look after her together *here*."

"I see." DI Macron looks at us in turn with an expression that's hard to read. Maybe he shouldn't have used the word *together*. Perhaps it's too soon for that. "Well, we'll come back to that. But firstly…"

"Why did you want *me*?" Their faces still aren't giving anything away. "You said you went to my house?"

Sergeant Wilson speaks now. "We've got a few more questions we need to ask you."

"But I gave you a statement. I've already remembered as much as I could." I shrug with as much nonchalance as I can muster. Hopefully, they just want to know why I didn't talk more about Ash. Then I'll just tell them the truth – that I was scared. That's all it will be.

Sergeant Wilson glances at Charlie, then back at me. "We'll speak with you at the station, if that's OK."

"What? But why? Why can't you just speak to me here?"

Something lurches within my chest. What if Ash has said something? What if he's trying to pin everything on me? Shit. Shit. Shit.

"If you could just come with us, please." DI Macron steps forward and, for a moment, I think she's about to snap handcuffs on me. "We've got the car waiting."

"You're arresting me?"

"Not at this stage."

Not at this stage. I can't move. What the hell are they going to ask me? I glance at Charlie and Darren who seem to be rooted to the spot as well. I try to catch Darren's eye. I need a sign that he believes in me. Otherwise, what's the point?

"There's a unit of officers waiting to search your house. So if we could have a key?"

"*Search my house? What for?*" My landlord's going to love this if he finds out. And what if all the neighbours see them going in there? Like things aren't bad enough.

"I want to be there if my home is being searched."

"Why do they want to search *your* house?" Charlie suddenly finds her voice and spins around to face me.

"Look, whatever this is, I'll sort it. I'll be back here before you know it." I load as much normality as possible into my words.

"We really need to speak to you Donna. As soon as possible." DI Macron comes right up to me now and rests her hand lightly on my arm.

"You're not going in my house. No chance."

"Why? What have you got to hide?" Charlie has never, ever looked at me with such hatred before.

"If you could leave our colleagues a key." Sergeant Wilson nods towards the door, "it would make life much easier than obtaining a warrant and breaking the door down."

"So it was *you* who killed my mum?" Charlie's voice is the

most hostile I've ever heard it. As I suppose it would be. What's happening here looks terrible.

"Don't be so stupid. There's obviously been some huge mix up." I wave my finger from one police officer to another. "I'll be taking further action for this you know. You can't do this to me. To *us.*' I turn back to Charlie. "Look, I'll go and answer their questions, and then I'll be back."

"I don't want you back here. Not if you've..." Her voice trails off.

"You must be able to tell me and my daughter *something.*" Darren's eyes are loaded with suspicion and it appears he can't even bring himself to look at me. "What's going on here?"

DI Macron still has me by the arm. I shake her loose. "Get your hands off me. I'm quite capable of walking by myself."

The neighbours on both sides are out as I walk behind the officers to the waiting police car. I swear that Helen's jaw visibly drops as she notices me.

"Is everything OK?"

"It's none of your damn business, right?" I glance back at the house as Sergeant Wilson opens the car's rear door. Darren's and Charlie's eyes bore into me. He slings his arm around her shoulder, making me feel more on the outside than ever. It would appear that he's suddenly morphed into father of the year.

"Your door keys, please." DI Macron stretches her hand towards me. "The quicker we can do this, the less time you'll have to spend in a cell after we've spoken to you."

"A cell!" My voice is a squeak as I drop the keys into her hand. I'm beaten. I'll do anything to get this over and done with as quickly as possible. There's a thud of misery in the pit of my stomach as I get a glimpse of my keyring. It's a silver half of a forever friends keyring. Lou bought it years and years ago and kept the other half on her keyring.

"Do I need a solicitor?"

"We'll sort that out when we get to the station."

As the car pulls away, I stare back at Darren and Charlie. One minute we were looking forward to brunch, well insofar as anyone can look forward to *anything* after what's happened to Lou, and the next, I'm as good as being arrested. Hopefully, the police will be grovelling later for putting me through this.

It's the first time I've been in a police car. We pass through the main street where Lou and I have spent many hours trawling the shops. Our local where we used to do quiz nights, and put the world to rights. Lou's hairdresser – well, my hairdresser as well now. The school I work at. The school she works at. *Worked* at. Why can't I stop thinking of her in present tense? It's as though I haven't accepted that she's really gone.

"Are you still holding Ash, er Bradley?" I hesitate at the side door of the police station. He's the last person I want to cross paths with.

"We can't tell you that." DI Macron glances back as I follow her in with Sergeant Wilson behind me. Her eyes are marble hard – there's certainly no trace of the sympathy that filled them on Sunday.

She swipes us through three sets of security doors then suddenly, I'm in the sort of area I've only ever seen on TV. I'm overpowered by the stench of body odour and sweaty feet. Everything's a putrid green. The walls, the floor, even the desk. It would give me a migraine if I worked here.

"Which room can we use Sarge?" DI Macron looks expectantly at a man with huge underarm sweat patches perched behind the high desk. He turns to a board on the wall.

"Room three ma'am." He gestures towards an open door into another sick-inducing green room. I hope it smells better in there than out here.

"Hang on." I stand still, instead of following them as they

start towards the door. "Without a solicitor, I'm not going in there. No chance." I don't care if it sounds like I have something to hide by taking this stance. They're searching my house. They're questioning me. I *need* a solicitor.

"We were coming to that if you'd given us chance." DI Macron slides the sign on the door to *engaged.* Sarky cow. I've no choice other than to follow her in, exchanging body odour for the slap of heat. She beckons for me to sit.

"Will you see about getting a fan Robin?" She nods towards Sergeant Wilson who springs back to his feet just before he sits. He's like her lapdog.

"Can I have some water?" I look at her as she hangs her coat on the back of the chair. "And a solicitor."

Sergeant Wilson turns back from the door. "Do you already have a someone in mind, or shall I call the duty solicitor?"

"Since I hadn't planned to get hauled in for questioning, no, I haven't got anyone *in mind.* How long will it take?" Plus, I don't add, *I won't have to pay for a duty solicitor.* I've made a massive dent already in the loan I took out. And it's not as if I know where any more might come from. Especially *now.*

I can't deny that I'm terrified. But as long as I say nothing that could dig me into a hole, I should be alright. A solicitor, even a duty one, should be able to give me some advice. I don't know what Ash has told them and that worries me. He's cleverer than I am, and more used to dealing with this sort of thing. Plus, he obviously wants some sort of revenge. He might think it was *me* who reported him last Sunday.

"It depends," Sergeant Wilson replies. "As we're getting towards the middle of the day, there may well be someone leaving court after the morning session. If we get them at a good time."

A good time. I don't know whether to laugh or scream.

45

NOW

"You do not have to say anything. But it may harm your defence if you do not mention when questioned something which you may later rely on in court. Anything you do say may be given in evidence." DI Macron clasps her hands together on the table and surveys me over the top of her glasses. The hard and cold expression she exhibited as we arrived here has been replaced with a look of seriousness. "Do you understand the rights I've just read to you, or do you need them explaining?"

"I understand." A bead of sweat slides from my armpit and down the side of my body. I've never felt in more need of a shower. The heat in here and the lack of anything to eat today are conspiring against me. My stomach is churning like a cement mixer with both hunger and nerves. I wish I knew what was going on and hope to God I get out of here. I'm scared. In fact, I'm terrified. I've never even been in a police station before, let alone an interview room. *What if they lock me in a cell? I'll go mad.*

"It is Friday August 28th. The time is 11:50 am, and this interview is being conducted by myself, Detective Inspector Susan Macron, at West Yorkshire Police Station. I am interviewing.... for the recording, can you confirm your full name, your date of birth and your home address?"

"Yes, Donna Marie Meers. The fourth of March 1983, and my address is 17 Chestnut Grove, Farndale Leeds."

"Thank you. Also present is..." She nods towards her colleague.

"Sergeant Robin Wilson of West Yorkshire Police." His wedding ring flashes in the light getting through the slit of a window, reminding me that people do live ordinary lives. It just didn't work out for me. Even at school, I was known as *the boyfriend stealer,* so I didn't really have any friends. Not before Lou came along.

"Also present is..." DI Macron nods towards the duty solicitor who looks barely out of high school. Still, she's got here quickly. As Sergeant Wilson predicted, the morning court had just finished when he rang the duty service. And at least I've been able to wait in here rather than in a cell. They'd have to arrest me to put me in a cell.

"Amy Smith. I'm a duty solicitor based at Bowman Donnelly and Co." I've had about fifteen minutes with her to fill her in. Not that I really know anything yet about exactly why they've hauled me in here. All I could tell her were the basic details of Lou's death, and that we'd had a major fallout earlier that day after what I did to her with Scott. I've told her everything, including the fact that our friendship was already hanging by a thread after what I admitted to about Darren.

Then there's Ash in the mix. He was threatening both of us – me *and* Lou. The solicitor has advised me to do a *no comment* interview unless they throw up any so-called evidence against me. I don't see what they could have, though.

"So Donna. You're attending here at West Yorkshire Police Station on a *voluntary* basis to answer some further questions regarding the death, which we are treating as murder, of your friend Louisa Ann Rhodes."

I nod. It's the word *murder*. A word loaded with hatred and darkness. I suddenly feel as though I can't speak. And hearing Lou's name spoken out loud too. Suddenly I'm enveloped by a sadness so raw, I wonder how I'm going to get through these questions. So far, I've suppressed it. I've been numb and going through the motions, but it's threatening to erupt. I'd give anything to have her back. *Anything.*

"For the benefit of the recording, can you ensure you verbally confirm your replies rather than just nodding?"

I swallow. Stupid cow. "Yes."

"At this stage in our investigation, you are not under arrest and are free to leave at any time. Do you understand this?"

"Yes." But her face suggests that if I tried to leave, they'd arrest me straight away. They've clearly got *something* or I wouldn't be sitting here.

"I'm going to start by reading out the statement that we took from you in the early hours of Monday morning, the 24th of August, three hours after Louisa's body was discovered in her garden."

"Yes." Like I have to relive that again.

I listen as the words I previously said swim through and around my foggy mind. Amy scribbles notes onto her pad. The early hours of Monday morning feels like such a long time ago.

"Can you confirm, Donna, that this is the statement *you* made, to myself and Sergeant Wilson, when we attended at your home in the early hours of Monday morning, the 24th of August?"

"Yes it is."

"And can you confirm that is your signature?"

I remember when Lou and I used to practice our signatures when we got our first credit cards. She could do mine and I could do hers. We'd practice putting our names together with the lads we were seeing.

"Yes." The churning in my stomach is making me feel sick. I hope I can hold up and get through this.

"Donna. We've brought you in to speak to us because it would seem that there are many omissions in the statement you made. Things you ought to have mentioned. Things we can't understand why you would have kept quiet about."

I stay quiet now and just look at her, waiting. Her eyes are full of accusations. But until I know exactly what she's referring to, I'm not saying a word. I definitely feel better having a solicitor in with me. To wait for her was the right thing. She might not be some top-notch legal eagle, but she knows far more than I do.

"As you know," she continues, "we're now on the fifth day of the investigation into Louisa's death and from the people we've spoken to so far, your name has come up time and time again."

"It's bound to have done. Lou and I were best friends." This sentence hits me like a punch in the chest. *Were* best friends. Maybe we always will be. In death and in life.

She and Sergeant Wilson look at each other.

"I'm not sure I'd want a best friend like you." DI Macron clears her throat and shuffles in her chair. Her expression says it all. I glance towards Sergeant Wilson. Though he's clearly trying to keep a professional front, he's thinking the same awful things about me.

I wait for her to continue. She obviously knows how I betrayed Lou. The solicitor waits too, pen poised. I've already told her the truth, so she'll know what's coming next.

"I have it on good authority that you spent many years in a relationship with Louisa's former husband, Darren Rhodes." DI Macron runs a pen down her page as she speaks. "A relationship which started before the time Louisa and Darren got together and beyond the time they were divorced. Is that correct?"

"No comment." Gosh this really is like something off the TV. I can't believe that I'm stuck in the middle of it.

"It would seem also that you coveted the life your friend Louisa led. I can see just by looking at you, how similar the two of you are."

"So?" Maybe I should have said *no comment,* but I want to know what she's getting at. Or more to the point, what she's accusing me of.

"I see a similar line of employment with you both, a car you recently bought exactly like the one Louisa drove. And I've also discovered that you've just moved around the corner from her house? Why is that?"

"She wanted me to move there."

"That's not what we've been told Donna."

"Why? What *have* you been told?"

"That not only could Louisa not trust you, but she was feeling suffocated by your behaviour. It was as though you wanted to *be* her. These are the exact words I've heard from two of our witnesses." Her voice rises. "Not the healthiest of friendships. Wouldn't you agree?"

"No comment." She's trying to rile me, trying to trip me up. I won't let her. If Lou had felt suffocated by me, she'd have said something. Who does this woman think she is, judging me in this way?

"You recently took a holiday to France with Louisa and her daughter Charlotte. Is that right?"

I nod.

"Is that a yes Donna?"

"Yes."

"A holiday during which you confessed about the relationship I've just mentioned - a long-standing sexual relationship with Darren Rhodes, the father of Louisa's daughter?"

"No comment." It sounds awful, what she's just said, out

loud in the cold light of day. Or the *hot* light of day given the temperature in here. I should have stayed well away from him, especially after he and Lou married, and Charlie was born. But the forbidden fruit has always proved too tempting for me.

"What I don't understand is why did you wait all these years to confess this betrayal to Louisa?" She stabs at her notebook with the pen, looking as though she'd stab me with it, given half a chance. "And why did you tell her when you were away on holiday?"

"No comment." I don't really have an answer to this, apart from that I was drunk. Very drunk. If I'd been sober, I doubt I'd have told her.

"On the morning of her death, Louisa caught you, in her home, engaged in a sexual act with her new boyfriend, Scott Lucas, someone she thought a lot of. Someone she thought she had a future with."

Shit. She knows. I'm not sure whether she's asking a question of me here or not. I felt such power when he succumbed to my advances that morning. But in hindsight, it's one of the biggest mistakes I've ever made.

"No comment."

They must have got this from Georgia. As far as I'm aware, she's the only other person who knows about Scott. Unless he's confessed. He's gone *very* quiet since it all happened. I hope the guilt hasn't got the better of him – maybe he couldn't keep it a secret anymore.

But I don't see how it would incriminate me with Lou's death, anyway. And in any case, if this information has only come second hand to the police, via Georgia, nothing can be proved.

"Was that the *only* encounter between the two of you?"

"No comment."

"Did you not consider the fact that Charlotte, Louisa's

daughter was in the house? You've told me yourself that you're her 'godmother,' and how much you care for her."

She draws air quotes as she says the word *godmother*. I feel like smacking her.

"No comment." *Shut up! Shut up!*

"Have you got children of your own Donna?"

I shake my head. "No." Charlie's face swims into my mind. Wearing the look she gave me this morning when she asked whether I'd killed her mum. That hateful expression on her face will always stay with me.

"From an outsider's perspective, and from what I've been told by everyone we've spoken to, I'd say it's safe to say you'd have liked to have swapped places with Louisa. Is that right?"

"No comment." Of course I would, but they don't need confirmation of this.

"You were never happy with your own life. You'd have preferred hers. What have you got to say about that?"

"No comment." It's true. I was always saying *it's alright for you.*

"You were jealous of her."

"No comment."

"You couldn't understand why she should have the trappings of the life she enjoyed, as well as the solid relationships she had with those around her."

"No comment."

"Whilst for *you*, *Louisa* was the only person you really had in your corner, wasn't she?"

"No comment." Tears stab at my eyes. She's right. Lou really was the only person I had in my corner. And now she's gone. If things don't work out with me and Darren, I don't know what I'll do. I can't be on my own. I'm tired of being on my own. My so-called father upped and left before I was born. My mother always treated me like an inconvenience, and I've never really got on with other women. Apart from Lou. She's the only real friend I've had.

"The only people you seem to attract into your life were married men and thugs. Isn't that right Donna?"

I stare at her. We must be getting to Ash now. I was wondering when he'd be mentioned. Though surely she's not supposed to refer to him as a thug? It's hardly very professional.

"Does the name," she glances at her notepad, "Bradley Harris, mean anything to you Donna?"

I wish she'd stop using my name so much. *Donna. Donna. Donna.* It's really patronising. "Yes. But he was calling himself something else," I reply. "Ash..." I stare down at the table. "He never actually told me his second name."

The solicitor frowns at me. Probably because I keep slipping up and answering questions when I'm supposed to be *no commenting.* It's hard though. Surely questions like that one, I'm alright to answer. It's straightforward enough.

"And how did you meet *Ash?*"

"No comment."

She looks disappointed, probably at my return to *no commenting.* "What did you know of Bradley's previous and current criminality?"

"No comment."

"I gather he attacked you. Don't be doing him any favours here. He's certainly not doing you any."

"What's that supposed to mean?"

The solicitor frowns again.

"Before we discuss that, let me first ask you about the day of Louisa's death." She reaches towards the fan and turns it up. Her papers flutter in the faster air. "You were present in Louisa's house when Bradley, or Ash, as you call him, turned up, wanting to speak to you earlier that day, weren't you?"

"No comment."

"But you let Louisa go out and face him instead, didn't you?

Alone. Even when you suspected the mood he was presenting in."

I want to tell her I didn't know about his exact background at that point. I knew he was a thug after how he'd treated me, but not the extent. It was only after speaking to Georgia and searching online that I knew. But I can't say anything. Not yet. Not until I know what they've got on me. Which might be nothing at all.

"No comment."

"Do you know what was said between the two of them during that conversation?"

"No comment."

"How well do you know Bradley's sister?" DI Macron runs her pen down a piece of paper. "Georgia Harris?"

Amy writes something down. She stifles a yawn, which sets me off too. I was up half the night with Darren. It doesn't feel right at all, having sex in Lou's bed, not now she's gone. But it'll feel like my bed before long. That's if he lets me back in.

DI Macron looks at me as though I'm diseased as I yawn for the second time. "Tired? Oh dear."

I stifle a third yawn. "I'm not sleeping. My best friend's just died."

"I'm not surprised you're not sleeping." Her voice has an edge I don't like. Earlier this week her words might have been loaded with sympathy, but here and now, they're filled with sarcasm. "I'll ask you again. How well do you know Georgia Harris?"

"No comment." I feel the usual stab of jealousy that I've always felt whenever Lou's had a friend that wasn't me. Especially *Georgia*. She was always going on about her. I imagine the conversation they must have had on Sunday afternoon - Lou confiding in her about what I'd done to her with Scott, and the way I'd put her 'at risk' from Ash that morning. But if she knew who he really was and what he might be capable of, she should never have gone out there.

If I'd known the day before, everything that happened wouldn't have. But for some reason, she sat on the information doing nothing. Really, it's partly *her* fault I got attacked again on Saturday night. And without that happening, Scott would never have taken me to hospital and we wouldn't have-

"We've taken a statement from Georgia." DI Macron's voice cuts into my muddled thinking. "She firstly confirmed the toxicity surrounding the friendship you had with Louisa. What was the word she used? Oh yes, *stalked*. She says that Louisa often felt *stalked* by you."

My fists bunch in my lap. "No comment."

"And she felt responsible for you. Like you depended on her for *everything*."

"No comment."

"She was always bailing you out, constantly having to listen to the aftermath of your mistakes, frequently needing to scoop you off the floor. *Georgia's* words, not mine." DI Macron's head is tilted to one side. There's a smirk playing on her lips as she waits for me to respond. She obviously enjoys being a bitch.

"No comment." Hopefully my *no commenting* is as infuriating to her as her questions are to me.

"She was planning to move away. Do you know that?"

I stare straight into her eyes. "No comment." It might as well just be me and DI Macron in this room. The other two are doing nothing apart from scribbling on their notepads.

"She *was* planning to move away from *you*. Well away from you. She didn't trust you anymore." Her voice is as hard as concrete. "She'd had enough of being dragged down by your behaviour. Again, we've had this from more than one witness."

"No comment."

That'll be her mum. And Scott. And obviously, bloody

Georgia. Wait until I get out of here. I'll make sure they all regret bad-mouthing me to the police.

"It must have been quite something when Louisa threw you out of her house on Sunday." The sarcastic edge in DI Macron's voice intensifies. She really is a totally different animal to the one I initially gave the statement to, and so sensitively dealt with Charlie. "I gather she told you she never wanted to set eyes on you again after what she walked in on."

"No comment."

"That must have been hard for you to take Donna. Being rejected by the person you relied on for *everything*. Even the roof over your head."

"How do you know about that?" I forget again that I'm supposed to be *no commenting*. Louisa promised that our guarantor arrangement was between the two of us and she wouldn't tell anyone. I didn't want others knowing that at the ripe old age of thirty-eight I needed a guarantor. I've always been useless with money.

"We also know about the loan. Is there something you want to tell us?"

"No comment." Shit. I'm done for here.

"The one for ten thousand pounds taken out in Louisa's name." She slides a sheet of paper towards me. "Whose is this signature Donna?"

I stare at it, the swirls blurring in front of my eyes. "No comment."

"For the benefit of the recording, I can confirm the signature on the loan application and acceptance match that on other official documents signed by Louisa Rhodes. But yet the application and supporting documents have been sent from your IP address."

Shit. Shit. Shit. If I could speak I'd lie and tell them that Lou did the application whilst round at my house. "No comment."

"Louisa had no reason to require a loan like this." It's as if the woman's a mind reader. "Nor did she have any reason for obtaining car finance for a car matching the description and registration of the one you're driving."

I can't believe they know about all this? It had all been so easy at the time. Too easy really. Especially with both things being mostly done online. I'd been able to use one of Lou's bank accounts that was sitting idle. I knew practically everything about her – what she had, where she kept things. She'd shown me. She trusted me. And now I feel as heavy as a helicopter at the extent to which I've betrayed this trust. I don't know how I'll ever forgive myself. What the hell is going to happen to me now?

"Were you not worried she'd find out about this fraud? Or didn't you care?"

"No comment." I wonder if DI Macron notices the wobble in my voice. The fact of the matter was that I was terrified Lou would find out. Especially after she'd mentioned she was going to check out her credit score, as she and Scott had been talking about joint mortgages and joint bank accounts. Everything I'd taken out in her name would be on there. When I took the money, I never really considered the aftermath. I was desperate. The only loan I'd have been able to get would have been a few hundred quid from a shark. I'm so sick of being broke all the time. I've never had any luck or support. Not like she had.

"Let's move on a few hours to the night of Sunday 23rd August, shall we?" She pauses and I don't know whether to be relieved that she's moving on or terrified of what's coming next. A bit of both I think. "Firstly, Donna, where were you between the hours of ten thirty and eleven fifteen pm?"

Here we go. They *are* accusing me of this. "No comment."

"Was anyone with you throughout the evening?"

"No comment."

I could tell her about the banging on the door and Ash's car on the street, but I need to wait. See what they already know. I could tell her that half an hour after that, there had been more banging on the door, but this time, Ash's car was nowhere to be seen. There'd been noises and scuffles from outside all night, but with the way I was feeling, I just wanted to be left alone.

I think of my mobile phone tucked into the pocket of my handbag. The police will probably, at some point, ask to go through it. I've deleted all the messaging that went on that night, the texts I had been sending Lou, hoping she'd unblocked my number, then between me and Ash, and there were the messages Liz was sending to me. Threats and name calling. *Slag* seems to be her favourite word. I suppose it would be after finding out about me and Darren.

Lou had years of nasty texts, so it was probably a novelty for Liz to shift her hatred onto me. Though I was beyond fuming that Lou had gone around there shooting her mouth off. Especially since she wasn't even with Darren anymore. Nothing good was ever going to come from her spilling the beans to Liz about our relationship.

"Have you any idea why we wanted to search your house?"

"No comment." Here we *really* go.

"So you're unable to give us a heads up on what we're going to find there?" DI Macron continues.

"It would go in your favour," Sergeant Wilson looks up from his notes and speaks for the first time during the interview. "If you told us first-hand what we're going to find."

"And also what you *really* know."

"No comment."

46

NOW

"Donna Meers. I am arresting you on suspicion of the murder of Louisa Rhodes. You do not have to say anything..."

DI Macron's words swarm around me as I dig my nails into the fleshy part of my palm. I dig so hard, I'll probably bleed.

"We're going to get you formally booked in, and then we'll resume the interview."

Booked in. They make it sound like a bloody hotel. This isn't happening. This really isn't happening.

"Do you understand why you've been arrested Donna?"

"No." More sweat drips from my armpits, down both the sides of my body.

"OK." They look at each other.

What the hell have they got on me? I look at Amy. She just sits there. She's going to get out of here, return to her office, to her normal life. She's supposed to be helping me. Instead, she's just sitting there, uselessly scribbling on a notepad. It's alright for her.

"The evidence I'm about to present points towards *you* as being the person who brutally ended the life of Louisa Rhodes on Sunday 23rd August. As I said before, you do have the right to stay silent, but I would suggest you answer my questions and respond to the evidence as fully as you can."

"Can I remind you Donna." Amy nudges me. "That you can stop this interview at any time if you're not sure of a question, or if you want to ask anything of me."

I nod. She's told me that 'no commenting' can go against me once I'm actually under arrest. But so can giving an ill-thought-out answer. We could talk when they left the room an hour ago. Amy told me that when they returned, they'd probably either let me go or arrest me. I can't believe it's the latter. The whole thing feels surreal, like it's not really happening to me. I'm really fighting for survival now. I've got to get out of here. Get back to Darren and Charlie. Be able to explain myself.

Sergeant Wilson points a remote control at a large screen to the right of where we're sitting. I blink in its glare after the gloom of this place for the last few hours. "We're going to show you a series of photographs Donna." His voice is gentler than that of DI Macron and I'm less irritated with his use of my name.

"As we go through them, we'll be asking you questions. As my colleague has already mentioned, you do not have to say anything, but anything you do say can be given in evidence. And, as your solicitor has stated, you can pause the interview and speak to her at any time. We will stop the recording and leave the room."

"Yes." I just want to see these pictures. The sooner we get through this, the sooner I'll get out of here. One way or another.

I stare at the words on the screen. *Case Number 53421 LAR WYP.* Lou's life has been reduced to a case number on a screen. I dig my nails into my palm again, as though I'm reaffirming this is all actually happening. A scene from when we were younger flashes into my mind, when Lou and I were discussing death and how the first to go would give the other a sign. Had anyone told us she'd be dead before the age of forty, and I'd be arrested on suspicion of her murder, we'd have told them they were insane.

"Right Donna. The items we have seized as evidence are being shown to you as photographs. This is because they are currently being forensically examined. We will check them for DNA against the swab you provided, as well as your fingerprints."

"The results of that will be checked against the forensics from the murder scene, and will inform whether you are charged," DI Macron adds, as though I'm thick. I might not be the high-flyer Lou was, but I know what they want my DNA for.

"How long will that take?" Amy's voice is almost weary. She probably didn't realise she'd be stuck here all day when she walked from the court. At least she knows she'll definitely be leaving this hell-hole of a place later. She's already told me they can hold me here for thirty-six hours without charging me. *Thirty-six hours.* I'll either boil to death, starve to death, or crack up.

"The lab is currently working at about six hours," Sergeant Wilson replies. "Unless something more urgent comes in, that is."

DI Macron nods towards him and he presses the remote. *Six hours.* I'm not eating the muck they'd probably give me in here, no matter how hungry I am.

"For the purposes of the recording," he begins, "we are showing Donna Meers a photograph, marked LAR1, an image of the dressing gown worn by the deceased, Louisa Rhodes, at the time of her death. Donna, do you recognise this dressing gown?"

"Of course I do." I let a long breath out. If this is the best they can do, I'll be walking out of here with my head held high after all.

"The garment bears DNA, which is neither Louisa's nor anyone related to her. However, it *has* been identified as female DNA. When we get the results back from your swab, do you think we'll find a match?" DI Macron leans back in her seat. Suspicion is written all over her face. She's already found me guilty and hung me out to dry.

"Most definitely." I can literally feel the weight of my shoulders sag as tension seeps from them. They really could be clutching at straws here. The media will push for someone to be charged. The longer this goes on, the worse it looks for the police. They'll want to charge *me*. Just to pin it on *someone*. "I'd borrowed the dressing gown from her on Sunday morning. After I'd slept the night there."

Despite my plausible answer, DI Macron looks smug, as though she's got something up her sleeve. What that might be is what I'm frightened of.

"We are now looking at photograph LAR2, which shows the murder weapon, a hammer, thirty-two centimetres in length, which has been found to bear fingerprints not belonging to Louisa Rhodes or anyone related to her. Again, according to our lab, these fingerprints are likely to be female. Have you seen this hammer before Donna?"

"It's just a hammer," I reply.

"But it's not just *any* hammer, is it?" She gestures towards the screen. "It just so happens to be a hammer that matches with a tool set found in your shed at 17 Chestnut Grove, Farndale, this morning."

"I- I don't know how it got there. To Lou's garden, I mean. It was in my shed the whole time." She bought me that toolset as a joke housewarming present when I first moved out of the flat we'd shared when we were younger.

"We are now showing Donna Meers photograph LAR3,

which shows the inside of the toolbox found at her home at 17 Chestnut Grove, Farndale. There's one item missing from it, which appears to be the hammer found in Louisa Rhodes's garden."

"She must have borrowed it from me." I stare at the hammer as though the longer I do, the more feasible the answer I will be able to give. "I don't know."

"We will now move on to item LAR4, a still taken from CCTV footage captured from the neighbour at *1 Millfield Road, Farndale*, three doors to the left of Louisa Rhodes's home. The image is from 10:51 pm on Sunday. It seems to depict you Donna, passing the house on your way to Louisa's home?"

"That's not me." I peer at it. Though there's no denying it looks like me. But like she alluded to with the word *seems*, it's not clear. The shot is in darkness and extremely grainy.

"The suspect in the image is darkly dressed and wearing a cap," DI Macron says. "I would suggest Donna, that if you were to take part in an identity parade, *you* would be picked out, since your height, build and gait matches the person in the recording exactly."

"Similarly..." Sergeant Wilson presses the remote again. "Item LAR5 shows the same person walking in the opposite direction at 11:13pm. This time they are moving faster and carrying something underarm." He looks at me.

"That isn't me. It can't be. I'm telling you. I was at home."

DI Macron frowns. "For which you have no alibi."

Shit. Shit. Shit. I look at Amy, who's writing something again. Probably her bill by the hour for this utter farce where they don't seem to know what to do with me. There's silence for a few moments other than a scratch of a pen against the page.

"Is Ash, erm Bradley still here?" My voice is shrill in the quiet. I don't know why this should make any difference, but part of me will feel a lot better if I know I'm not the only suspect still in this. And that he's suffering as much as I am.

"Like I said before," she replies, "we can't tell you what's going on with anyone else. All we can repeat are things he's said that relate to you and this investigation."

"Such as?" He'll have told them all sorts probably. I wish I'd never clapped eyes on the man. The relationship I've had with him, if it can even be called that, has caused so much trouble. I just want to make a go of things with Darren now. If I get the chance.

"He told us how furious you've been about the rejection you've been experiencing." She arches an eyebrow.

"What rejection? From *him*? He's done me a favour."

"The rejection from Louisa," she replies. "He said you didn't know how you were going to deal with it."

"I hardly even discussed it with him." I'm sure he'll have been bad-mouthing me as much as he can. "We were getting through it, me and Lou. She was forgiving me. She sent Scott to help me when I was in trouble. The night before she died. And she let me sleep at her house." I wish she hadn't now. I wish she'd sent me home.

"Bradley has told us he knows first-hand how you like your own way. To the point where you get possessive about people."

"That's not true."

"He said that when you *can't* have someone, or your own way with someone, you get nasty. What was it he called you?" DI Macron gives an expression like she's trying to remember, when in reality, she knows full well what she's going to say.

Amy sits up straight. "I object to this line of questioning. In fact, I wouldn't even call it questioning."

I feel like applauding her. Finally, she's got my back. I'd forgotten what her voice sounded like. Maybe I should use some of that loan money to pay for a better solicitor, but who knows if I'll even be allowed to spend the rest of it now?

"Fair enough." DI Macron lowers her tone. "But I will repeat one thing Bradley has alleged about you." She looks at me pointedly and the pause before she speaks again is clearly designed to infuriate me. "He alleges you were worried that she'd find out about what else you'd been up to."

"What do you mean?" From how she's speaking, it sounds as though she's on his side. Sergeant Wilson has an expression on his face that suggests he is too.

"I'm talking about the loan you'd taken out in Louisa's name. Which we've already mentioned."

Shit. I might have known I couldn't trust Ash. He found the paperwork in my bedroom when he stayed over and hadn't believed me when I said they were Louisa's documents. He'd seen straight through me. I suppose going red and stuttering didn't help.

"You also thought it was likely she would go back on her agreement to act as your guarantor. That's what you told him."

I must have been drunk when I've mentioned *that* to Ash. I don't even remember. That's been happening a lot lately. Drinking. Saying things. Doing things. Being unable to remember.

"And..." DI Macron looks almost joyful at whatever she's going to come out with next. "Bradley has mentioned that you asked him whether he knew anyone who'd get Louisa out of the picture for good."

"That's not true." I raise my voice. "That's just not true. I said one or two things to Ash, I mean Bradley, about things being strained between me and Lou, but *nothing* like that. He's lying."

"But," DI Macron continues. "Bradley's testimony and the CCTV footage is not enough *on its own* to warrant the CPS charging you."

I relax *slightly* until I realise she hasn't finished speaking.

"However, they may take a different view when presented with further items recovered at your home address of 18

Chestnut Grove, Farndale, earlier today." She gestures towards Sergeant Wilson to continue.

He clears his throat. "LAR6 shows a dark coloured cap with a white stripe at each side, identical to the cap pictured in the CCTV. For the benefit of the recording, we are showing Donna Meers each item we have recovered side by side with the video stills. LAR7 shows a black pair of lycra leggings, size 12, and LAR8 shows a black long-sleeved lycra top, displaying a large Adidas logo. Finally LAR9 shows a pair of Nike size 6 black trainers, again identical to the training shoes worn by the suspect in the CCTV."

I blink in the screen's glare. *Where is this going? Where the hell is this going?*

"The pattern on the sole of these trainers..." DI Macron speaks now, "matches the footprints found in the blood stains on the patio where the killing took place, and were also walked into the kitchen of Louisa's house."

Sergeant Wilson drains the water from his plastic cup. I'm going to have to ask for some more soon. I run my tongue round my parched lips. My mouth feels as though something has died in there.

"I am now showing item number LAR10 which shows the sole of a shoe, side by side with an image of a bloodied footprint taken from the scene."

I take in a sharp breath.

"The items of footwear and clothing in pictures LAR6 to LAR10 were found laundered and stacked in a basket. A basket which was in the kitchen of your home, Donna. This can be seen on item number LAR11."

"They're just my gym clothes. That wasn't me in the CCTV. What happened to Lou has *nothing* to do with me."

"A further search of the upstairs of your home, yielded the discovery of the following two items." He presses a button on the remote control again. "Item LAR12, which is a purse belonging to Louisa Rhodes, containing one hundred and forty-four pounds in cash, and four debit and credit cards." He glances from the screen to me and back again. "Then item LAR12 is a jewellery box, again belonging to Louisa Rhodes, the contents of which have been itemised in our report. What have you got to say about these findings in your home Donna?"

"I don't know how they got to my house. Maybe she left them there? Or they were planted there." My mouth is even drier. "I don't know how they got there. I really don't."

Ironically, it was me who originally bought both items. She had been coveting the Radley purse for about six months. And she would often joke about her childhood having been deprived as she'd never had a musical jewellery box with a ballerina twirling before the plastic mirror.

"Item LAR13," his voice slices back into my thoughts, "is another still from the CCTV footage, this time, it can be seen," he points at the screen, "the subject carrying an item which is the same shape and size as a jewellery box, under their arm. Can you see what we're getting at here Donna?"

"It's not me. Why aren't you listening? It can't have been me. I was at home." Although I'm doubting myself. How much had I drunk that night? I'm sure it wasn't that much? Though I was so pissed off after what had happened with Scott, and that Lou had fallen out with me.

"We're scrutinising CCTV from two more houses between your house and Louisa's house." DI Macron's voice is gentler now. "But as Sergeant Wilson alluded to before, you can make life easier for all of us, especially yourself, by telling us the truth right now." She tips her head to one side. Everything about this woman infuriates me.

"I knew *nothing* of her death until Scott got in touch with me." I'll never forget that phone call as long as I live. Though I wonder what he's told the police. Perhaps Lou told him about her being a 'guarantor' for me after all. If both he *and* Ash have talked about it, things are looking even worse for me.

I jump as there's a knock at the door.

"Come in," calls DI Macron.

The desk sergeant curls his head into the room. "Sorry to disturb you ma'am, but there's a telephone message you might want to see."

"Right you are." She reaches towards the recording machine. "Interview with Donna Meers, suspended at 15:42. If you could just excuse us one moment."

"Can I have some more water please?" This is turning into one of the longest days of my life. Longer even, than the day after Lou's body was found.

"Certainly. I'll bring it in for you." The desk sergeant sounds slightly friendlier than the two officers who've been interviewing me.

"Me too please." Amy dabs at her brow with her scarf. Surely there are laws about how hot these rooms can be. Though that's the least of my worries right now.

"We'll be back in a few minutes." Sergeant Wilson gets up too and follows DI Macron to the door. I thought he was good-looking when I first saw him. Now I've decided he's a weasel.

"What are you thinking?" I turn to face Amy as the door falls closed behind them.

She pushes her hair back from her face. Her mascara has run. "They haven't got enough to charge you with Donna. Not from what they've presented so far. But things will hinge on a few factors now."

"Like what?"

"Well, they'll be examining that clothing they found in the laundry basket. If there're any traces of Louisa's blood..."

"There can't be," I reply quickly, shaking my head.

"They could get clearer CCTV footage from one of the other houses, or match more of your DNA at the crime scene.

We'll know more when they've analysed the swab you gave them. Things such as what your boyfriend said are difficult to prove. They're just his word against yours."

"He's not my boyfriend." Like that matters one iota right now.

Just a few hours ago, I was waking in Lou's lovely house, looking forward to brunch and a day pottering around with Darren and Charlie. We might not have been a conventional family, but we'd have made it work. It was the life I wanted, the life I deserved. I wonder what Darren and Charlie are doing now, what they're thinking. Surely they don't think I'm capable of this?

We sit in silence for a few moments. What the hell is the telephone message? I really can't take much more today. I just want to go home. Whatever *home* is. Darren might not let me back into Lou's after this. Charlie may never speak to me again. And I might not even be able to go to my house if they're treating it as some sort of crime scene.

I stare at the scratches all over the table. Words such as *help me* and *let me out* have been gouged into it. Desperation that mirrors mine. My life feels as over as Lou's is right now.

47

NOW

I jump as the door opens, heralding the return of the two police officers. They place two cups of water on the table. I reach for the cup before me, almost choking on my urgency to get the tepid water down my throat.

DI Macron presses a button and a long beep echoes around the room. "Interview resumed at 16:02. Still present are DI Susan Macron."

"Sergeant Robin Wilson."

"Amy Smith, duty solicitor."

"And..." She nods at me.

"Donna Meers."

"Before we charge you Donna, I'm going to give you an opportunity to answer to something new that's been found in your home."

"What? *Charge me?* Why?"

They can't charge me. How can they charge me?

"Can you explain..." she pauses and glances at Amy who's sitting with her pen poised, "why our team has found traces of Louisa's blood in and around your shower?"

"You can't have." I rack my brains, trying to remember when

she was last at my house, or some other plausible reason she might have been in my shower. "I don't know what you're talking about."

"Donna Meers. You are charged with the murder of Louisa Ann Rhodes. You do not have to say...."

I don't hear anymore. Whether it's the heat, the stress, or lack of food today, the room turns black, and I'm gone...

DARREN

ONE YEAR LATER

I N THE YEAR we've lived here, we've *painted Lou out,* just like she did with me when we first broke up. The house didn't really need repainting, but I understand how Liz might have wanted to put her own stamp on the place.

We've been getting on better than we used to, definitely more so when Charlie's not here. When she is, I try to take her out, or she spends time in her room. But there's always an atmosphere. I wish I could do something, *anything,* for the two of them to thaw out with each other.

However, I'm grateful that Liz seems to have buried her resentment about my relationship with Donna, to some extent. She's gone from throwing it in my face hourly, to daily at the most.

Carole hasn't forgiven me though, and probably never will. It turns out she was the one who made sure the police knew about it.

She even told me to stay away from Lou's funeral. I didn't though. I slipped in at the back and left just before the end. Charlie was standing at the side of the coffin before the curtain went around. She looked so small, and it was all I could do not to charge forward and comfort her. Scott did that instead. Like *he* had any more right to be at the funeral than me. He was just as bad as I was really.

"We've really got things as we wanted now, haven't we?" Liz strides into the kitchen and passes me a glass of fizz. "Cheers."

"Erm, what are we celebrating exactly?" It's a year since Lou's body was found and Liz is passing me a glass of bubbly. It doesn't sit particularly comfortably.

I was furious with Lou the day before she died, especially after she ridiculed me in front of her boyfriend, but I didn't wish her dead. Never. She was still the mother of my daughter, no matter what. And I always respected her. I was a crap dad back then and left it all to Lou. And she rose to it. Always. I'm not sure I've ever truly respected Liz.

"We're celebrating life, of course." She smiles but it's the smile she has when she's up to something. "We got your house back. We no longer have to put up with your grasping ex-wife, or that tart Donna. And we've got more money at our disposal than we could ever know what to do with." She holds her glass aloft.

"That's Charlie's money." I can't bring myself to toast with her. No way. "Most of that money's meant for her upbringing."

"We put a roof over her head, don't we? Shoes on her feet?" Liz's voice is shrill and echoey in the newly-painted kitchen. "Clothes on her back?" It's the same line she trots out to anyone who'll listen. Especially the next door neighbour who she once bullied. They've become as thick as thieves since we moved in here.

"She spends most of her time at her grandma's anyway." It's true. But I wish Charlie were here more. I've got to a point where I'd like to spend more time with her. But Liz gets jealous.

Even now Lou's gone. It's as though she can't separate Charlie from her.

"Thank God she does," Liz replies. "Like I've always said to you, if I'd wanted kids, I'd have had my own."

"I always hoped you'd come around one day. Be a proper stepmum to her. Apart from Carole, you're her main female role model." *God help her,* I stop myself from adding, though I'm still hopeful that things might improve in time. It *has* only been a year.

Liz sighs as she sinks to the chair where Lou always used to sit. "Two years does feel like a long time to wait until she can have her own place."

"Who said anything about Charlie having her own place? Give over." I can't believe Liz is talking about my daughter moving out as soon as she turns sixteen. Over my dead body.

"Charlie. Charlie. Charlie. I'm sick to death of hearing about her." Liz's mouth is set in a thin, hard line. It's a look I know well. Clearly, my lack of feeling celebratory has well and truly pissed her off.

"What the hell's up with you Liz? How much of that stuff have you drunk?" I walk to the window, staring at the spot where my ex-wife apparently ended up. Poor Lou. How could we ever have known when we bought this place how things would ultimately turn out?

I still can't get my head around the fact that Donna was responsible. She was a lot of things, but I thought I knew her. It gutted me when she was found guilty. Absolutely gutted me. I'd never have had her down as someone who could be capable of violence on that sort of scale. There were often ructions between Lou and Donna, but deep down, they loved the bones of each other.

"You're thinking about *her* again, aren't you?" Liz comes up behind me. She's slurring her words. She *is* drunk. It's not even lunchtime. Bloody hell. I might go out for a bit. Pick Charlie up from Carole's. Do something with her – today of all days. It's what I *should* be doing. Honouring the silent promise I made to Lou at her funeral.

"A bit. I don't normally think about her love. It's only because it's the anniversary today."

Plus, I've heard today that Bradley Harris is being released on an electronic tag next month. A spot of plea bargaining and the information he gave about Donna was enough to reduce the time they sent him back to prison for. So that's playing on my mind as well. I can't talk to Liz though. She is only interested in herself...

"Don't you think I heard enough about your ex wife when she was alive? Lou this. Lou that." Liz's voice is rising. I've seen this kind of mood far too many times. "And if it wasn't *her*, it was that slag, Donna. It's no wonder I flipped."

A silence hangs between us for a moment.

"What do you mean, *flipped*? When?" I place my glass on the kitchen counter and turn to face her.

"Forget it."

"No. Go on. I want to know more about you *flipping.*"

"All those years of your bloody ex threatening us. If it wasn't with the Child Support Agency, it was with something else. Do you know," Liz slops more prosecco into her glass, "she once told me she could click her fingers anytime and you'd go running back to her." She knocks back half the glass in one swig,

She's right. I would have run back to her. Anytime. Lou was the love of my life. But I screwed up. Or more to the point, I screwed Donna. My silence seems to anger Liz more. I suppose I should have replied straight away. I should have said something like, *of course I wouldn't.*

I just haven't got the energy to deal with her shit anymore. After all the drama in my life, I've had enough. Especially over the last year, to be honest, I just feel shellshocked.

It began with Lou's death, then the aftermath with Donna, the trial, the media, trying to bring Charlie through it all, fighting with Carole, appeasing Liz, doing this place up. I'm knackered. I've really, really had enough.

"You definitely would have gone running back to her, wouldn't you?" Liz sounds more subdued suddenly.

"No. No. I wouldn't." I drain my glass. The cheap prosecco is difficult to swallow. God knows why I'm drinking it.

"Why won't you look at me when I'm talking to you?"

"Give it a rest Liz." This is one of those occasions when I'm so glad Charlie's not here. I suspect she'd have been around a lot more if me and Donna had... If she hadn't...

"I'm so pissed off Darren." Liz's voice now rises to shriek level. Bloody hell, she's truly on one. "I've got them both out of the way, and for what?"

I've got them both out of the way? I bang my glass down and stare at her. "What on earth is that supposed to mean?"

"Nothing." She turns from me and spins on her heel as though she intends to walk away.

I catch her by the arm. "No, tell me what you're talking about Liz. What does *getting them both out of the way* mean?"

I try to smile at her. I need her to trust me here. The drink has truly loosened her tongue.

"Don't act as though you didn't know, Darren." She folds her arms and gives me a knowing look as she says my name.

"Didn't know *what?*" She truly has me baffled here. Not to mention worried.

"I couldn't understand, at the time, why you'd told the police I never moved from the house all night."

A hint of a smile plays on her lips. *What the hell is she about to tell me?*

"I said as far *as I was aware,* that you hadn't moved from the house. They knew I was sleeping in the car. And I told them I was drunk."

Her gaze falls from my face and her voice lowers with it. "I never planned what happened you know. It sort of just did."

"Do you mean us falling out like we did? It was my fault too."

She can't stop now. I have to make her believe I'm a safe outlet for whatever tale she's telling here.

"No, I mean what happened with *her*." She looks back at me again. "But I did it for you. I did it *all* for you."

"Did what Liz? What is it you're telling me?"

Part of me doesn't want to hear this. Because once I have, *everything* changes.

"I couldn't be happier that Lou and Donna aren't here anymore, but I'm only human Darren. I *do* feel guilty at times. Especially now we're living here." She gestures around the kitchen. "And especially on days like this." This time, she tilts her head towards the patio doors. "A year on."

"Guilty for *what,* exactly?" I need her to spell this out. Maybe I should reach for my phone and record whatever she's about to say. But I hardly think she'll allow me to do that.

I now know what the saying *blood running cold* means. Surely she isn't *really* trying to tell me what I think she is. I wasn't lying when I told the police that I didn't see her leave the house that night. I really didn't see her.

"You know how angry I was. Not to mention drunk. So I came to see her." Liz looks me squarely in the eye. Whatever she's about to come out with, I mustn't break this moment. I daren't even blink as we eyeball each other.

"Lou? You mean the night she died?" *Died* sounds better than *murdered.* I can't do or say anything which might jeopardise this conversation.

"Yeah. You can't ever repeat *any* of this Darren. You can't. I'm trusting you." Her eyes narrow. "And if you go to the police, I'll make sure I drag you down with me. You'll have no evidence anyway. You'd just make yourself look stupid."

"You can trust me. Of course you can. How long have we been together love?" *I'll drag you down with me,* she says. Oh. My. God. She killed Lou. It was her. Not Donna. That's what she's trying to tell me. Donna's been serving time for something she didn't do. I always thought the police and the media pinned everything on her too easily. She was an easy target. They got their conviction, then left her to rot.

"It was *Donna* I went to see that night, at least to begin with." Liz points in the direction in which Donna used to live.

She only ended up living there for two or three weeks before they remanded her.

"But she wouldn't answer the door, would she? So, I helped myself to some stuff from her washing line, along with the trainers she'd left at the back door."

I think of the clothes that were passed around the jury as evidence during Donna's trial. Donna's clothes. But seemingly, she *hadn't* been the person wearing them. And there's little wonder Liz might have passed for Donna on the CCTV.

I've definitely got 'a type,' and they're literally the same height and build as each other. "So, where did the hammer come from?" I'm trying to keep my voice level.

"A toolbox in Donna's shed. Have you *honestly* never suspected it was me? I was convinced you really knew."

"It was all planned then, was it? What happened to Lou, I mean?" I'm choosing my words carefully. *What happened* sounds calmer than *what you did to Lou.*

"By that point, yes. But not before I left the house. I'd gone round to have it out with them both. It was all *your* fault. *You* put me in the middle of it." She points at me as she hisses the word *you.*

"I'm sorry for what I did. I can't say it any more times."

"Anyway, it was only when I got hold of the clothes and the hammer from Donna's that it all came together in my mind. All her blinds were down, so I was sure she hadn't seen me. She'd have been out there if she had."

"And then you came *here?*" I sweep my gaze over the garden as bile rises from my gullet. I'm desperately trying to blink away images of my wife bludgeoning the mother of my daughter to death, but this is something I've no choice other than to face.

There'll be more questions, another court case, the press, Charlie... My God, Charlie was even in the house when it happened. "Why are you even telling me this Liz? Why now?"

"I wanted to make her go away. Properly go away. For good. For ever. *And* Donna, after what I'd found out. I couldn't get beyond it. After I'd finished with Lou, I was going back to Donna's to do the same to her. I didn't even care at that moment if I got caught. I was wired. Really wired. And very drunk."

"But you *knew* what you were doing?" Part of me wants her to say *she didn't*, that it was temporary insanity or something. How can the woman I've lived with for all this time be capable of killing one woman and then framing another to take the blame? It's all mental.

"So what happened next?"

"I was hiding behind Donna's car as she came out of the house. She didn't even lock her front door. She just headed off round the corner towards here." She draws the shape of a corner in the air.

How can she be so calm, so considered? Though I suppose she's had a year to come to terms with what she's done.

"When she'd gone, I went in."

I stare at her. "And?"

She grins. "I had a washing machine to learn how to use. You know how I am with domestic appliances."

"You washed the clothes you were wearing?"

"Too right. But no amount of washing or showering would have ever of got rid of the amount of blood there was. I knew that. It was only a matter of time before they came after Donna."

I try to remember the other evidence against Donna. I think I always knew in my gut it couldn't have been her. Although she was miles away in the courtroom's dock a few months ago, our eyes met occasionally. It was as though she was imploring me to believe in her. But I honestly didn't know what to think.

"Donna must have raced round here after Scott rang her? Whilst you used her shower? And planted the other stuff?"

"Corr-ect."

The way she elongates the word makes the hairs stand up on the back of my neck. She's so assured, so sarcastic.

How have I been so blind? How could I have not known?

All that matters now is me getting out of here, away from her. I'm going to finally get justice for both Lou and Donna. Not to mention Charlie. She's going to be in bits when all this comes out. *How could I not have known?*

My eyes suddenly fall on the hammer that I've been using to put up new shelves. Without proper intention, I step in its direction.

But Liz has followed my gaze. We both lurch towards it.

At the same time.

EPILOGUE
LIZ

"ARE *YOU* SCARED OF DYING?" I look at Helen. Since I've lived here, in what was Lou's house, I've become quite friendly with the woman who lives next door. I'm not proud of the way I treated her when we were younger but things have changed now.

She looks thoughtful for a moment. "Not so much scared of dying itself." Helen reaches for a cushion which she lays across her lap, almost protectively. "More of how it will happen."

"Me too." I reach for my wine. It's looking like we'll have to open a third bottle. Though I should be careful. Too much alcohol loosens my tongue. And it makes me do things I regret.

"And I'd be worried about what and who I'd leave behind," she continues. "My dog, my sister. Wouldn't you be the same?"

"Like who?" I roll my eyes. "Who've I got to leave behind?"

Helen opens her mouth to say something. I should change the subject. I don't want to talk about who I have or haven't got. It's dangerous territory.

"So what about me?" I look at her.

"What do you mean?"

313

"You mentioned your dog and your sister... if you died. But you never mentioned me. I thought we were friends now?"

Her face breaks into a smile. "Of course I meant you too Liz. Gosh, I wouldn't have said *that* a few years ago, would I?"

"So would you cry if I died?" I go on, surprising myself. Since Darren's *departure*, I've become more needy. I can't even bear being on my own. Especially in this house. Charlie's moved in with her grandma full time since she finally resigned herself that her dad's not going to get in touch. Thank God.

But it's the only home I've got now, and if anyone ever finds out that Darren's not coming back from his work 'down south,' I'd be out on my ear anyway.

Helen looks taken aback. "Of course I'd cry "

"Just promise me." I glance around the room, imagining Lou and Donna probably sitting in here, doing the same thing as us, once upon a time. Chatting. Drinking. Putting the world to rights.

"Promise you what?"

"If you die *before* me, you'll give me a sign."

Helen laughs, which seems to break the mounting tension. "What do you mean?"

"Just a sign to let me know there's somewhere else. Somewhere after this shitty life. Somewhere better than here."

She laughs again. "Oh, it's not so bad, is it?"

"Nah. Not anymore."

"Don't worry." She reaches for my hand then, possibly sensing the rubbish feelings that are swirling around inside me. "If I go first, I'll give you a sign, I promise."

I squeeze her hand back. It's so nice having a friend at last. A proper friend. *And* money. *And* a nice place to live. I'll do whatever it takes to protect what I've accomplished.

"Anyway," Helen's voice rises. "What a maudlin conversation! I think we've had too much wine this evening."

"Possibly." I reach for the bottle.

"Let's talk about something happier, shall we?"

I raise my glass towards her. "What's that saying... something like, *a neighbour will keep you company, a friend will keep your secrets, but a true friend will help you hide a body.*"

We both laugh.

Before you go...

Thanks so much for reading Frenemy - I really hope you enjoyed it and will consider leaving me a review on Amazon and/or Goodreads as this makes such a difference in helping other readers find the book.

Frenemy is the first book in the Dark Hearts Series. Next in the trilogy is The Fall Out, followed by Nemesis.

Join my 'keep in touch' list to receive a free book, and to be kept posted of special offers and new releases.

Find out more about me via www.mariafrankland.co.uk and find out more about my other psychological thrillers by visiting my author page at Amazon.

BOOK CLUB DISCUSSION QUESTIONS

1. Discuss the phenomena of those who go after relationships with people who are unavailable, as Donna did.
2. Talk about the factors where two siblings who've had the same upbringing might turn out so differently, as with Georgia and Bradley. (Ash.)
3. Discuss what made Donna so attractive to men. What would happen after that? What would she have to do in order to change?
4. Why did Lou put up with Donna's behaviour?
5. Which characters did your sympathies lie with? Did these alter over the course of the story?
6. What is best for Charlie in the future? Why?
7. What would justice for Lou look like? What is the likelihood of it now?
8. Talk about the step family dynamic in the story. Would Scott have been a decent stepfather if Lou's hopes for the future had come to pass?
9. What was the influence of Donna on Charlie?
10. Where should 'the line' be in a friendship?

11. What aspects of Lou's life did Donna crave? How were these lacking in her own?
12. What suspects did you have in mind as the story reached part two? What were your reasons for each one?
13. What is the glue that holds a friendship together? Think of some examples to illustrate this.
14. Talk about how friendships may differ between genders. Female/female, male/male, male/female.
15. Discuss the ending. How much do you think Helen knows?

LAST ORDERS - PROLOGUE

WE HAD some good times in this place. I can't believe they're going to demolish what's left of it. But apparently, what's left to demolish is merely a shell. I scan the fencing around the perimeter, my eyes falling on a sign saying, *demolition site, keep out.* I can't imagine who could possibly want to go in there after what happened. Kids or ghouls - that's about it. The inside has been totally gutted by all accounts. It's eerie, standing here, staring at the boarded up doors and windows, and the blackened brickwork. This pub was the centre of our world, our sanctuary, and for some of us, our second home.

Being out in the sticks, it was too far from where we lived to walk here, so a taxi was the norm. We'd pull up outside, anticipating the evening ahead as the appearance itself invited us in. It was your typical semi-rural pub, though larger than most. Log fires, lamplit windows and everyone knowing each other. There'd be disco nights, quiz nights and lock ins. Always a fund raising event going on. The family who owned the place were great, we got really friendly with them - until everything turned sour. Really sour.

One minute the landlady was letting me in on the plans for

their silver wedding, the next there was venom flying. Absolute ructions. Apparently *she* had cheated and was planning to leave. Personally, I felt sorry for their two kids, stuck in the middle of it all. Although they were practically grown up, it still hurts when your parents' marriage is falling apart. Especially so publicly. But what came next , you wouldn't wish on your worst enemy, let alone on two people starting out on their adult lives.

Rumour has it that what happened on New Year's Day *wasn't* an accident. At first, there was speculation whether a group of kids might have started it. Then gossip turned to whether it could have been an insurance job gone wrong, or something even more sinister. But surely what happened that day couldn't have been intentional - they didn't seem like those sort of people.

Though when that charred body was dragged out, I couldn't help but recall the warning...

Watch this space. I'll give you all something to gossip about...

Find out more via Amazon.

INTERVIEW WITH THE AUTHOR

Q: Where do your ideas come from?

A: I'm no stranger to turbulent times, and these provide lots of raw material. People, places, situations, experiences – they're all great novel fodder!

Q: Why do you write domestic thrillers?

A: I'm intrigued why people can be most at risk from someone who should love them. Novels are a safe place to explore the worst of toxic relationships.

Q: Does that mean you're a dark person?

A: We thriller writers pour our darkness into stories, so we're the nicest people you could meet – it's those romance writers you should watch...

Q: What do readers say?

A: That I write gripping stories with unexpected twists, about people you could know and situations that could happen to anyone. So beware...

Q: What's the best thing about being a writer?

A: You lovely readers. I read all my reviews, and answer all emails and social media comments. Hearing from readers absolutely makes my day, whether it's via email or through social media.

Q: Who are you and where are you from?

A: A born 'n' bred Yorkshire lass, with two grown up sons and a Sproodle called Molly. (Springer/Poodle!) The last decade has been the best ever: I've done an MA in Creative Writing, made writing my full time job, and found the happy-ever-after that doesn't exist in my writing - after marrying for the second time just before the pandemic.

Q: Do you have a newsletter I could join?

A: I certainly do. Go to https:www.mariafrankland.co.uk or click here through your eBook to join my awesome community of readers. I'll send you a free novella – 'The Brother in Law.'

facebook.com/writermariafrank

instagram.com/writermaria_f

tiktok.com/@mariafranklandauthor

ACKNOWLEDGMENTS

Thank you, as always, to my amazing husband, Michael. He's my first reader, and is vital with my editing process for each of my novels. His belief in me means more than I can say.

A special acknowledgement goes to my wonderful advance reader team, who took the time and trouble to read an advance copy of Frenemy and offer feedback. They are a vital part of my author business and I don't know what I would do without them.

I will always be grateful to Leeds Trinity University and my MA in Creative Writing Tutors there, Martyn, Amina and Oz. My Masters degree in 2015 was the springboard into being able to write as a profession.

And thanks especially, to you, the reader. Thank you for taking the time to read this story. I really hope you enjoyed it.

Printed in Great Britain
by Amazon

40754738R00189